More Praise for *Outlawed*

"*Outlawed* stirs up the Western with a provocative blend of alt-history and feminist consciousness. The result is a thrilling tale eerily familiar but utterly transformed . . . In North's galloping prose, it . . . turns the sexual politics of the Old West inside out."
—Ron Charles, *The Washington Post*

"Anna North presents a far different perspective on the [Western] genre, one forged by women, Black, and nonbinary people looking for the freedom, space, and right to exist in a world that largely doesn't want them . . . The vividness with which she writes this world is one that's captivating and hard to put down." —*USA Today* (Best New Books)

"Fans of Margaret Atwood's *The Handmaid's Tale* are in for a stellar ride where gender roles, sexuality, agency, and self-discovery come together, making North's story as experimental and novel as it is classic." —*The Boston Globe*

"The heroes of the traditional Western were always sure about what made them the way they were; what made a man a man. For Ada and the other 'outlaws' of this spirited novel, the frontiers of gender and sexuality beckon to be explored." —Maureen Corrigan, NPR

"A thoroughly gripping, genre-subverting and -defining marvel of a novel." —Refinery29 (Most Anticipated Books of the Year)

"From the author of the Lambda Literary Award–winning *The Life and Death of Sophie Stark* comes an alt-history feminist Western . . . Think *Foxfire* by way of Mattie from *True Grit*, yet North's swashbuckling saga is wholly her own." —*O, the Oprah Magazine* (Best LGBTQ Books of the Year)

"North's knockout latest chronicles the travails of a midwife's daughter who joins a group of female and nonbinary outlaws near the end of the nineteenth century . . . The characters' struggles for gender nonconformity and LGBTQ rights are tenderly and beautifully conveyed. This feminist western parable is impossible to put down." —*Publishers Weekly* (starred review)

"2021 is already a year that could use a little joy. Here to provide some is the scrappy new feminist Western novel *Outlawed* . . . It's an absolute romp and contains basically everything I want in a book: witchy nuns, heists, a marriage of convenience, and a midwife trying to build a bomb out of horse dung." —*Vox*

"There is something both thrilling and intimidating about the first book of the year to receive rave reviews, and we didn't have to wait long for it in 2021. Published during the first week of the new year, Anna North's *Outlawed* sets a high bar for the twelve months of publishing still to come . . . It upends the tropes of the traditionally macho and heteronormative genre while also being a ripsnortin' good read, too." —*The Week* (Most Anticipated Books of the Year)

"A western unlike any other, *Outlawed* features queer cowgirls, gender nonconforming robbers, and a band of feminists that fight against the grain for autonomy, agency, and the power to define their own worth." —*Ms.*

"Earns its place in the growing canon of fiction that subverts the Western genre by giving voice to the true complexity of gender and sexual expression, as well as race relations, that has previously been pushed to the margins of traditional cowboy or westward expansion tales. A genre- (and gender-) bending take on the classic Western." —*Kirkus Reviews*

"A lovely slow draw in the world of the Old West, a story about the people who don't belong, portraying a realistic, close-minded world that only accepts women willing to fit into a specific mold . . . It's exciting to read a Western tale that features such a range of women and queer characters, and Ada herself is a bold protagonist whose desire to learn more about the female reproductive system and how it actually functions runs fiercely in her veins. Perfect for fans of Sarah Gailey's *Upright Women Wanted*." —*Booklist*

"This book has me, and you should have this book." —*Glamour* (Best of the Month)

"A gender-bending, genre-hopping yarn that's part frontier novel, part *Handmaid's Tale* and all ripsnorting fun . . . North easily subverts expectations as her characters struggle to find their identities in a patriarchal world." —*BookPage*

"Anna North has written a captivating Western unlike any other, with unique rhythms, dusty lands, and characters like new friends brought in on high winds. A grand, unforgettable tale." —Esmé Weijun Wang, author of *The Collected Schizophrenias*

"I'm dazzled by this feminist Western about a world in which women's worth and right to live are determined by the vagaries of fertility. Set in an alternate past, one all too similar to our today, *Outlawed* is terrifying, wise, tender, and thrilling. A masterpiece."
—R. O. Kwon, author of *The Incendiaries*

"*Outlawed* flips the script on the beloved Western genre and gives us the iconic heroine-on-the-run we deserve. Anna North is a riveting storyteller . . . Reader, you are in for a real treat." —Jenny Zhang, author of *Sour Heart*

"A moving and invigorating complication of the Western, highlighting chosen family, love, and survival among outcasts in another American timeline. As she mines the genre for vital new stories, North beautifully shines a light on our real past and conveys a warning for the future." —Lydia Kiesling, author of *The Golden State*

"Fans of Margaret Atwood and Cormac McCarthy finally get the Western they deserve in *Outlawed*, but Anna North doesn't just reimagine a damsel-in-distress as her own savior. She plays with the promise and danger of the frontier, introducing us to an America we never knew—and one we know all too well." —Alexis Coe, *New York Times* bestselling author of *You Never Forget Your First* and *Alice + Freda Forever*

"This ain't your grandpa's Western. Yes, there's gunslinging, hosses, banks to rob, and a no-good sheriff. But then no, this novel is as if *The Handmaid's Tale* had a baby with the real Butch Cassidy . . . It's rough, and soft. Profanely sweet with wide-eyed openness, and an exciting culmination that ricochets off the bulk of the tale . . . Start *Outlawed* and just try to put it down." —*Sidney Herald* (Sidney, Montana)

OUTLAWED

OUTLAWED

A NOVEL

ANNA NORTH

BLOOMSBURY PUBLISHING
NEW YORK · LONDON · OXFORD · NEW DELHI · SYDNEY

BLOOMSBURY PUBLISHING
Bloomsbury Publishing Inc.
1385 Broadway, New York, NY 10018, USA

BLOOMSBURY, BLOOMSBURY PUBLISHING, and the Diana logo are
trademarks of Bloomsbury Publishing Plc

First published in the United States 2021
This edition published 2022

This is a work of fiction. Names, characters, and places are the products of the
author's imagination. Any resemblance to actual persons, living or dead, or actual
events is purely coincidental.

ISBN: HB: 978-1-63557-542-2; PB: 978-1-63557-824-9;
EBOOK: 978-1-63557-543-9

LIBRARY OF CONGRESS CATALOGING-IN-PUBLICATION DATA IS AVAILABLE
Names: North, Anna, author.
Title: Outlawed : a novel / Anna North.
Description: New York : Bloomsbury Publishing, 2021.
Identifiers: LCCN 2020023175 (print) | LCCN 2020023176 (ebook) |
ISBN 9781635575422 (hardback) | ISBN 9781635575439 (ebook)
Subjects: GSAFD: Western stories. | Adventure fiction.
Classification: LCC PS3614.O774 O88 2021 (print) |
LCC PS3614.O774 (ebook) | DDC 813/.6—dc23
LC record available at https://lccn.loc.gov/2020023175
LC ebook record available at https://lccn.loc.gov/2020023176

Typeset by Westchester Publishing Services
Printed and bound in the U.S.A.

For my family

CHAPTER I

In the year of our Lord 1894, I became an outlaw. Like a lot of things, it didn't happen all at once.

First I had to get married. I felt lucky on the day of my wedding dance. At seventeen I wasn't the first girl in my class to marry, but I was one of them, and my husband was a handsome boy from a good family—he had three siblings, like me, and his mama was one of seven. Did I love him? We used to say we loved our beaus, my girlfriends and I—I remember spending hours talking about his broad shoulders, his awkward but charming dancing, the bashful way he always said my name.

The first few months of my marriage were sweet ones. My husband and I were hungry for each other all the time. In ninth form, when the girls and boys were separated to prepare us for married life, Mrs. Spencer had explained to us that it would be our duty to lie with our husbands regularly so that we could have children for baby Jesus. We already knew about the children part. We had read Burton's *Lessons of the Infant Jesus Christ* every year since third form, so we had heard about how God sent the Great Flu to cleanse the world of evil, just like he'd sent the flood so many centuries before. We knew that baby Jesus had appeared to Mary of Texarkana after the sickness had killed nine of every ten men, women, and children from Boston to California, and struck a covenant with her: If those who remained were fruitful and peopled the world in His image, He would spare them further sickness, and they and their descendants forever after would be precious to Him.

But in ninth form, we learned about lying with our husbands, how we should wash beforehand, and put perfume behind our ears, how we should breathe slowly to relax our muscles, and try to look our husbands in the eyes. How we'd bleed.

"Don't worry," Mrs. Spencer said, then, smiling at us. "It only hurts in the beginning. After a while you'll start to like it. There's nothing more joyful than two people joining together to make a child."

My husband did not know what to do at first, but he took his responsibility seriously, and what he lacked in experience he made up for in ardor. We lived with his parents while he saved for a house; in the mornings his mother made little jokes about how soon I'd be eating for two.

During the day I still attended births with my mama. I was the eldest and the only one who actually wanted to learn about breech births and morning sickness and childbed fever, so I was the one who would take over for Mama when she got too old. When I came on rounds with my new wedding ring, the mothers-to-be winked and teased me.

"It's good you're learning about all this now," said Alma Bunting, forty years old, pregnant with her sixth child and suffering from hemorrhoids. "Then you won't be surprised when it's your turn."

I just laughed. I was not like my friend Ulla, who had eight baby names picked out, four boys and four girls. When I was ten and my sister Bee was two months old, my mama had gone to bed and stayed there for a year. So I had already been a mama—I had changed a baby, fed her from a bottle when Mama couldn't nurse, soothed her at night when I was still young enough to be afraid of the dark. I was not in a rush to do it again. I knew from working with Mama that sometimes it could take months, even for a young girl like me, and I was happy to sleep with my new husband and still sneak off sometimes to drink juneberry wine behind the Petersens' barn with Ulla and Susie and Mary Alice, and not have to worry about anyone except for me.

But then it was six months since our wedding day, and my husband's mama was lingering in the kitchen while I put the breakfast dishes away.

"You know," she said, "after you do it, you can't just get right up and go about your day. You have to lie still for at least fifteen minutes to give everything time to work."

She had a way of talking to me like we were girls the same age gossiping after school, but this wasn't gossip and we weren't friends. I kept my voice light and happy.

"Mama says that doesn't matter so much," I said. "She says the most important thing is the time of month."

"Your mama's a very smart woman," she said. She had never liked my mama. "But sometimes every little bit helps."

She took the teacups from my hands.

"I'll finish this," she said. "You get ready for your work."

I didn't take my mother-in-law's advice—I'd never liked lazing around in bed. But I started marking my period carefully on the calendar so I'd know exactly when my fertile time was coming. Still I didn't worry—Mama had said it took her eight months to get pregnant with me, and my daddy almost left her, but after that Janie and Jessamine and Bee were easy. My husband made fun of his mother when we were alone—he said she meddled so much in his older brother's marriage that his sister-in-law banned her from their house. Six more months we were happy and then it was a year.

"There's only one thing to do now," my mama said. "You'll have to sleep with someone else."

Half the time, she explained, the man was the one who was barren.

This shocked me. Mrs. Spencer had taught us that the most common reason for failing to conceive a child was not lying with one's husband often enough, and the second was forgetting one's prayers. If a woman did her duty by her husband and baby Jesus and still did not become pregnant, then most likely she had been cursed by a witch—usually a woman who, barren herself, wanted to infect others with her malady.

I knew from Mama that there was no such thing as curses and that sometimes the body simply went wrong all on its own, but I had never heard of a man being barren before. When Maisie Carter and her husband couldn't have a baby, it was Maisie who got kicked out of the house and had to live down by the river with the tinkers and the drunks. When Lucy McGarry didn't get pregnant her family took her back in, but when two of her neighbors miscarried the same summer, everyone looked to Lucy for the cause. I was eleven when she was hanged for a witch. I had not yet started going on rounds with Mama; I had never seen a person die. It terrified me, not the violence of it but the swiftness, how one moment Lucy was standing on the platform and the next she was dangling limp below it. I tried to imagine it myself: what it would be like to see and think and feel and then suddenly plunge into blackness—more than blackness, into nothingness. It kept me awake that night and for many nights after, the dread of it. But at the gallows I cheered with everyone else; only Mama did not cheer.

"I don't want to sleep with someone else," I said. "Can't we just try a little longer?"

Mama shook her head.

"People are already starting to gossip," she said. "My patients are asking me if you're pregnant yet."

She would find someone for me, she said. There were men who did this for money, men whose virility was proven and who knew how to keep a secret. When it was the right time of month, I'd meet with one of them during the day for a few days running.

"Don't think of it as being unfaithful to your husband," Mama said. "Think of it as keeping yourself safe."

The man was a surprise to me. We met at my mama's house, where he posed as a repairman (he really did repair Mama's stove). He said I could call him Sam, and I understood that was not his real name. He was Mama's age and ugly, with a scraggly mustache the color of mouse fur, a big belly, and skinny legs. But he was kind to me, and put me at ease.

"You ever want me to stop, you tell me," he said, taking off his socks.

I did not want him to stop. I wanted him to do what he had to do quickly so I could go back to my husband with a baby in my belly and never be afraid again.

After our fourth meeting, when I was waiting to see if what we had done had worked, I asked Mama what really made women barren. Mama knew many things that Mrs. Spencer and the other people in our town did not know. She knew, for instance, that the Great Flu that had killed all eight of her great-grandparents was not, as everyone else said, a judgment from baby Jesus and Mother Mary. Mama's teacher Sarah Hawkins, a master midwife, had taught her that the Great Flu had come to America on ships along with spices and sugar, then spread from husband to wife and mother to child and trader to trader by kisses and handshakes, cups of beer shared among friends and strangers, and the coughs and sneezes of men and women who didn't know how sick they were and went on serving food and selling cloth and trading beaver pelts one day too long. Sarah Hawkins said the Flu was just a fever, a sickness like any other, and the only reason people put a meaning to it was that otherwise their grief would have overwhelmed them. Mama said Sarah Hawkins was the smartest person she had ever known.

But when I asked Mama about barrenness, she just shook her head.

"Nobody knows," she said.

"Why not?" I asked. I'd never before asked Mama a question that didn't have an answer.

"We don't even know exactly how a baby forms in a mother's womb," she said. "How can we know why sometimes her womb stays empty?"

I looked down at my hands and she could tell I was disappointed.

"I know one thing," she said. "It's not witchcraft."

"How do you know?" I asked.

"People cry witchcraft whenever they don't understand something," she said. "Remember, the town ladies said a witch had put a curse on Mayor Van Duyn, and when he died the doctor found his lungs all filled up with tumors. The only curse on him was that pipe."

"So why don't you tell people?" I asked. "Everyone listens to you."

Mama shook her head.

"I used to tell my patients," she said. "Every woman worries about a curse if she's not pregnant two months after her wedding. 'That's just a silly story,' I'd say. But they didn't believe me, and what's more, some of them got suspicious, like maybe I had cursed them."

Mama delivered all the babies in the Independent Town of Fairchild and cured most of the illnesses besides. She had set more bones than Dr. Carlisle and heard more confessions than Father Simon. Her reputation was so secure that even when she took to her bed after Bee was born, her patients were all but lined up at our door the day she got well. Nobody was suspicious of Mama.

"I don't understand," I said. "Why didn't they believe you?"

"When someone believes in something," Mama said, "you can't just take it away. You have to give them something to replace it. And since I don't know what makes women barren, I've got nothing to give."

I didn't get pregnant that month, or the month after. At my husband's house my mother-in-law watched me all the time, like she might catch me in the act of witchcraft. Once she came into our bedroom while I was washing and began making small talk with me, forcing me to answer politely as I washed my underarms and private parts. I felt ashamed of my body then as I never had before, of my small breasts, stomach flat over an empty womb. She began to make me pray to baby Jesus in the mornings; we knelt together and asked him to send our family a child. My mother-in-law was not a particularly religious woman. She kept a crèche above the hearth and a copy of Burton on the shelf like everyone in Fairchild, but went to church only on holidays or when she was seized with a desire to appear pious. The fact that we were praying now—in stumbling words I imagined she half-remembered from some childhood catechism—showed me how desperate she'd become.

At night my husband would touch me only during my fertile week; he was tracking me himself now, as though he didn't trust me to do it. When I reached for him late in the month he told me his mama had said it was better to save our energy for when it counted, and I was not surprised that he talked to his mama about such things, but I was still disgusted by it.

My meetings with Sam, strangely, became a refuge. In Mama's house no one watched us. Afterward he did not pester me to lie still or put my legs up the way my husband did; he put his clothes on and said goodbye and left me alone so that I could lie in my childhood bed and pretend that I had never married.

Sam and I didn't talk much, but in the third month of our meetings he asked if I wanted him to touch me while we did it.

"It might help you relax," he said. "Some people say that makes you more likely to conceive."

By that time I trusted Sam. He had never tried to do anything I didn't want, had always behaved like a friend helping me with something—perhaps a dish on a high shelf I couldn't quite reach. So I said yes, he could touch me, and that was the beginning of the end.

When it came to married life, we girls had other sources of information besides Mrs. Spencer. We had the older married girls and the web of gossip and advice they wove to keep us safe. From them we knew it was dangerous to sleep with someone too many times before you were married—if you didn't get pregnant after a few months of fooling around, he'd never marry you. Worse, he might spread the rumor that you were barren. We knew, too, that if you married someone who turned out to be cruel, the best thing to do was to have children as quickly as you could. A woman with three children could divorce her husband and she would probably find another man to marry her—she had never said as much, but I knew that was why Mama had waited until after she had Janie and Jessamine to leave our daddy and bring us to Fairchild, where the old midwife had recently left town. A woman with four children could do as she pleased, marry or not, and I knew that was one reason no one spoke ill of Mama when she chose not to take another husband after Bee's daddy left.

There was also a book that circulated among the girls and younger women of Fairchild, succinctly titled *Fruitful Marriage*. The book was more explicit than Mrs. Spencer's lessons, and it was mildly scandalous to be caught reading it, though not altogether forbidden. When Susie's mother had found the book while cleaning, she had not reprimanded Susie but had merely replaced the book under her bed in such a way that made it seem likely she had read some of it.

Fruitful Marriage included drawings of men and women naked together, locked in embrace. The author, one Wilhelmina Knutson, also discussed something called "climax," which she described, frustratingly, as "a moment of indescribable pleasure." The ability to feel this sensation, Mrs. Knutson said, was the sign of a physically and psychologically healthy individual who was ready for motherhood. And Mrs. Knutson was very clear on one point: climax could only occur when a man's "member" was deep inside a woman's body.

I had never experienced climax with my husband, and in recent months, I had come to believe that my inability to do so was yet another sign of my bodily deficiency. But when Sam touched the top of my vagina with his fingers, rhythmically and patiently, for an amount of time that might have been two minutes or two hours, I experienced a sensation so extreme that I thought it must either be climax or something very dangerous, possibly fatal. It was something like what I had felt a few times when, awakening from a sweaty dream of hands and mouths, I touched myself under the covers of my bed. But what I felt with Sam was much more intense, and when he took his leave that day I was still shaking slightly, and absolutely sure that this time, I must be pregnant.

I was still thinking about it when I met Ulla and Susie at the barn a week later. Mary Alice was four months pregnant with her first baby so she wasn't meeting us anymore; Ulla was two months married, and Susie was engaged to be married in November during the harvest feasts. At first we joked and gossiped about our former classmates and their courting the way we always did, but soon I was too curious to keep quiet.

When it was my turn with the bottle I took a deep drink.

"Have you ever had a climax?" I asked my friends.

Susie knitted her brows for a moment, considering.

"I think so," she said, "a small one."

Ulla laughed. She had a gap between her front teeth that always made her look mischievous, like nothing would shock her.

"With Ned it's like this," she said, miming a hammer pounding in a nail. "Mostly I just feel sore. But my mama says not to worry, you don't need a climax to get pregnant."

She took a swig from the bottle.

"Why," she asked, "have you?"

"I think so," I said. I should have stopped there, but my confidence buoyed me on. My period was a day late and I knew that what Sam and I had done must have worked at last.

"And do you know," I said, "I think a man can make you climax with his fingers."

Ulla looked incredulous.

"With his fingers," she said.

"That's right," I insisted. "He touches you between your legs, above the opening. And then it's just like Mrs. Knutson says—a little hard to describe, but very powerful. Almost like fainting."

"Your husband did this?" Ulla asked. "Just by touching you?"

"That's right," I said, in what I hoped was a convincing tone. Ulla shook her head.

"That's not possible," she said. "Everyone knows a woman can only climax from deep inside. Mrs. Knutson says so."

"Well," I said, affecting a tone of pride, "maybe my husband knows better than Mrs. Knutson."

She looked skeptical.

"Where did he learn it, then?" she asked.

It began to dawn on me that I had made a mistake.

"What do you mean?" I asked, stalling for time.

"I mean I highly doubt Mr. Vogel taught the boys about this form of climaxing, if none of us have ever heard of it before. And he certainly didn't learn it from *Fruitful Marriage*. So how did he know how to do it?"

"From another book," I said, "that only the boys have."

"Really?" Ulla asked. "What book?"

"It's called *Fruitful Marriage for Men*," I said, cursing myself even as I said it. "It's quite rare. One of my husband's visiting cousins had a copy."

Ulla took another drink, all the while looking me in the eye.

"Well," she said, "I'll have to track it down. Ned could use a copy."

I'll never know who put two and two together, whether it was Ulla or Susie or both who understood that the experience I was describing was much more likely with an outsider than with one of our town boys, young and inexperienced and raised on all the same folk wisdom as we had been. All I know is that when I came back to my husband's family's house after my rounds with Mama one evening, my husband was gone and his mother and father were sitting at the kitchen table.

"You know," said my mother-in-law, "I stuck up for you."

"What's going on?" I asked.

Mama's old suitcase, the one I'd used to bring my clothes and medical books to my husband's house, was standing next to the stove.

"Malcolm thought you'd be a bad match. He said your mama was unstable. He said if it wasn't for the charity of your neighbors, your little sister would have died."

My father-in-law looked vaguely pained. He had never spoken more than three words to me. It was hard for me to imagine him saying all this to his wife.

"That's not true," I said. "I took care of Bee myself while Mama was sick. She was never in any danger."

"That's what I said," my mother-in-law went on. "And I told him your mama still delivers every baby within ten miles of here. That has to count for something, I said."

She waited like she expected me to thank her. I didn't say anything.

"Are you listening?" she asked. "I'm trying to tell you why it hurt me so much to find out you betrayed us. To find out you chose to be with another man when my son loves you so much, he was willing to wait another year if that was how long it took."

I imagined the conversations they must have had about my failure to conceive, the same ones in which she told him to save himself for my fertile days. I doubted either he or she would have waited a year.

"I didn't want to sleep with him," I said. "I just wanted to give you a grandchild."

My mother-in-law rolled her eyes.

"Well, did it work? Are you pregnant now?"

I shook my head. I'd started to bleed that morning, while I was mixing mallow and beeswax for a baby's rash.

"Of course not," she said.

Was she disappointed? What would have happened if I'd said yes? Would we have raised the child, my husband and I, together? Would I have done it again? Sometimes I still wish for that life, and everything it would mean.

My mother-in-law nodded at her husband and he picked up my suitcase and handed it to me.

"Leave your wedding ring on the table," she said.

That night I had dinner with my mama and sisters like nothing was wrong. Janie and Jessamine were excited to see me and told me everything that was happening in seventh form: how Arthur Howe said his daddy had gone to the high country to join the Hole in the Wall Gang, but everybody knew he had just taken up with a woman two towns away, how Agnes Fetterly had started her monthlies already but nobody wanted to court her because she was an only child, how Lila Phelps had tried to fake hers with chicken blood so her mama would let Nils Johansson come to court her, but her mama caught her pouring the blood onto her bedsheets and made her do all the laundry in the house for a month. It hurt, almost, to remember what I'd been like at their age, not so long ago, a woman-child—my body beginning to change, my mind, like theirs, still full of tricks and gossip. The darkness of the grown-up world just starting to seep in.

All the time our sisters were talking, Bee was stealing looks at me. I could tell she already knew something was wrong. Bee was eight years old that spring. Mama said we were like two sides of the same coin. When I was her age I'd been chatty, always asking questions. Bee was quiet—she picked up what she needed to know by watching and listening.

Jessamine and I were washing the dinner dishes when Sheriff Branch came to call. He was friends with Mama and often came just to chat, bringing barley candy or Babies' Tears for my sisters. He'd tell us stories, too, tall tales about Jesse James or the Kid, the leader of the mysterious Hole in the Wall Gang. The Kid was nearly seven feet tall, the sheriff said, and as strong as three ordinary men put together. His eye was so keen he could shoot a man dead from a mile away, and his heart was so cold he'd steal the wedding ring from a widow or the silver spoon from a baby's mouth. Unlike the common cattle rustlers who plied their trade in sweat-stained hats and filthy dungarees, the Kid was known for his vanity—he wore a wide-brimmed pinch-front hat in the Colorado style, and his face was always covered with a fine silk scarf.

The sheriff himself had never personally squared off against the Kid. But he assured us that when they finally met, that villain's days of riding roughshod over the laws of the Dakotas would be over.

Susie's daddy and some of the other men in town told stories about outlaws to scare their children. But Sheriff Branch never aimed to terrify us; he always promised that while he was the law in Fairchild, no outlaw or anyone else would harm a hair on our heads.

"As long as you mind your mama," he'd add, winking. "If I hear you've been giving her a moment's trouble, I'll drag you down to the courthouse to stand trial."

I had always loved Sheriff Branch and his visits. He rode a quiet horse named Maudie, and when he came to call he let us pet her mane and feed her lumps of sugar or carrots from the garden. But this time I remembered Lucy McGarry, and I was afraid. I knew I was right to worry when the sheriff refused coffee and Mama's spice cake.

"I can't stay long," he said. "Maybe the three of us grown-ups could talk?"

Mama told Janie and Jessamine to take Bee upstairs, and only then did Sheriff Branch accept a seat at our table. He took off the white hat he always wore when he was working, stared at the brim of it, and made as though to brush some dirt away although there was no dirt there. Despite his work, Sheriff Branch was a shy man.

"I heard there's been trouble in your marriage," he said finally.

Mama didn't wait for me to answer.

"It's Claudine," she said. "She never liked Ada. She made that house a hell for her. Stress isn't good for conceiving children, Sheriff. You know that."

Sheriff Branch had just one child, a daughter. He would have had no children and maybe no wife if not for Mama. The sheriff was friends with Dr. Carlisle, and had asked him to attend the birth of his first baby. But Dr. Carlisle had little experience with births, and when Liza Branch's labor stalled, the baby's head halfway down the birth canal, he began to panic, pacing around the house and muttering to himself while Liza howled in pain. Finally he called Mama, who was able to turn the baby's head from front to back so Liza could push her into the world. Sophia was born blue and barely breathing, but Mama revived her; another half hour stuck inside Liza, Mama said, and the baby would have been beyond help.

Since the birth, Liza had been unable to conceive again. Mama had visited many times to give tonics and massages, but nothing had worked—finally, she had told the Branches that perhaps they were not meant to have more children. Sheriff Branch became distant from his wife after that, but doted on his daughter as if she were five children.

"Claudine can be a handful," the sheriff said. "But I've started hearing complaints. Greta Thorsdottir says she saw Ada walking the fields at night carrying a dead hare. Agatha Dupuy says she and her daughters have all come down with womanly ailments in the last month."

Mama shook her head. She looked completely calm.

"Sheriff," she said, "you've known Ada since she was a child. How could you possibly suspect her of what those women are suggesting? You know Aggie and her daughters are always coming down with something, usually imaginary."

The sheriff nodded. His brows were knit. He kept twisting his wedding ring around on his finger.

"True enough," he said. "Ada, you've always been a good girl. As long as you stay with your mama, and stay out of trouble, you won't hear any more from me."

He turned back to Mama.

"Of course, she can't attend births anymore," he said. "She'll have to find something else to do."

Bee came down the stairs as Mama was seeing him off.

"That's ridiculous," Mama said, "but all right. She'll help me at home with the herbs and tinctures."

The sheriff stood, taking his hat in his hands.

"I'm sorry," he said. "I didn't want to make this call."

"So why did you make it?" Mama asked. She kept her voice even but I could see how angry she was.

"Evelyn, you know what I always say is the most important part of my job."

"Protecting children," Mama said. "But my daughter hasn't harmed anyone. She's barely out of childhood herself."

The sheriff nodded. "And hopefully she never will harm anyone. But if there's even a chance that she'll hurt a baby, or keep a baby from being born—I couldn't live with myself."

His voice was cracking.

"You understand, don't you, Evelyn? Of all people?"

"We'll do what you ask, Sheriff," Mama said, standing up and moving toward the door. "That's all I can promise."

For weeks I lived under a kind of house arrest. In the mornings I woke, made breakfast for my sisters, then sat and read in my bedroom while Mama went out on calls. Sometimes in the afternoons I'd bake corn muffins so that the house would smell good when my family came home. It was not an unpleasant life, especially after my husband's house, and I might have lived a long time that way, except that at the beginning of March, the town had an outbreak of German measles. In one week, three pregnant women lost their babies. One was Lisbeth, the mayor's niece; one was Mrs. Covell, who taught the lower forms at the school; and one was Rebecca, the new wife of Albert Camp, who worked in the bank, and who had been widowed the year before.

School was canceled; my sisters stayed home. Janie and Jessamine plaited each other's hair and told increasingly outlandish stories about what they would do once they were allowed outside. Bee sat by the window and watched the empty street. Mama still made her rounds, but when she came home at night she was troubled, and circled the house doing small tasks as though trying to outrun her mind.

"The general store is closed," she said, "and the bank. The church is empty—Father Simon visits once a day to light candles for the babies. Even the saloon is deserted."

She didn't say it, but I knew what she was afraid of: too many lost babies at once, and people would start looking for the witch. I was not the only barren woman in town. Maisie Carter was still alive, still young even; if she'd been fertile she would still be having children. But no one saw her, she came into town only rarely and bothered no one. I was the one whose expulsion from my husband's home was a fresh scandal, whose barrenness was news.

After a week, though, the sick began to improve. None of them died; the measles that had been so deadly for babies in the womb turned out mild for those already on the earth. The saloon started serving again, the congregants returned to church. The general store and the bank reopened for business. Then Mama came home ashen-faced: Ulla had lost her baby.

"I didn't even know she was pregnant," I said.

Mama ignored me. "They sent me away," she said, shaking her head. "They had Dr. Carlisle attending her. If she bleeds out, it will serve her stupid mother right."

"Why did they send you away?" I asked.

Mama looked at me with weariness and sorrow in her eyes and I saw the answer before I heard it.

"Ulla is saying you put a curse on her. She's saying you made her lose the baby."

"I haven't seen Ulla in months," I said.

"It doesn't matter," said Mama. "Now her family will want you charged with witchcraft. And with the others, too, the sheriff won't be able to protect you."

I knew it was useless to argue. I saw already that my time was up and what little I had left would be taken from me. But I argued anyway.

"You said it was the measles. You always say German measles is dangerous for pregnant women. You tell everyone about it. Why would they think it was witchcraft?"

"They want to know what caused the measles," Mama said. "Maybe if it had been just one woman, two, even three. I thought for a day or two we might be all right. But another loss right when people were starting to catch their breath—they'll want someone to pay, Ada. They'll want it to be you."

We sat on the bed Bee's daddy had bought for Mama before he left in the third month of her sickness. It was twice the size of her old one, with a heavy headboard made of rock maple all the way from Vermont. Bee and Janie and Jessamine loved to pile into Mama's bed, but it always made me think of the nights of her sickness, when I sat with her after Bee was asleep, terrified to be with her in the dark when she had become almost a stranger to me, but terrified that if I took my eyes off her she might just give up, just quit breathing the way she'd quit dressing and cooking and getting out of bed. Every night I fell asleep in the chair next to Mama's bed, and every morning I woke up and she was just the same, until one morning I woke up and she was better.

"So what do I do?" I asked Mama.

She smoothed a strand of hair behind my ear.

"I know a place," she said. "You won't like it, but you'll be safe there."

That night as I tucked Bee in, I told her I was going away for a while. She just nodded, those wide eyes taking everything in.

"You're going to have to help Mama," I said. "In a few years, you're going to have to start learning the business from her."

"Janie and Jess are older," Bee said.

"Jess faints at the sight of blood," I said. "And Janie can't focus long enough to darn a sock, let alone stitch a wound. It has to be you."

Bee nodded. She had dark brows like her daddy, who was half Polish, half Ojibwe and handsome—not like my daddy, whose long pale hatchet face I still remembered, though I remembered little else about him. Bee's daddy had tried with her in the beginning, he really had, but only I could soothe her. And he still sent money every couple of months, and letters for Bee, which was more than my daddy ever had.

"Don't worry," I said. "You'll be good at it. Most of it is just listening to people, and you already know how to do that."

I wanted to give her a head start, so that in time, when she started to learn in earnest, she'd remember me. I taught her the song Mama had taught me to memorize the seven most important medicinal herbs and their uses. I showed her how to count a pulse and explained what it meant if it was fast or slow. I was halfway through explaining the early symptoms of the six childhood fevers when I saw that her eyes were wandering and her brows were knitted close.

"What's wrong?" I asked her.

"Aren't you scared?" she asked.

"Scared of what, Honeybee?"

She dropped her eyes from my face.

"I know people die sometimes," she said. "Mama didn't talk about it, but I know Sally Temple died."

Sally Temple had lived on the outskirts of town with her husband, who was a ratcatcher. She was very young—just fifteen, some people said—and her baby came so fast that he ripped her all apart inside. Mama was finally able to stop the bleeding, but Sally had lost too much, and she died in her childbed with her new son screaming in the next room. I was there when she died and for weeks I dreamed of her, her little pointed face draining of color, the confusion and then anger and then panic in her eyes. Then Mama explained to me how she went on, knowing it could happen anytime.

"Mama says at every birth, death is in the room. You can try to ignore it, or you can acknowledge it, and greet it like a guest, and then you won't be so afraid anymore."

Bee looked skeptical.

"How do you greet it? 'Hello, Death'?"

"She pictures the last patient she lost," I said. "The death that's freshest in her mind. She pictures that woman standing right there in the room with her. She looks the woman up and down. She doesn't say anything, but sometimes she gives a little nod. Then she's ready for the birth."

"Does it work?" Bee asked.

I had seen Mama enter a birth with fear in her heart, if the baby was early or breach or the mother was sick with sugar or high blood pressure. Mama's face was as confident as ever but still everyone in the room could feel something was wrong; the aunties' hands would begin to shake as they wiped the laboring mother's brow. And then Mama's eyes would focus on a point in the empty air, and she would nod, and then the whole room would pull together around her, and the birth would go as well as it could possibly go, because she was in charge.

"It works," I said.

I bent to hug Bee, more for myself than for her. She smelled like soap and cedar, just like she had ever since she was a baby.

"When I'm grown," she said into my shoulder, "I'm going to come find you."

I pulled back to look her in the face.

"Bee," I said, "I'll be back before you're grown."

"Okay," she said, not believing. "But if you're not, I'll get a horse, and a map, and I'll come help you, wherever you are."

CHAPTER 2

The Mother Superior of the Sisters of the Holy Child said I
could have sanctuary as long as I accepted baby Jesus into
my heart. Baby Jesus had not helped me conceive a child, but
neither had drinking four glasses of milk every day or keeping
my legs above my head or lying down with Sam or anything else
I had tried. I had nothing against baby Jesus.

"I accept Him," I said.

The Mother raised an eyebrow.

"You'll have Bible study with Sister Dolores," she said. "In six
months, if she thinks you're ready, you can take your vows. Then
you'll be one of us."

In the meantime, Sister Rose introduced me to Goldie, Holly,
and Izzy. Sister Rose was a skinny girl with a gummy smile. She
shared my room at the convent—two narrow beds, two chamber
pots, a washbasin, and a crèche.

She was a natural with animals. The cows calmed visibly when
they saw her, and when she touched their backs and cooed to
them she was almost graceful. Holly, the Holstein, was the only
one who let me near her. The others switched their tails or
kicked or jerked their dugs out of my hands. But Holly was
quiet, her eyes big and droopy, almost like she felt sorry for

me, and Sister Rose showed me how to squeeze so I didn't hurt her, so milk ran in a clean stream from her teat to the bucket.

Milking was a good time to cry. I was hardly ever alone at the convent; at matins and breakfast and Bible study and vespers and dinner, I was surrounded by sisters. But at milking time, Sister Rose was focused on Goldie or Izzy, and the wind blew across the meadow and shivered the barn windows and hid the sound of my cries.

I cried out of pure sorrow. I kept remembering the softness of Bee as a little baby, the way Janie and Jessamine filled the house in the mornings with their voices. I cried, too, out of anger. I had never done anything in my life as bad as what Ulla had done to me. I knew that Ulla had only been trying to save herself—her mother-in-law was meaner than Claudine, her husband weaker than my husband, and she had been considered a risky match because she had only one sister, who had a clubfoot and breathing troubles. For some families one miscarriage was enough to kick a new wife out, even if it happened during a sickness. But none of this made me want to forgive Ulla, who had been my best friend since we were smaller than Bee, who had slept in my bed whenever her mother's rages became too much, who had cried at night as I stroked her hair.

When all the sorrow and anger were wrung out of me and I was almost hoarse from sobbing, then, like the thunder that follows lightning, came the fear. I knew Mama was right, that the families who had lost babies would want someone to pay, and I was afraid they would turn on my sisters in their grief. I had seen it before—when Lucy McGarry's neighbors miscarried, suspicion fell on her whole family, even her littlest sister who was barely five years old. Some people said Lucy ran a coven out of her mama's house. But when she was hanged the rumors dissipated, and her family went back to their lives—her sister eventually married the mayor's nephew.

I knew Mama must have thought it all through. She must have believed she could keep herself and my sisters safe once I went away. Probably she decided her position in town was secure enough that she could weather whatever came—people could whisper about her for a while, but eventually they'd realize Dr. Carlisle didn't know the first thing about birthing babies, and they'd be forced to come back to her. But what if, instead, the mayor decided to send for another midwife? I didn't know, I realized, what had happened to the one before Mama. But if Fairchild could find her, then it stood to reason they could find someone else, if their fears for their future babies came to outweigh her record of healthy babies born.

And once I had been down this list of frightening thoughts, I always came to the worst of all—that Mama must have been down the list too. That she knew it was dangerous to send me away instead of letting the sheriff take me, and she did it anyway, balancing her safety and the safety of my sisters against my life. Deciding my life was worth risking all of theirs.

When I was finished crying there was always a time when I stared blankly up at Holly from my milking stool: her strong shoulder, her calm, contented eye, her pale pink udder already filling again with milk, the simple rightness and sufficiency of her. It was in this position that Sister Rose found me, and though I could have wiped my tears quickly and pretended nothing was wrong, I was tired of being so lonely and instead I let her see.

"Do you miss your family?" she asked.

I nodded.

"Don't you?"

Sister Rose sat cross-legged on the barn floor. Our dresses were made for this, dark cloth to absorb dirt and spills for six days, until Sister Dolores and Sister Socorro washed them all in enormous steaming tubs on Saturdays and hung them up to dry in the washroom, drips pinging on the stone floor.

"I was married," Sister Rose said. "He was nice when we were courting. He used to bring me flowers from his mama's garden. But after we got married, I couldn't stay pregnant. I miscarried three times in a year, so he kicked me out. And my daddy wouldn't take me back. He knew he'd never find someone else to marry me. Luckily our priest was friends with the Mother Superior, and she took me in."

Sister Rose smiled. "This is my family now."

Every sister had a story like this. Sister Mary Grace's husband divorced her after five childless years. Sister Dolores started sleeping with the neighbor boy when she was fifteen—when they were seventeen he told everyone in town that she was barren, and then nobody would marry her. Sister Clementine had been married two years with no pregnancy when a baby on her street was born with a hard black crust over its face and neck. The sheriff arrested her for putting a curse on the baby, but because she was just nineteen (and maybe also because she was pretty and sweet and claimed to pray to baby Jesus every day), he let her go to the convent instead of jail.

Sister Rose was right—these girls and women without families were a kind of family of their own. Sister Mary Grace took care of Sister Teresa, who couldn't use her arms. Sister Socorro was like a daughter to Sister Dolores, who had taught her Latin and Greek and laundry. Sister Rose was not my sister, but in the mornings I let her brush and braid my long hair, like my sisters used to do.

In time I learned to milk Goldie, and even Izzy, who was trouble, and Sister Clementine taught me how to strain the curds out of hot milk to make cheese. Everyone was kind to me except the Mother Superior.

One day as we filed into the chapel for morning prayer, the Mother asked in her loud voice, "Trying to be stylish, Ada?"

I didn't understand what she meant. I looked down at my dress, my heavy brown shoes.

"Sister Rose," said the Mother, "after service, show Ada how to tie her headscarf properly."

"She can be a little stern," said Sister Rose later as she helped me knot the scarf at the back of my neck, under my hair. "But don't worry. She's like that with everyone."

"She isn't," I said. "She loves you and Clementine."

I'd seen the Mother whisper to Sister Rose as she gave her communion. At breakfast, I'd seen her scoop the applesauce from her own plate onto Sister Clementine's.

"We've been here for years," said Sister Rose. "It'll be different for you when you take your vows."

I wasn't sure I believed her, but in the mornings I went to catechism and learned from Sister Dolores about the lives of Saint Hannah, Saint Monica, and of course Mother Mary herself. Sister Dolores made us memorize Burton and recite him aloud, and I felt like a child mouthing those familiar words: "and the orphaned infant she had suckled at her breast was Jesus Christ Himself, come to preach a new gospel to her." But I allowed the stories to comfort me like everything I had ever learned by heart—the letters of the alphabet, the names of the medicinal herbs, the days of the week, the months of the year.

We also read a book by a pastor, the Reverend Alfred Byrd, called *The Justice of the Blessed Infant on Earth*. Reverend Byrd had been born in slavery on Mount Haven plantation in the state of Georgia in the United States of America, but by the time he was twelve none of those places existed anymore. The plantation lasted the longest—the old owner survived the Flu and hung on for years after the governor and the president died and the state-house was turned into a hospital, then a morgue. But with his strong young sons dead and the town's police force gone, it was only a matter of time before the people he had enslaved rose up, burned down his huge empty house, and fled. Reverend Byrd and his parents settled in one of the Independent Towns near the Kansas River like many other former slaves. Land was everywhere—fields lay fallow and farmhouses empty for the taking, if you were willing to bury the bodies left inside. But the former slaves had no money for seed corn or cotton, horses or plows. Most of them—Reverend Byrd's parents included—had to hire themselves out as farmhands to the remaining white farmers, and as they got poorer the white farmers got richer and began to cultivate the land the dead had left behind so that within a generation Kansas country looked like the old Southern states, except on paper the black people were free.

Reverend Byrd wrote that white people who cheated black people and treated them like slaves had forgotten the lessons of Jesus. "When a child is born to a black household," he wrote, "all the townsfolk, black and white, assemble to receive the blessing. And yet the same white townsfolk who gather to kiss the child's feet forget that black men, too, are blessed by baby Jesus."

In Fairchild there were no huge farms like in Texas, and the few black people in town were tradesmen and small farmers like white people. But it was true that all the black families lived on the far side of the river, in a part of town called Coralton where the land was marshy and worse for farming.

I had thought little of this fact when I still lived at home, but now, removed from the unspoken laws that governed that place, I could see them more clearly: how the children of Benjamin

Rockford, the cooper, did not attend our school though they were of age to do so; how Rockford himself ran his cooperage out of a shed adjoining his family's home rather than a store on Main Street; how I saw his wife at the dry-goods store and the butcher's and the baker's but never having tea at Ulla's house or Susie's house or, for that matter, at ours.

And it was true, too, that when a baby was born in Coralton, the white families gathered just as they did for a birth in Fairchild proper, though across the river the houses were smaller, so that people often had to stand out on the front steps, waiting their turn to receive the baby's blessing.

On Saturdays Sister Dolores was busy with the laundry, so instead of catechism I had free time in the library. Technically I was supposed to study theology—Burton or Viletti or *The Diary of Eleanora Funt*, which was about a lady who decided baby Jesus spoke to her and went around telling everyone, mostly important mayors and priests. But the library had thousands of books, more than I'd ever seen in one place. It had herbals better than Mama's, almanacs better than the ones in the headmaster's office at the school back home, and histories of the colonies, the United States, the Flu years of the 1830s, the fall of the governments, and the founding of the Independent Towns west of the Mississippi. My favorites, though, were the natural science books, with their beautiful and complicated etchings of the insides of people and animals. I saw a slice of kidney, a cross section of an eye; I saw the four valves and four chambers of the heart; I saw the twenty-seven tiny interlocking bones of the hand. I saw, too, the penis cut open to reveal the spongy flesh inside, and all the tiny tubes of the testicles. I saw a woman splayed as I'd seen countless times, but with each fold and furrow frozen by the draughtsman's pen, so I could confirm with a hand mirror what I had suspected: that on the outside at least I was like any other woman. And I saw a woman's insides—the stretchy purse of the womb, with and without a child inside it, the tubes with their frilly fingers, the ovaries like little stones.

But no book explained the why of it. Even Burton, who had an explanation for everything, was silent on the question of why some women could have children and some could not. He spoke of "those whose bodies reject the blessing of a child," but said also that Jesus personally loved and cared for every single descendant of the Flu survivors. If Jesus loved us, why would He let our bodies reject His blessing? I knew that Mrs. Spencer's explanation would involve the evil workings of witches against Christ's design, but hadn't He sent the Flu to cleanse the world of evil? Why did he leave witches behind? It wasn't that I didn't believe in baby Jesus—I prayed like anyone, I always had, when I was afraid or grateful or in pain. The year Mama was sick I had prayed every day. It was only that I found the lessons of baby Jesus insufficient to explain the world.

One book in the library did claim to explain the origins of barrenness and other conditions. It was by one Dr. Edward Lively, whose name I'd heard before—some of the town ladies had a pamphlet he'd written on exercise and mental hygiene. This book, however, was called *On the Heritability of Maladies*, and initially, I found it interesting. Dr. Lively posited that barrenness, clubfoot, and many other ailments were passed down from grandmother to mother to child in the blood. "When a woman is barren," Lively wrote, "we commonly find an aunt or close cousin who was barren as well, suggesting a kind of familial contagion."

This made me worry for my sisters, and I hoped nobody back in Fairchild happened upon Lively's book. In later sections, however, Lively made claims I knew were untrue, like that babies born to one black parent and one white one were frequently feeble and sickly due to "incompatible bloodlines." As proof, the doctor offered a series of etchings of deformed sheep and goats, whose ailments he claimed were caused by crossing noncomplementary breeds.

I had seen Mama deliver two babies in Coralton with a black mother and a white father, and both were strong and healthy infants. Moreover, I knew that having two white parents was no protection against feebleness or deformity, since many children born to white families in Fairchild did not survive their first year. The more I read, the more Lively's book reminded me of the superstitions of some of the town ladies, who claimed that simply sharing a meal with a black person could give a white person the flu. I tucked *On the Heritability of Maladies* away on a back shelf, next to a book on the benefits of oat flour.

"Can we get more science books?" I asked Sister Thomas, the librarian.

She was in her forties, with a face that changed from ugly to pretty in different lights. Sister Rose didn't know why she had come to Holy Child, but had heard she was brought in handcuffs, by a sheriff.

"I built this library myself," Sister Tom told me. "It has every book the medical students in Chicago use, and more. What else do you want?"

"I need to know what causes different diseases," I said.

"Rawley's *Handbook of Flu Transmission* should be over by the window, under the death records. He's got one for rheumatic fever too."

"Not those kinds," I said. "I want to know what causes barrenness."

Sister Tom rested her elbows on her desk.

"The bookseller can get us the latest tracts on problems with the reproductive system," she said. "But they cost money."

Mama had given me twenty golden eagles when I left, but the wagon driver had taken all of it. The fee, he'd said.

"I don't have any money," I told Sister Tom.

"That's okay," she said. "You can work for it."

The library had a basement storeroom I'd never seen before, cooled by the earth around it, the small window at ground level looking out on grass and dandelion heads. Wooden boxes were stacked floor to ceiling, full of records dating back to the convent's founding and books too rare and fragile to keep on display. In the center was a desk, lit brightly by a phosphorus lantern, with an inkwell and a sheaf of papers and a hand-bound book lying open to the middle.

"The big monasteries like Saint Joseph's," she said, "they have printing presses. But when I want to make books, I have to copy them out by hand. Then the bookseller buys them from me, or we do a trade."

I shut the book to look at the cover: *On the Regulation of the Monthlies.*

"My mama taught me about this," I said. "She was—she's a midwife."

"Good," said Sister Tom. "Then you should find this interesting."

After that I spent all my free time in the storeroom, copying the book onto a stack of loose-leaf paper so thin I had to be careful not to tear it with the pen. It was three days before I realized what I was copying.

The book started innocently enough, with a chapter on cramps and irregularity. At first it made me angry to read about women whose biggest problem was a little pain a few days out of the month, but copying down the names of familiar herbs soothed me. The second chapter was about remedies for hot flashes and melancholy during menopause. But the third one was called "Remedies for a Late Period," and I didn't have to read long before I knew what I was looking at.

I was twelve when Susan Mill came to see Mama. I'd seen scared girls before—girls with sores between their legs, pregnant girls bleeding, girls with black eyes and bruises on their arms. But Susan—funny Susan, usually chatty, just that year old enough to court—she scared me. She looked like a ghost in our house, walking so softly her feet made no sound, her eyes focused on nothing.

"I'm a month late," she said. "Can you help me bring down my period?"

I didn't know what she meant then but Mama did. She said, "Are you sure, Susan? If it's money you need—"

"I don't need money," Susan said.

"If it's a married man, it's all right, you know. His wife might be mad, but now that you're pregnant, everyone will support you. He'll have to take you into his house, if that's what you want. You have the power now."

Then Susan gave Mama a look I'll never forget, a look of total contempt.

"If you can't help me, Mrs. Magnusson," she said, "just say so."

I expected Mama to get mad—she never liked people mouthing off to her—but instead she just nodded once and said, "Remember this, because I'm not going to write it down."

Then she explained how to get to a hairdresser's in Oxford, and told Susan to ask for a woman named Saphronia there, and to bring fifty golden eagles, which was five times what Mama got paid for a birth.

Afterward, when I asked what Susan was going to do, Mama explained that despite what we'd been taught in school, there was a way to end a pregnancy, but it was dangerous, because anyone who did it or had it done could go to jail, or worse. And so when someone wanted to do it, it usually meant something very, very bad had happened to her.

"What happened to Susan?" I asked.

Mama said she didn't know yet, but for the next three days I saw her whispering with her friends from town, Mrs. Olsen and Mrs. White and Mrs. Barrow, and when Susan came back from Oxford, Mama helped her meet a man who was a miner, and that man married her and took her out to silver country with him, and she never came back to Fairchild as long as I lived there. And whenever people said what a shame it was that the Mills didn't get to see their only daughter anymore, Mama's eyes went ice-cold.

"I know what your book is about," I told Sister Tom. She was reshelving the biographies of the saints. Sister Clementine always got them out of order.

"And?"

I wasn't sure if I should be afraid of Sister Tom. It was possible she was trying to trap me somehow, get me in trouble with the Mother. My position at Holy Child was still uncertain—before I took my vows, I knew the Mother could simply kick me out if she wanted to, and then I'd have nowhere to go. So I gave what I thought was the safest answer I could.

"Does the Mother know?" I asked.

Sister Tom just smiled—not a cruel smile, but not one I could understand.

"You'd be surprised what the Mother knows," she said.

That didn't do me much good.

"I don't want to get sent away," I said.

She motioned for me to sit. It was almost time for vespers. The library was empty except for us and the light in the windows was low. A few strands of Sister Tom's hair had escaped from her headscarf. They were the color of wheat.

"Do you know why I came here?" she asked.

I shook my head.

"I was learning from my mama, just like you," she said. "But my mama was the opposite of yours. Girls and women came to her when they were in trouble, and she gave them abortions."

I nodded like I wasn't surprised, but I was. I had thought everyone at the convent was barren, like me. And when I imagined Saphronia, the woman Susan had gone to in Oxford, I had imagined an old witch like in the picture book I used to scare Janie and Jessamine on October nights, with long fingernails and snaggleteeth. But of course an abortionist could be a woman like Mama, could have a child of her own.

"The sheriff made me watch when they hanged my mama," Sister Thomas said. "All the girls in town had to watch. My mama was an example of what happens when you leave the path of baby Jesus and Mother Mary."

Her voice was so cold it chilled my blood, so bitter I could taste it.

"But the sheriff gave me a choice," she said. "The convent or the jail. He didn't care which one I chose. Either way, no man would ever marry me, I would have no child. I would never go among ordinary people as long as I lived."

Sister Tom smiled then. "This is jail," she said. "You don't have to worry anymore. You're already here."

I could've refused, of course. I could've told Sister Tom to find someone else, and spent my free hours with Sister Rose, working my way through *An Unmarried Woman's Book of Daily Prayers*. But

I was curious—I wanted to know what the woman in Oxford knew that was so secret and dangerous Mama couldn't even talk about it. And so I began my criminal career there in the house of God, with a leaky pen instead of a pistol and books instead of silver for my reward.

In Sister Tom's book I read about a woman in Rapid City who was courted by a man she did not want to marry, who forced himself on her and made her pregnant; she drank black root and miscarried at thirteen weeks, and went on to have two healthy boys with another man. I read about a woman sick with sugar-in-the-blood, whose midwife said a baby would surely kill her; she took a mix of tansy oil and clarified butter, and she miscarried, and she lived. I read about a woman whose father made her pregnant, and I understood why Susan Mill had looked at Mama the way she had, and why she had gone away.

I read, too, about a woman who drank lye to end her pregnancy and died. I read about a woman who drank turpentine to end her pregnancy and died. I read about a woman who could find no one to help her, though she went to three different towns and inquired with seven midwives, an herbalist, and even a dentist, and so she tried to end her pregnancy herself with a knitting needle, and hemorrhaged, and died. I had not thought I could ever feel lucky again, but sitting safe in the storeroom as I read about how that woman bled all day long and into the night, I did.

When I had copied a full book, Sister Tom traded it to the bookseller who drove his wagon up and down the road between Denver and Chicago for *On the Causes and Treatment of Female Disorders*, by Father Boniface Malvey, who was a priest and a doctor. Sister Tom let me cut the pages myself; my heart was in my throat as I opened the cover.

But quickly Father Malvey began to disappoint me. He said the proper cure for uterine fibroids was to drink a solution of one part water and one part bacon grease, which I knew was no cure for anything. He said going outside on a full moon night could cause a pregnant woman to give birth early, which even the old wives in Fairchild knew was just a silly superstition. And when it came to barrenness, he listed the following possible causes: frigid or irresponsible mother, wearing boys' clothes at a young age, too many spicy or bitter foods, idleness, and excessive focus on unwomanly pursuits like bookkeeping.

"I knew of a girl who, because her father was a ne'er-do-well and a drinker, was forced to keep all the records for her family's farm," Father Malvey wrote. "She was unable to conceive a child until her father was prevailed upon to assume his responsibilities, whereupon she fell pregnant and was soon the happy mother of twins."

"I don't think Father Malvey knows what he's talking about," I told Sister Tom.

"The bookseller told me he's the best there is," said Sister Tom. "The medical school in Chicago just bought five copies."

"What luck for the bookseller," I said, "and for Father Malvey."

Sister Tom gave me a half-smile.

"I think I need something by a master midwife," I said. "Someone who's delivered babies."

"I'll see what I can do," said Sister Tom. "But if the bookseller has to hunt it down, it'll cost extra."

It took me three weeks to copy enough books to earn Mrs. Alice Schaeffer's *Handbook of Feminine Complaints*, and another six for the bookseller to bring it to me on his way back from Denver. Spring turned to summer at Holy Child. On Sundays we had services outside in the meadow so we could see the fertility of the earth, and afterward the Mother let us gather geraniums and black-eyed Susans and put them in pitchers and drinking glasses all around the dining room, and that small brightness made us giddy with joy, giggling into our nighttime tea at jokes that would have been nonsense to my friends back home, about Sister Martha's clumsy catechism, the time she guessed that Saint Ignatius was the patron saint of weasels. All the while my mind moved along two tracks. I came to feel at peace in the convent; I no longer woke each morning expecting to see my sister still asleep in the next bed, and I no longer cried when I milked the cows. I looked forward to taking my vows in September and changing my gray shift for a black robe. But I felt a lack in my head and heart, which I understood that Sister Clementine and some of the other devout sisters filled with baby Jesus, but which no story could fill for me, especially not one in which I could play no part, I who could neither carry a child nor, locked away in the convent, even do what my mama had trained me to do and help bring children into the world. Instead I thought about what I might learn from Mrs. Schaeffer.

Of course a part of me thought maybe Mrs. Schaeffer had a cure for barrenness. I imagined gathering herbs and barks from the woods near Holy Child and steeping them in alcohol like Mama used to when she needed something the herbalist didn't have. But how would I know a cure had worked? I would have to find a man again and be with him at the right time for several months, and if nothing happened I wouldn't know if the problem was the tincture or him or me. And even if I was cured, if I conceived and bore a child, would I want to return to my old life? Would I go back to Fairchild with my baby on my hip, triumphant? I could imagine just how my mother would look if I brought a grandchild home to her—the shock and confusion that would play across her face before she let delight break through. It made my chest hurt to think of it. But when the surprise wore off, when the sheriff and Ulla had asked for my forgiveness and my husband had begged me to take him back (probably I would refuse him, though some nights I wavered in my certainty on this point), and I was living a comfortable life as a wife and mother, I did not think I would be satisfied.

I wanted to understand what barrenness was—how a child was conceived inside a woman and what it was, inside or out, that got in the way. Then I could feel the quiet that only comes with knowing what you need to know. And I could teach other people what I knew. I remembered what Mama had said, that you couldn't just take away something people believed in. You had to give them something in its place.

I knew I liked Mrs. Schaeffer as soon as I read her section on miscarriage. "Some say a woman can cause a miscarriage by going to bed with a man who is not her husband," she wrote. "This is nonsense. It matters not at all to the baby whom his mother takes to bed, though it may matter a great deal to her."

From Mrs. Schaeffer I learned that severe cramps could be caused by the blood-rich tissue of the womb growing elsewhere in the body, and that ground flaxseeds added to cereal or coffee could help if taken regularly. I learned that a woman who has cancer of the breast should not eat flaxseeds or soybeans or alfalfa sprouts, and that the best treatment was to remove both breasts at once, not simply to remove the lump the way Dr. Carlisle back in Fairchild had done for Mrs. MacLeish, who died the following summer. I learned that if a woman's labor does not progress, and she or her baby is in danger, then it is possible to cut open the womb with a very sharp knife, lift the baby out, and sew the mother back up, and that Mrs. Schaeffer had performed seventeen such surgeries successfully in the course of her career. When I got to the section on barrenness, my heart began to race.

"Failure to conceive a child is more common than most people believe," she wrote.

I myself have seen more than a dozen women with this condition. Many people believe it has supernatural causes, which explains why so many childless women have been imprisoned or hanged for witchcraft, even today when the populace fancies itself educated and modern. I believe the complaint has many causes, all of them natural. Girls who are undernourished routinely lose their monthlies and thus cannot carry children; proper diet will nearly always remedy the problem. Other cases are more complicated. At our surgery in Pagosa Springs we once saw a woman of twenty-one who had been unable to conceive a child after five years of marriage. Though healthy and well-nourished, she had never begun her monthlies, and examination showed unusual formation of the vagina. We have also seen five women who seemed to have no physical complaints themselves, but whose husbands had suffered from mumps or rheumatic fever in boyhood. Three of these women went on to have children by other men, suggesting that fevers in early life may cause a kind of barrenness in men. Unfortunately it has been difficult to test this theory since no man has yet made himself available to us for examination.

In most cases of failure to conceive, however, we have found nothing unusual either in the woman's medical history or in that of her husband. We are continuing to study this complaint and hope to include our discoveries in future handbooks. We invite any woman or man who has failed to conceive a child after a period of one year or more to visit our surgery for examination.

I dropped the book on Sister Tom's desk.
"Where is Pagosa Springs?" I asked.

"Out west, in the mountains near Ute country," she said. "Why?"

I sat in the chair in front of her. I looked behind me before I spoke. I knew the sisters gossiped, because I knew who smoked cigarettes and who kept a secret stash of communion wine. But I didn't know anyone who wanted what I wanted.

"Could the bookseller take me there?" I asked. "I'd pay him. I'd copy as many books as he wanted."

Sister Tom smiled, but shook her head.

"There's not enough money in the world to make that worth his while," she said. "What if someone finds out where you came from? Everybody knows why girls go to convents, Ada. That's why they don't usually come out."

"So there's no way," I said.

"I didn't say that," she said. "The bookseller can't help you. I can't help you. But the Mother might help you, if she wants to."

Just that week the Mother had scolded me for bringing in the milk in two small buckets instead of one large one.

"You're always trying to be different," she'd said. "Now Sister Mary Grace has more buckets to wash."

"I don't think the Mother wants to help me," I told Sister Tom.

She just shrugged. "You don't know until you ask."

The Mother's cell looked like the one I shared with Sister Rose: the bed in the corner, neatly made; the crèche above it carved from rough wood, Mary and Joseph little more than curved shapes around the infant Jesus; a small window looking out on the cow pasture. The only difference was the desk where now she sat, the hard chair in front of it for me, and, on the wall opposite the crèche, a painting of Saint Joan of Arc in her armor, kneeling in prayer. This was unusual; some of the older sisters had devotional paintings on their walls, but generally they showed Saint Monica or someone else from the list of mother-saints I'd had to memorize in catechism. The only reason I even recognized Saint Joan was because of Mrs. Covell back home in Fairchild. Her people were Quebecois traders, and she taught us about Saint Joan who died for her God when she was almost as young as us. Later I heard that some parents complained, and Janie and Jessamine never learned about Saint Joan.

"That's a beautiful painting," I said to the Mother.

"Saint Joan wasn't beautiful," she said. "What do you want, Ada? I know you wouldn't visit me just to talk."

All my time in the convent I had done nothing but obey. I had read the Bible and learned dozens of verses by heart, including Proverbs 31, even though I could not become a wife of noble character or any other character. Every day I got up before sunrise to milk the cows; at matins, lauds, and vespers I bowed my head in prayer. I kept my cell neat and my shift spotless. I wanted to tell the Mother I was sure it was a sin to hate someone for no reason.

Instead I said, "I've been doing some studying."

She raised her eyebrows. "So I hear."

"I've been reading a book by a master midwife who's been researching my condition," I went on. "The thing is, she lives in Pagosa Springs."

"And?"

I forced myself to look her right in the eye.

"I'd like to go there, Mother," I said.

"Why?" she asked.

"I want to find out why I'm barren," I said.

"You mean you want to find a cure," she said.

"No," I said. "At least, not for me. I just want to understand."

"That's very noble," she said. "Have you considered that it might be a better use of the talents baby Jesus gave you to understand the scriptures instead?"

"Mother," I said, "I saw a woman hanged for being barren. If I'd stayed at my family's house, I would've been hanged. Imagine if people understood barrenness, even a little. Think how many women could live."

The Mother took her glasses off. Her eyes were smaller without them; her face looked older and softer. She rubbed the bridge of her nose.

"When I entered the sisterhood," she said, "I was going to start a school. The sisters were going to be the teachers, so boys and girls would learn reading and writing and catechism from barren women. I thought if we became schoolteachers, the children would learn not to fear us, and then when they were grown and became sheriffs and mayors and mothers, more of us would be safe."

"Did it work?" I asked.

The Mother raised an eyebrow.

"Do you see any children here?"

It was hard to imagine—girls laughing in the silent halls, boys playing sheriffs and outlaws in the meadow. Holy Child a part of the world, not hidden away from it.

"Three boys and four girls came to study with us," she said. "They were all from poor farming families far out in high country. Most of them had never been to school. One girl was thirteen and didn't know how to read.

"Three months we taught them, from the end of the harvest until the snow came. Even in that time they learned so much, they were hungry for it. That girl could read the twenty-third psalm.

"One day early in the new year the sheriff came up from Laramie with three deputies. We were in the middle of catechism. It was just three of us then: me, Sister Dolores, and Sister

Carmen—you never knew her. They put us in handcuffs in front of the children. They said we were not women, we were witches sent by the Devil to corrupt their minds. I saw how quickly the children believed them. As they led us away that thirteen-year-old girl spit in my face."

The Mother in handcuffs—I could barely imagine it.

"Did you go to jail?" I asked.

"We were there five years," she said. "Sister Carmen got tuberculosis and died there. After that they let me and Sister Dolores go. When we came back to Holy Child someone had smeared shit all over the walls. It took us days to clean it. Do you understand what I'm telling you?"

"I'm sorry," I said. "I'm not sure I do."

"Knowledge can be very valuable," she said, "but only if people want it. If they don't, it can be worse than useless."

"I understand," I said, even though I didn't.

She waved her hand to shut me up.

"You have a choice," she said. "You can stay here and try to lead a godly life, or you can go up to the high country, to Hole in the Wall."

I thought of the stories I'd heard about the Hole in the Wall Gang, outlaws who robbed banks and wagons all around the territories.

"What do you mean?" I asked. "How could I go to Hole in the Wall?"

"Soon after we got back to Holy Child, a young man came to us, maybe twenty years old. He asked for sanctuary. We didn't know what to call him—he refused to accept a Christian name or tell us his given one—so we hit upon the Kid."

I remembered Sheriff Branch's stories about the Kid, a man tall as a pine tree and as strong as a grizzly bear, who once shot a deputy's hat off his head while riding backward on his horse.

"Did he rob you?" I asked.

The Mother looked annoyed.

"Why would he rob us? We had nothing of value except food and shelter, which we gave him freely. He stayed with us a few months, then he went on his way. But we haven't forgotten him, or he us. Every now and again I send someone out to Hole in the Wall. You're young and healthy and stubborn—they might take you."

I was not sure what the Hole in the Wall Gang would want with a young girl, but none of my guesses were pleasant ones.

"I mean no disrespect, Mother, but I can't be a proper wife to any man, even an outlaw."

The Mother smiled a little then.

"You wouldn't be a wife, Sister Ada. You'd be an outlaw too."

She stood up then, so I stood up with her.

"It sounds like you've already been doing some business with the bookseller," she said. "He can take you up there if that's what you decide. I hear his rates are reasonable."

"Thank you," I said, not knowing what else to say.

"Don't thank me," she said. "I'm not doing you a favor. And remember, before you go: You may not like this place, but you're safe here. If you go up to Hole in the Wall, you won't be safe anymore. And other people won't be safe from you."

I smiled. "I don't think I'm much of a threat," I said.

"Take your prayer book with you," she said. "I'd like to feel we taught you something."

CHAPTER 3

I rode to Hole in the Wall with two hundred copies of *A Young Bride's Tale* by Mrs. Eglantine Cooper (a woman's new husband turns out to have five brothers, each more strapping and depraved than the last; many acts depicted were anatomically improbable or even impossible but I read it very quickly), one hundred copies of *A Season in the Rocky Mountains* by Geoffrey Cragg (boring, except for the chapter about killing and eating a marmot), assorted less prominent works of fiction and nonfiction, and fifty-nine copies of *On the Regulation of the Monthlies*, all of which I'd copied myself. In my satchel I had a copy of Mrs. Schaeffer's *Handbook of Feminine Complaints*, which Sister Tom had let me take and which I held close to me, the way Bee used to hold a doll that Mama had stuffed with dried lavender and pine needles to give it a calming smell.

Three nights I slept hidden among the books while the book-seller drank beer and ate potpie at roadhouses. On the morning of the fourth day he woke me from a dream in which I still lived with my husband, who had locked me in the henhouse until I gave him a child. All around me the hens were clucking and fighting, pecking each other to pieces. One hen was pecked almost clean.

"You know a Sheriff Branch?" the bookseller was asking me. The name frightened me fully awake.

"Why?" I asked.

"Somebody in there at Albertine's said there's a Sheriff Branch from Fairchild offering three hundred golden eagles for the capture of a witch. Said she goes by Ada. Isn't your name Ada?"

I tried to think quickly.

"I'm from Spearfish," I said. "And Ada's not my birth name, it's my convent name. For Saint Ada, the patron saint of midwives."

I had no idea if Saint Ada existed, and hoped the bookseller didn't either. He had a slender, nervous face, and he was looking at me with a new scrutiny, his eyes narrowed.

"If I was running from a sheriff, I might go to a convent," he said. "Or I might go to Hole in the Wall."

I had no money to offer the bookseller, certainly not three hundred eagles.

"I told you, I don't know any Sheriff Branch," I said, buying time.

All I knew about the bookseller was that he bought Sister Tom's books, and that not very many people owned books like *On the Regulation of the Monthlies*, much less were willing to copy them. Such books, I realized, might be valuable—perhaps worth far more than what Sister Tom was getting for them.

"Listen," I said, "say I am the witch he's looking for. Say you manage to find Sheriff Branch, and you turn me over to him. That's ten gold pieces you just made. But do you think Sister Tom's going to be happy when she finds out she paid you to take me someplace, and you sold me instead? There are other booksellers, you know. She can find another buyer for what she's selling, maybe at a better rate. Can you find someone else to make what you need?"

I tried not to show my fear as he considered. I thought about whether I could hurt him if he tried to grab me, gouge out his eyes or knee him between the legs and make an escape. But then where would I go?

"Get back behind the *Bride's Tales*," he said finally. "We've got a lot of ground to cover today."

All that day I crouched in the wagon worrying. On the one hand, if Sheriff Branch was looking for me, maybe that meant I still had the town's attention, and my neighbors had not yet transferred their anger over to my mother and sisters. But on the other, if the sheriff was searching this far afield—farther from home than I or my sisters or any of my friends had ever been—then he might not stop until he found me. Even Hole in the Wall might not be far enough away.

Toward nightfall, I heard wooden slats beneath the horse's hooves, and peeked out the back of the wagon to see that we were crossing a wide, calm river. Past the far bank—powdery gravel that crunched as we passed—the land began to climb. Red rocks jumped out of the prairie at strange angles, and large birds wheeled between the hills, dark above, light below, and songless. The road grew narrow and poorly kept, and for hours the wagon shuddered over rock and scrub in land so wild I saw not even a fence post to mark a man's claim to it. Finally we stopped, and the bookseller turned in his seat and said, "This is where we part company."

I looked out. Behind the wagon was all darkness, the only light coming from a cat's claw moon.

"We're in the middle of nowhere," I said.

"They don't allow me to approach their camp," the bookseller said. "Usually they send a scout up to the road to meet me. Tonight they didn't. You'll have to find your way down there on your own."

"How do I even know which way to go?" I asked.

"Well, it's not that way," he said, pointing back to the road behind us. "So it's probably that way."

He let me take two strips of pronghorn jerky and a handful of dried buffalo berries.

"Baby Jesus keep you," he said, not unkindly, and then I was walking in the blackness.

After a while my eyes adjusted, and I saw that to my left the roadside fell away into a silkier, deeper black, a valley whose depth I couldn't measure. I kept close to the right, on the rocky margin where the road met the hill. I heard the hoofbeats of the bookseller's horse in the distance, then nothing but the sawing of summer locusts and the pounding of my own blood in my ears.

The road seemed to wind down toward the valley floor, and after a while the hillside gave way to flatter land. I felt a chill in the air and a change in the shape of the darkness; I saw the stars reflected in the still surface of a pond. I had not had a drink of water since the bookseller had come back from the roadhouse that morning. I knelt with cupped hands. The pond tasted like dirt but I drank deep. I sat on the soft ground by the water's edge and ate the berries and one of the strips of jerky. A frog hopped away from me, its croak like a plucked string. Then I heard the rustling of something much larger in the tall grass, something that scared more frogs into the water and sent a duck flapping and quacking into the air.

Mama always said wild animals were afraid of human voices, so I shouted and waved my arms. But in town the only wild animals were black bears and the occasional coyote—out here could be grizzlies and wolves and mountain lions. I had been walking for what felt like hours and I had seen no sign so far of any human life. I began to wonder if the bookseller had lied to me, if it had always been his plan to collect my books, drop me off in the middle of nowhere, and move on.

"Hello?" I called.

Nothing but a scuffling in the scrub near the road, more night animals fleeing or approaching. I began to run. I called and ran and ran and called until my throat was hoarse and my legs were spent. Then I knelt on the road—by now a horse track just wide enough for my two knees together—and gasped and ate the second piece of dry jerky, and ran and called some more.

My throat was scraped raw and my whole body aching when, out in the black to the left of the road, I heard someone playing a fiddle. The music was lively and dreamy at the same time, a tune I'd never heard but that reminded me of stories Mama told us when we were very little, about pirate ships in the time before America, about elves and goblins meeting at midnight in the woods. I was afraid my senses might have left me and I might be dreaming or imagining the sound, but with nothing else to guide me I had no choice but to follow the song.

I scrambled down a steep hill and through thick brush that scratched my legs, but the fiddle grew louder, and soon I saw a flicker of firelight in the distance and even heard voices shouting and laughing. A few minutes more and I saw the fire, tall as a man and wide as a wagon, and the fiddler, standing in its light, eyes shut and face upturned as though in prayer, bow hand moving furiously. The fiddler was black-haired and brown-skinned, and garlanded head to toe with wildflowers, black-eyed Susans and bluets and sweet William. I took a few steps nearer, not sure how or if I should announce myself, and against a tree not ten yards from my shoulder I saw two people kissing and touching each other with a hunger I remembered only dimly from the early days of my marriage. The woman was short and wide-hipped, with thick dark hair and a crown made of flowers. Her lover was tall and slim and pale, his fingers in her hair almost delicate in their movements.

I ducked behind a tree; I knew enough not to surprise a pair of kissing strangers in a place I'd never been. Peeking out around the trunk, I could see the shadows of dancers cast giant-size by the firelight on the ground below, and then the dancers themselves: a tall man in a buckskin jacket trimmed with bells, and a woman in a calico dress with her hair in two neat braids. The woman, in particular, was a masterful dancer, leaping and twirling in her partner's arms and then, when he released her, turning a series of backflips that had even the lovers turning around to cheer. When she finished her acrobatic routine she landed as easily on both feet as though she'd been playing hopscotch, her face in the light of the bonfire both serious and full of joy.

Finally, sitting in a wooden rocking chair at the edge of the firelight, I saw a handsome, dark-skinned person dressed in a top hat and tails like the mayor of Fairchild wore on festival days. Flowing around this person's shoulders and down onto the ground below was a cape made entirely of flowers, yellow and orange and blue and purple, so large and complex that it must have taken many days and many hands to stitch it all together.

The person was drinking from a champagne glass, and when the dancer with the bells approached to refill it, and both leaned a little into the firelight as he poured, I saw that the person's hat was a Colorado pinch-front like the one the Kid was said to wear. The person took a sip, laughed at something the dancer with the bells said, and gave a theatrical roll of the eyes. Was this the Kid, and these people his gang? Or had I stumbled upon some other group celebrating in Hole in the Wall territory? I was planning how to approach to resolve these questions when someone grabbed me by the wrist and dragged me into the firelight.

"Look at this," she shouted, a redheaded woman with a brightly made-up face and the low-necked, full-skirted dress of a showgirl. "I've captured an infiltrator!"

The fiddler stopped. The dancers stared. The couple turned from each other's faces to look at me.

"I'm not an infiltrator," I said. "My name is Ada. I come from the Sisters of the Holy Child. The Mother Superior sent me. She said—"

The person in the cape set the champagne glass down in the dirt. "Agnes Rose, be neighborly. I've been expecting this young lady a long time." The person stood and extended an elegant, long-fingered hand.

"Sister Ada, welcome to Hole in the Wall."

"Are you the Kid?" I asked.

The person laughed, a full and mellifluous sound.

"I have gone by many names," the person said, "but that is the one by which, today, I am most commonly known."

"And the others?" I asked. In the stories I'd heard, the Kid rode with a gang of at least a dozen strong men—hardened outlaws, the reward for whose capture was five hundred gold eagles each.

"We are as you see us," said the Kid, arms spreading wide, "in all our glory."

"Who is this?" asked one of the lovers, the woman with the flower crown. "You didn't tell us anything about a new recruit."

"That's because she's not a new recruit yet," the Kid said. "I told the Mother we'd receive her as a guest, and consider whether to keep her on."

"And you didn't think maybe you should tell the rest of us?" she asked. "If we do keep her, that's one more mouth to feed, and one more person riding around the territories on our horses, getting spotted by ranchers and lawmen and who knows who else. And that's if she's trustworthy. How do you know she's not one of Sheriff Dempsey's people? After what you pulled last month, he's sure to have bounty hunters on us."

"I like the look of her," said Agnes Rose, the one who had dragged me out of the dark. "I could teach her a thing or two. You ever play cards, convent girl?"

"I'm not teaching her how to ride," said the acrobat. "It took me three months to teach Aggie and she's still terrible. I'm not going through that again."

The Kid stood, flower cape swirling in the night breeze.

"Cassie, Lo, my comrades, my friends," the Kid said, "do you remember what Christ says in Luke about judgment?"

"It's not Sunday, Kid," said the woman with the flower crown. But the others had gone still and silent, as though on command, though no such command had been uttered.

"'Judge not,'" the Kid went on, "'and ye shall not be judged. Condemn not, and ye shall not be condemned. Forgive, and ye shall be forgiven.'"

Though high, the Kid's voice was rich, loud, and soaring, fit for a great cathedral. The woman with the flower crown looked on in frustration.

"'Give, and it shall be given unto you,'" the Kid said, "'good measure, pressed down, and shaken together, and running over, shall men give into your bosom. For with the same measure that ye mete withal it shall be measured to you again.'"

The Kid turned to the woman with the flower crown. "Whenever we've had a new mouth to feed, haven't we found the means to do so? And haven't we always gained more than we laid out? Look around, Cassie," the Kid said, gesturing at the champagne glasses and flowers. "Good measure, wouldn't you say?"

"We've had a run of luck," said Cassie. "But if we keep growing—"

The Kid went to Cassie and lifted her up by both hands, danced her around the fire.

"If, if, if," the Kid said, one arm around Cassie's back, the other leading her by the left hand. " 'Sufficient unto the day is the evil thereof,' Cassie. 'Take therefore no thought for the morrow' "—the Kid dipped Cassie low and her flower crown slid into the dirt— " 'for the morrow shall take thought for the things of itself.' "

The Kid released Cassie, bent to retrieve the crown, dusted it off, and replaced it on her head.

"You're right, of course," the Kid said. "You're always right. We must be judicious in our growth, we must be cautious in our charity. Tomorrow we'll decide what to do with Sister Ada here, whether to make her one of us or send her back out from whence she came. But tonight—surely tonight we can spare a little champagne for our guest."

Cassie looked at the Kid with a helpless expression— exasperated, affectionate, resigned. She rose, disappeared into the dark, and returned with a bottle and a glass.

Mama had always told me never to drink anything offered to me by a stranger, but I was thirsty and exhausted and confused and I took the glass and drank. I'd had champagne only once before, on my wedding day, and this was different—sweeter, spicier, with a strong poisonous scent like paint thinner. I drained the glass and Agnes Rose cheered. She took the bottle from Cassie and refilled my glass. The others seemed, if not to accept, then at least to ignore my presence. The fiddler began to play again, slower this time, and the dancer with the bells began to sing in a rich contralto, very beautiful, with humor and sorrow in it.

> *O Mistress mine, where are you roaming?*
> *O stay and hear, your true love's coming,*
> *That can sing both high and low.*
> *Trip no further pretty sweeting.*
> *Journeys end in lovers' meeting,*
> *Every wise man's son doth know.*

That's the last thing I remember clearly from that night: the dancer's mournful, beguiling voice, the bells on that jacket glinting in the firelight.

When I woke, the sun was already high in the sky. I was lying on top of a bandanna quilt below a sloped ceiling of knotty pine; reaching up, I could brush it at its lowest point with my fingers. As I gathered my wits, I saw I was on a kind of lofted sleeping porch, so narrow that if I rolled to one side I would plunge down into the great room below. Wooden beds lined the porch, some made up and some disheveled; below in the great room were more beds and a cast-iron stove and a long couch over which was draped the Kid's flower cape, its colors beginning to fade. Heavy-shuttered windows on the ground floor let in the late-morning light. Both porch and great room were deserted.

I was barefoot, I discovered, and the sturdy clogs I'd been wearing were nowhere to be seen. I had no choice but to walk shoeless down the creaking staircase and out to the firepit, where the company had gathered as on the night before, but altogether more subdued.

No one was wearing flowers anymore. The acrobat with the braids had on a simple dress of brown muslin picked out with white dots; Agnes Rose wore a high-necked frock of sky-blue cotton. The lovers, the fiddler, and the dancer with the beautiful voice were dressed in men's dungarees and work shirts, and the Kid had traded tails for a wool suit in a slim cut, its jet black clouded only slightly at the hem of the pants with red dust. All sat around a fire much reduced from its stature the night before, a small, tame blaze for heat, not light.

"Sit," said the Kid. "Cassie, give Sister Ada some breakfast."

Cassie stood reluctantly, went into a smaller cabin next to the bunkhouse I'd just exited, and came back out with a cracked blue china bowl of porridge. It was salty and savory, flavored with bacon fat, and I ate it hungrily, until I noticed that everyone around me was staring. I looked around the circle. It was clear to me now that the dancer with the beautiful voice was a woman: she was tall as a man, with broad shoulders, but I saw the curve of breasts beneath her cotton shirt, and she had a fluid, graceful way of moving that reminded me of some of the older girls back home, the ones who had already had one or two children and seemed more at home in their bodies than I would ever be. Looking at some of the others, I was not as sure. Whispering something to Agnes Rose, the fiddler looked one moment like a roguish young man, the next like a gossiping girl. And I saw now that the person I'd taken for Cassie's beau wore a diamond earring in each ear.

"Thank you again—" I began, hoping to give an accounting of myself, but the Kid cut me off.

"Can you shoot?"

"I can clean and load and unload a rifle," I said.

"So no. Can you ride?"

"I used to ride my neighbor's pony sometimes."

"No again. What can you do, little Sister?"

I began to grow nervous.

"I can milk a cow," I said. "I can make soft cheese and I'm learning to make hard cheese."

"We don't have cows here," Cassie said.

Until now, I had not thought of the possibility that the gang might turn me away. If they did, I knew I'd never find the bookseller again. Sheriff Branch was looking for me. And even if I hadn't had a price on my head, a woman traveling alone makes everyone suspicious. I couldn't pass near a town without attracting the attention of the sheriff or, worse, a gang of young men out looking for trouble. Once Lucas Saint Joseph and the two younger Petersen boys had come upon a woman on the Buffalo Gap Road, and even though she told them she was running from her husband who beat her, even though she showed them the bruises on the sides of her neck, the boys raped her one by one to break her of her witchcraft. They would have gone free, too—the mayor was on their side—except she had people in Fairchild who vouched she was a mother of three back in Buffalo Gap, and pledged to take her in and find her a better husband. I was many days' ride from home now, with no one to vouch for me. I had to think of what would make me worth feeding and protecting.

"My mama is a midwife," I said.

"What luck," said Cassie. "We'll be sure to call you when we want to deliver a baby."

In the convent they had tried to teach me humility. Sister Dolores told us worldly knowledge and accomplishments are nothing to baby Jesus; they are like a cloth that falls away, leaving us naked as infants before him. But she also said baby Jesus would use us to do good in the world, and I didn't understand how He could use us if our knowledge didn't matter to Him, if we were nothing more than defenseless babies in His eyes. And so when the sisters asked us to pray for humility, to ask forgiveness for our pride and self-love, I said my own prayers to remind myself who I was and where I came from, so I would remember even if I pretended to forget, even if I took the vows and habit and lived my life under another name.

"I can set a bone," I said to the Kid. "I can bind a wound. If you get a chill, I know the herbs to warm you, and if you get a fever, I know the herbs to cool you down. I can stitch a cut, I can drain a boil, I can dress a burn so the skin heals clean. I can grind a medicine to put a man to sleep, and if I grind enough, I can make him sleep forever."

The strangers were quiet. The Kid looked at me for a minute, like measuring, then smiled.

"Texas, find the good doctor a horse she can handle."

And that's how I joined the Hole in the Wall Gang, in 1894 when I was eighteen years old.

At first it seemed like I might make a decent outlaw. Texas made me clean the stables and wash and brush all the horses before she would teach me to ride, and even then she was surly and expected me to be terrible, but we were both surprised at how good I was with the horses. They weren't so different from children, I realized, and I'd spent years convincing children to trust me enough that I could take their temperature or remove their splinters or lead them away from the room where their mother lay laboring.

Soon I learned the horses' names and their idiosyncrasies, the way they liked to be brushed and talked to and fed. Prudence, a black mare with a white blaze across her forehead and snout, was strong-willed and stubborn. Temperance, a bay, was sweet but flighty, afraid of loud noises and sudden moves. Charity, a sorrel, was sociable but could be jealous, grumbling in her stall when we tended to the others instead of her. Faith, the horse Texas rode most often, was small and brown-haired like her, but boisterous where Texas was quiet. Every morning Faith greeted Texas with a great whinnying and shaking of her mane, at which Texas only nodded and patted her flank. But when the two went out on a ride, Texas's whole face seemed to open up, her joints to loosen, and I saw in her the same joy I'd seen when she danced with Lo at the firepit, a joy at all other times obscured by her furrowed forehead and her clipped and parsimonious speech.

One horse in particular took to me, a dappled gray mare named Amity. She was alert, always the first horse to notice when someone new came into the barn, or when a field mouse skittered across the floor. She reminded me of Bee, the way she seemed to be always watching and listening.

Within three weeks I could guide Amity through a passable walk, trot, and gallop, and Texas, though still not exactly warm toward me, was forced to admit I was a better student than Agnes Rose.

One morning she woke me when it was still dark out, and handed me a chunk of the pressed, cured meat they called pemmican.

"Come on," she said, "time for a trail ride."

Texas hadn't mentioned anything about a trail ride before, and I was nervous as I saddled Amity. I could tell she noticed—she shifted back and forth on her graceful hooves, and shied her head away when I tried to adjust her bridle. I whispered to her and stroked her neck, and eventually she let me pull the straps tight.

Out in the summer air—still morning-cool, but with the promise of heat in it—Amity seemed to calm. We rode north, down into the valley and away from the towns the bookseller had carried me through. The road narrowed to no more than a horse path, dotted everywhere with stones and punctured by prairie dog burrows. Tall grass grew on either side, obscuring the way forward, and the path kept twisting and forking and crossing over dry streambeds that looked like paths, so it was all I could do to keep Amity on track. I held her reins tightly, trying to prevent her from tripping on a rock or turning her ankle in a burrow. But she rewarded my caution with annoyance, stopping and starting and finally, at a place where the road forked and Texas guided Faith down the left-hand path, refusing to move at all.

I leaned forward and squeezed with my legs the way Texas had taught me, but Amity wouldn't budge.

"Come on," I said, then felt ridiculous.

I squeezed again. Texas and Faith were receding in the morning twilight. Behind me, I could no longer see the bunkhouse or the stables, just grass and scrub and red rocks rising in the violet sky. I started to panic. I did what Texas had told me never to do, which was to kick Amity in the sides with my heels. I didn't do it hard, but she whinnied in rage and I could feel her whole body stiffen beneath me, resisting my very presence on her back. Texas turned Faith around and began making her way back to us.

"Look at your hands," she said when she was back in earshot. "Why are you choked up on the reins so much?"

"The path doesn't look so good," I said. "I just don't want her to hurt herself."

Texas came alongside me, rolling her eyes.

"How long have you been in this valley?" she asked.

"About a month," I said, "a little less. Why?"

Amity shifted angrily from hoof to hoof. Faith switched her tail but stood obediently in place.

"I brought Amity here when she was a foal. That was four years ago. She grew up on this land. You learn it from her, not the other way around."

I loosened my grip on the reins. Texas nodded.

"Okay, Am," she said. The horse relaxed beneath me.

Texas clucked her tongue and Faith began to walk. With no prompting from me, Amity followed.

"Horses hate a know-it-all," Texas said over her shoulder.

After that I held the reins as loosely as I could, just enough to let Amity know I was paying attention, and let the horse do the rest. Texas was right; Amity easily avoided the holes and hillocks that dotted the path. What was more, she clearly knew the way, ignoring the false paths cut by rainwater and choosing without hesitation when the way forked, even when Faith was too far in the distance to easily follow.

For the next week, Texas took me on a trail ride every morning, and Amity drew a map of the valley in my mind. At the northern end, where the valley floor sloped up to meet the pass, were the horse pastures and the bunkhouse and the other buildings where the gang kept their gear. Two creeks flowed through the valley, one along its western edge and the other to the east, bending at the valley's halfway point and running westward about a mile before ending in a heart-shaped pond. Near the bend was a small cabin where Texas kept some shoeing equipment and an extra bridle and saddle; she called it the cowboy shack. Beyond the shack was a small rise overlooking a wide salt flat where we sometimes spotted a badger or coyote, and once, a family of grouse, moving fussily with their heads held high like fancy, overdressed ladies. And always, rising above it all, was something that still shows up in my dreams: a wall of bright red rock many stories high, stretching from one edge of the valley to the other.

The wall kept its own time, its own matins, lauds, and vespers. The rock rose in jagged layers, each casting shade across the one below, so that even when the valley floor was bright with morning, the wall was striped and splotched with shadow. The shadows stretched and slid as the day wore on; with each quarter hour a new section of rock blazed flame red, and another plunged into ochre darkness. In the evening, the setting sun made the stone glow a living pink as though blood coursed through it, even as the warmth and light drained away from the valley floor.

I had been studying the wall and its transformations for a few days when I asked Texas, "Where's the hole?"

Texas looked at me like the question surprised her. Then she pointed.

"See that notch?" she asked.

Wind and water had carved chutes and furrows down the height of the wall, and I could see five or ten things that might qualify as a notch.

"No," I said.

"Yes you do," said Texas. "About three o'clock, the place where the shadow is."

We were watering the horses at the bend in the creek. To the southwest, I thought I could make out a spot where two rock faces, bending backward, met each other in darkness.

"It doesn't look like much," I said. "Not to name a gang after."

Texas shook her head.

"Cassie and the Kid didn't pick this place for looks," she said. "You climb up to that notch, you can see everything and everyone for ten miles in any direction. It's the best place in all of Powder River country to defend against an attack."

"Why did they come here?" I asked.

Texas looked annoyed.

"I just told you," she said.

"No," I said. "I mean why did they start the gang? Why did they become outlaws?"

Texas took a breath.

"I don't know the whole story," she said. "What I do know is they traveled for a while as husband and wife. Then something happened, and they decided they needed somewhere safe, far away from any towns or people. So they came here. They hunted and fished for a while, but the Kid always had big plans. And big plans mean money. So they started stealing from people, and people turned into stagecoaches, and stagecoaches turned into banks. Now we spend every spring and summer robbing up and down the Powder, and then we come back here and hope nobody follows us."

The wind was picking up. I could see the shadows of clouds racing across the valley floor.

"Have you ever been attacked?" I asked.

"Not yet," said Texas.

She looked up at the sky.

"We should get going," she said. "It's going to storm."

Once I had become a passable rider, it was time for me to learn to shoot. Elzy, whose tall form I remembered embracing Cassie against the tree the night I arrived, was the gang's best sharp-shooter, so the Kid assigned her to be my teacher. At first she was kind, if unconventional.

"Look, this is easy," she said. "I'll show you."

We practiced in the tiny orchard behind the bunkhouse, planted by some optimistic farmer in the days before the Flu. On a stump in the middle of the orchard she placed two rock-hard pears from a tree nearby. She stepped back about thirty paces, then lifted her revolver—so sleek and handsome compared to Mama's old shotgun—cocked it, and fired. The pear on the left exploded. It did look easy. It looked so easy anyone could do it.

Elzy showed me how to cock the gun. She showed me how to hold it and how to use the sights.

"Whenever you're ready, just pull the trigger," she said.

I had never longed to hold a revolver, never argued about Colts and Eagletons like the boys in school, or made my fingers into a gun to shoot noises at my friends. But now, the gun smooth and heavy in my grip, I felt like Justice herself, the blindfolded woman who stood cast in bronze outside the courthouse in Fairchild. I would not sentence barren women to die like Judge Hammond, whose mind was addled by drink and age and who did whatever the mayor and the sheriff told him to do. My gun would protect the innocent. I would be dangerous only to the wicked.

At first I thought I might have fired from an empty chamber. I pressed the trigger and a sound came out and then nothing, the pear and the stump unscathed, a few birds complaining in the summer air.

"Okay," Elzy said, "let's try a little closer."

I couldn't hit the pear at twenty paces, or at fifteen, and at ten Elzy began rolling her eyes and looking up at the bright blue sky like she was praying to baby Jesus to make me less useless. When I finally hit it—the bullet blowing the stem and neck off the pear, leaving an apple shape behind—I turned grinning to Elzy to receive her approval.

"The pear could grab that gun out of your hand from here," she said. "Now try farther back."

But all that day and the next I could only hit the stump from ten paces—even eleven threw my aim wild and I peppered the ground with bullets. On the third day Elzy showed me how to load and unload the gun, then gave me a box of bullets.

"Shoot until you finish these," she said. "Then I'll give you more."

Three days later I could hit the pear at eleven paces about a third of the time, but firing still felt like rolling dice—I looked at the sights and tried to hold the gun straight, but whether I hit the target was up to the bullet, not to me.

"How did you learn?" I asked Elzy at the firepit on the third night. We were all gathered drinking dandelion wine as News, the fiddler, played a lively rendition of "Simple Gifts."

"My daddy showed me when I was small. 'In case a fox comes for the chickens,' he said."

"And he taught you the same way you're teaching me?" I asked.

Elzy knitted her brows.

"He didn't really have to do much teaching," she said. "I suppose I took to it naturally."

The answer annoyed me. When Mama was training me, she had made me memorize the four stages and ten stations of labor, the seven medicinal herbs, and the four phases of the menstrual cycle before I was even allowed to go with her on a visit. Once I asked her how she had become so skilled in so many ways of healing the body, and she said she had always kept her eyes and ears open, and never missed a chance to learn. Mama did not believe in natural talent; she believed in wisdom.

"How about the others?" I asked. "How did they learn?"

"Well, News learned from cowboying, I know that. Texas grew up on a horse farm so she learned from her daddy, same as me. Lo, I showed her when she came, but she was a quick study. Aggie Rose, I tried to show, but honestly her marksmanship is still shit. The Kid learned from the Kid's husband."

"He—she—the Kid had a husband?" I asked, trying to keep my voice low.

"Not he, not she," Elzy said. "The Kid is just the Kid. And of course. Most of us here were married. Otherwise how do you think we found out we were barren?"

She reached out to rub Cassie's back, and Cassie briefly dropped her head to Elzy's shoulder. Elzy kissed her hair. I knew Elzy was a woman now—the others called her "she" and I'd heard Cassie refer to her once or twice as Elizabeth.

I surmised that the two must be like Diana Jesperson and Katie Carr, who were inseparable when they were in ninth form, always holding hands and, it was rumored, doing more under cover of night—though at the time, none of us understood what more might be. Both were from good, big families, so they were married when the time came, and then Diana's mother-in-law forbade her from seeing Katie, believing that Katie was distracting her from her wifely duties. Soon both were pregnant, and then mothers, and no one talked about their friendship any longer, but Diana especially lost the sense of humor she'd had as a girl, and frequently called on Mama for medicine to help her sleep. I wondered, for the first time, what would have become of them if they had not married, if they would be inseparable still.

"Did you have a husband?" I asked Elzy.

" 'Did *you* have a husband?' " She parroted my question back to me with mock incredulity. "Did anyone ever tell you that you ask too many questions, Doctor?"

"Yes," I said, chastened. "I'm sorry."

Elzy laughed then, a sweet sound, and tickled me beneath the ribs.

"I'm teasing you," she said. "No, in fact, I never had a husband. Does that satisfy your curiosity?"

It did not begin to. Across the firepit, the Kid was showing Texas something on a map. Texas was watching and nodding; the Kid wore a suit, a silk cravat printed with roses, and an expression of complete self-assuredness. It was impossible to picture the Kid as someone like me, a frightened wife, cast out of the house for failing to bear a child. I did not understand how any of them had become what they appeared to be now: strong, high-spirited, masters of their various crafts. It made my heart lift to think of it—perhaps I would not be green forever.

Elzy stretched and reached for the wine bottle.

"You're just going to have to keep practicing," she said. "I don't know what else to tell you."

I was out by the stump with a fresh box of bullets the next afternoon when I saw the Kid walking up the path from the bunkhouse. The Kid always looked tall to me from far away. Up close I was taller, but the effect remained, something about the Kid's carriage and stride that made you want to look up instead of down.

"What's Elzy been teaching you?" the Kid asked.

"She showed me how to aim and shoot," I said. "I'm just not very good at it."

"How exactly did she show you?"

"She shot a pear from thirty paces," I said. "Then she had me try. I've been trying ever since."

The Kid smiled. "Like asking a wild horse to teach someone to run. Very well. Show me your progress, Doctor."

I fired a shot off somewhere into the orchard.

"Again," the Kid said.

This time I saw the bullet hit a hummock of dirt and grass behind and about six feet to the left of the stump.

"Again," the Kid said.

I shot the rest of the magazine.

"I see what we're up against," the Kid said. "Tell me something, Doctor. If a young medical professional like yourself hopes to assassinate an underripe pear, where should she rest her eyes as she takes aim?"

The Kid's voice both beguiled and confused me.

"I'm not sure I understand," I said.

The Kid sighed.

"Where do you look when you shoot?"

"At the pear?" I ventured.

"Wrong," the Kid said, unholstering a revolver with a handle made of bone.

"This is the front sight," the Kid said, pointing to a small crest of metal at the mouth of the barrel. "And this"—the Kid pointed to a notched piece of metal where the barrel met the handle—"is the rear sight. Now, when you take your aim, you line the front sight up with your target, in this case your pear. Then you line the notch in the rear sight up with the front sight. Then you forget the pear exists. The front sight is all that matters. You watch that front sight like it's the only water in an endless desert, and you're dying of thirst."

The Kid lifted the revolver and squinted an eye. "Now, once you have your enemy—in this case your pear—in your sights, what do you do next?"

"Pull the trigger?" I asked.

"Very good," the Kid said. "You pull the trigger. But when you do, you don't move your hand—if you do, the gun will move, and you'll miss your shot. You don't move your arm—if you do, the gun will move, and you'll miss your shot. You don't move your shoulder—if you do, the gun will move, and you'll miss your shot. The only part of your whole God-given body that moves is your solitary index finger, and if you can manage that, and you keep your eye on the front sight like it's water in the desert, why then your unlucky pear will soon have breathed his last."

The Kid's shot rang in the quiet orchard. It was not as perfect as Elzy's—the bullet clipped the side of the pear, sending it spinning off the stump and onto the ground. But it was much better than anything I could manage.

"Your turn," the Kid said.

I set up a fresh pear and took eleven paces back. This time I lined up the sights and tried to forget about the pear. I tried to hold my hand still.

My shot fell low, boring into the soft wood of the stump, leaving a pale scar behind.

"Again," the Kid said.

This time the bullet sailed above the pear and into the trees at the edge of the clearing, frightening a squirrel.

"Stop," the Kid said. "At this rate, your pear's friends are going to form up a posse and capture you before you harm a hair on their leader's head."

I would have found the Kid amusing if I wasn't so exhausted from trying to do something I clearly couldn't do.

"I'm sorry," I said, tears gathering in my throat.

"Assassins never apologize," the Kid said. "Time to try another tack, Doctor. Put down your gun and point at the pear."

I didn't understand, but I did as the Kid asked.

"Now focus your eyes on the tip of your finger. Desert, water, et cetera."

I looked at my fingernail, black-rimmed from cleaning the firepit the night before.

"Now focus on the pear."

I looked at the fruit, pale green splotched with scabby brown, a small thing grown tough in a hard place.

"Now your finger again."

Back and forth we went, I don't know how many times, but I know that when the Kid finally told me to try again with the gun, I understood how to let the target go and focus only on the sight, and I hit the pear square in the belly.

"Excellent," said the Kid. "Your first kill. Now do it again."

I had forgotten the calm of it, another person's voice guiding me. The Kid sounded nothing like Mama—Mama's voice was soft, with a roughness in it that she said came from childhood whooping cough, and the Kid's was clear and loud, like the voices of the twelfth-form boys who got picked to read aloud from the almanac at the beginning of every school day. But unlike those boys, both the Kid and Mama could make me feel hypnotized, as though their words moved my very limbs, as though my hands were their hands.

Hours passed in the orchard and when dark began to fall I could hit a pear at fifteen paces nine times out of ten. I didn't think I would ever be a great shot, and I was right about that, but now I knew how it felt to aim and fire true, and I sensed—and I was right about this, too—that the knowledge would never leave me.

Soon after the sun fell behind the rocks, I heard Cassie banging a pan lid with a spoon to call everyone to the firepit for dinner.

"Just a moment," the Kid said to me. "I have a question for you."

I holstered the gun and came close. The Kid's expression was difficult to read—layers of bluster and confidence slipped to reveal something softer and more uncertain below.

"Your medical experience," the Kid said. "Does it extend to the treatment of insomnia?"

"Of course," I said. "It's one of the most common problems during pregnancy. Usually we'd tell the woman to start with hot milk before bed—"

The Kid cut me off.

"But suppose, hypothetically speaking, a person were to suffer from insomnia of a chronic nature. Suppose that this person found it impossible to sleep for months, even years. Suppose it seemed, at times, that this person had never slept."

I remembered now that I'd woken more than once in the middle of the night to see the Kid's bunk in the great room empty.

"One man in our town had terrible insomnia," I said. "Mama made him a tea out of valerian root. She also told him to stop drinking whiskey—it makes you drowsy, but then you wake up in the middle of the night, worse off than you were before."

"Did it help?" the Kid asked.

"It did," I said. "But this man—"

I paused. I wasn't sure how to explain what had troubled Edward Carrier. It was not unlike the sickness Mama had suffered after Bee was born, except that Edward Carrier was not a mother, and instead of lying in his bed all day he paced his house all night, frightening his children.

"This man was sick at heart," I said finally. "Nothing brought him any joy, not even his baby son. Once he told Mama that the flowers his wife planted smelled ugly to him, that they smelled like vomit."

A look crossed the Kid's face. It was fleeting, but I recognized it as fear.

"What happened to this man?" the Kid asked.

"He was sick for months," I said. Actually Edward had suffered for two years, but I didn't want to tell the Kid that. "Then he started to get better. By the time I left town he was sleeping well and playing with his children again."

The Kid nodded and began walking back to the firepit.

"Tell Agnes Rose to get some valerian next time she goes to see the trader," the Kid said. "And any other herbs you need to treat common ailments. You should have a fully stocked pharmacy at your disposal."

*

My last lessons came from Lo. In the storage shed between the bunkhouse and the barn, I stood shirtless in my dungarees as she looped a measuring tape around my chest above, then across my breasts.

"It's good you're so flat," she said. "You won't need much binding."

Half of the shed was given over to ammunition and other gun paraphernalia: a case of bullets, another of gunpowder, a third of rods and rags for cleaning. The other half was Lo's country: a makeshift wardrobe, knocked together out of rough pine boards, held fur-lined parkas, a crinoline, leather chaps, several women's traveling coats, and countless dresses of muslin, gingham, and lace—tucked between two of them I noticed the Kid's suit and tails. On pegs were hats of every kind and character: cowboy hats with wide and narrow brims, folded in cattleman's and cutter styles; several winter hats of beaver fur; and ladies' hats and fascinators trimmed in ostrich and peacock. Shirts, dungarees, and lacy underthings peeked out of trunks lined up along the walls. Lo rummaged in one of these and extracted a strip of sturdy cotton, six inches wide and several feet long.

"Hold still," she said.

She wound until the cotton was tight against my skin, then secured it under my arm with safety pins.

"Can you breathe?" she asked.

I nodded.

"Good," she said, sliding a finger under the cloth to test the snugness. "Too loose and it'll slide off. Too tight and you're liable to pass out on us."

I buttoned my shirt and looked at myself in the mirror hanging on the wardrobe's door.

"I look like a little girl," I said.

"That's because you carry yourself like a little girl," Lo said. "You have to learn to move like a man."

I thought of my husband, how when he was nervous, he would scratch one forearm, then the other. How he would wash his face and then run the water backward with his fingers through his hair. I looked at myself in the mirror again. Nothing I remembered seemed like enough to go on.

"First things first," Lo said. "You have to stand on both feet."

"I am standing on both feet," I said.

Lo kicked my left heel. I lost my balance and stumbled forward into the wardrobe, clinging to the coats to keep from falling on my face.

"Sorry, little colt," said Lo, laughing. "But you see what I mean now. Your weight's all in your right foot. Men stand with their weight on both feet equally."

With both feet planted I felt both too heavy and too casual, a big clumsy kid about to barrel down a hill.

"It feels strange," I said.

"It's supposed to feel strange," said Lo, crossing behind me. "Now hook your left thumb in your belt loop."

I did what I thought I had seen boys and men do, talking to one another at the feed store, loitering against the wall at a dance. Then I felt another kick and stumbled again, this time backward, pinwheeling my arms before regaining my balance.

"You took the weight off your left leg," Lo said.

"I didn't."

"If you hadn't, little colt, you wouldn't have fallen over. Now go ahead: do it again."

This time I was slower and more deliberate.

"Good. Now the right—"

Again I concentrated on holding my body in its odd new shape.

"Very good. Now both thumbs."

The kick made me jump.

"Ow!" I shouted. "Is this how you taught the others?"

"It's how I learned," Lo said.

"Who taught you," I asked. "The Kid?"

Lo laughed. "Please," she said, "I taught the Kid and everyone else here. It's a wonder they weren't all hanged for witches before I came along. No, I learned from the best—Naaman Theophilus Harrow and his traveling players."

"They came to Fairchild when I was twelve," I said. "I saw them do *Antigone*!"

"That was one of my favorites," Lo said, coming alongside me and smiling into the mirror. "Do you recognize me?"

A visit from a troupe of traveling performers was a big event in Fairchild—once or twice every summer, a group of jugglers, dancers, or actors would set up tents on the riverbank south of Coralton and put on a show for two or three days before moving on. For those few days a festival atmosphere would take hold, almost as wild as Mothering Monday—Edgar Winchell and his sons John and Jonas would sell beer and sweet wine outside the dancehall before the show, and afterward couples would stagger off into the woods together. The spring after a show typically brought at least one fatherless baby, its mother watching it as it grew for signs of skill with pirouettes or juggling pins.

I remembered *Antigone* well—I had seen it twice, once with Ulla and once with Janie and Jessamine, who grew bored and began playing baby's cradle with a loop of string they'd found on the floor of the hall. Antigone and Ismene had been played by women so alike they might really have been sisters: tall and raven-haired, they were sought after by local boys and men and warded them off with identical wedding bands. Eurydice and the nurse, meanwhile, were played by old women, their faces deeply lined.

Lo looked to be around Mama's age, not old and not young. She was a head shorter than me, large-breasted and broad-hipped, and she wore her hair in blonde curls cut close to her scalp.

Lo saw my confusion. As quick as slipping on a coat, she changed the set of her shoulders and the focus of her eyes, stooping over and gazing above the frame of the mirror as though at something far away.

"'This is the way the blind man comes,'" she said. "'Lock-step, two heads lit by the eyes of one.'"

I laughed aloud. In the play, the old prophet Tiresias had worn a long white beard and hobbled across the stage supported on one side by a cane and on the other by a young boy, chosen from the fifth form at our school for the privilege. He had worn long, flowing robes that concealed his body, but I had never thought to wonder if he might have been played by a woman.

"They let you play a man?" I asked.

"The male roles were the most prestigious," Lo said. "Lean your shoulders back and pitch your hips forward."

I squared off my legs and, trying to keep them square, hooked a thumb in each belt loop. I braced myself but the kick didn't come.

"And I was the best of all the players," Lo went on.

"Why did you leave?" I asked.

Lo gave me a sad smile. "You know why I left, little colt," she said.

I had known girls who had babies by traveling players, but I had never thought about the players themselves marrying and having babies, or marrying and failing to have them.

"Did your husband kick you out?" I asked.

Lo chuckled to herself. "I didn't have a husband," she said. "None of us did. We believed in free love, or at least Naaman did. Make a fist for me."

I showed her my clenched hand.

She shook her head.

"Thumb outside your fingers," she said. "Good. Now put your fists up."

I delayed, wanting to hear the story.

"So, did Naaman—"

"Come on," she said. I assumed what I thought was a fighting stance.

She came close, lifted my left fist a little, then my right.

"My mama taught me, same as yours," she said. "Don't sleep with the same man too many times without a wedding ring, just in case. But I was young and dumb, and I was so in awe of him. Show me a punch."

"What happened?" I asked.

"Come on," she said. "Hit me in the stomach."

"I don't want to hurt you," I said.

"You won't, little colt. Come on."

I jabbed half-heartedly at her red plaid shirt with my right hand. She caught my fist with her hand.

"He always told me the troupe would never survive without me," she said. "'You're our soul,' he said. But when it came time for me to go he couldn't even tell me himself. He had one of the new girls bring me my things in an old feed sack."

She released my fist. "Hit me again," she said.

"I'm so sorry," I said.

"Don't feel sorry for me," she said. "Now, come on, hit me."

I jabbed with my left. She caught my fist with one hand, and with the other, punched me in the stomach hard enough to take my breath away.

I gasped and staggered, my eyes watering.

"What was that for?" I asked.

"That was your first real fighting lesson," Lo said. "Odds are, every time you fight, you'll be fighting a man. He'll be bigger than you, and he'll be stronger. If you fight fair, you'll lose every time. So you have to learn to fight dirty."

A week later I had learned how to gouge eyes and kick balls, how to punch a man in the throat and shatter his Adam's apple, and how to use the back of my skull to break a man's nose. A week after that News and Texas stole the cows.

In the two days they were gone no one would tell me where they were.

"On a job," was all Lo would say.

She was distracted that morning; everyone was. At breakfast we heard a rustling in the bushes by the firepit and the Kid leapt up, face alight with excitement or fear. Then a jackrabbit hopped across the red dirt and back into the scrub on the other side. At dinner I heard Cassie talking to the Kid about a search party.

Then, just at sunset, the sound of hoofbeats. We ran up to the road to greet them. I had never found cattle beautiful before, but here they were, pink and gold in the dying light, at least a dozen of them, more, News riding tall at the center of the herd, Texas in back, her guidance holding them all together. In the upper pasture, the two dismounted and we held them, all of us together in a knot, the cattle grumbling around us. When we pulled apart News was crying a little.

"Are you all right?" Agnes Rose removed her cowboy hat and stroked her cheek.

"I'm just so happy we did it," she said. She looked at the Kid, joy in her eyes. "You said we could do it and we did."

The Kid embraced her again, spun her around—though News was taller and bigger, the Kid lifted her as though she weighed nothing.

"Of course you could do it," the Kid said. "You can do anything, you know that."

The Kid threw an arm around Texas, too, crowing: "My loves, your powers are limitless."

It was past midnight when the moaning woke me from my sleep. I had forgotten where I was and I leapt out of bed, sure that Mama or one of my sisters was hurt. But when I blinked and rubbed my eyes I saw, not my mother scrubbing her hands in scalding water, but Texas pulling on her cowboy boots by the light of a kerosene lamp. I followed her down the stairs and out into the cool night.

The cow's keening rang loud in the dark pasture, a terrible desolate sound. The steers had formed a circle around her, mooing softly with concern.

"Shit," said Texas quietly.

"What's wrong?" I asked.

"Don't ask me," she said. "I can manage a drive, but I don't know anything about taking care of cows."

She laid her head against the cow's belly, listened to her heart.

"If she were a horse, I'd say colic," Texas said.

The cow moaned again, even louder this time. The sound was too familiar to ignore. I dropped to my knees and reached down, carefully, to feel her udders. They were hard as rocks.

"Get me a bucket," I said.

At first she screamed when I tried to milk her. We had to warm water on the stove in the kitchen cabin, use it to soak rags, and apply those to her swollen udders, massaging downward, before her milk would flow.

"You separated her from her calf?" I asked when the stream finally hit the bucket.

"I didn't think so," Texas said. "I didn't see any calves with her. But we peeled them off from the herd in the narrows out by Douglas. The calf must have gone on before."

We were both quiet for a moment, the only sound the milk fizzing against metal.

"Will it die without her?" Texas asked.

"Maybe not," I said. "Another cow in the herd could nurse it."

Texas stroked the animal's back. "I know we're selling her off to slaughter," she said, "but I hate to see her in pain."

I thought of Sigrid Williamson, whose baby had died at two months of a fever. How, as she wept, my mama brought her a neighbor's baby to nurse so she wouldn't develop mastitis.

"I'll milk her in the mornings till we sell her," I said. "She'll be all right."

Texas nodded and turned to walk back to the bunkhouse. I pressed the cooling rags to the cow's udder one more time. Her moaning was a quiet lowing now. This cow was more woman than I would ever be.

"Texas," I said.

She stopped.

"What is it?"

I paused, then rushed headlong into my question.

"Do you ever wish you were a mother?"

Texas laughed. "Baby Jesus, Ada," she said.

"I'm sorry," I said.

"It's all right," Texas said. "I used to. But I don't think about it much anymore."

"What changed?" I asked.

"I met the Kid," she said.

I remembered how the two had embraced, the pride with which the Kid praised her.

"And now the gang is your family?" I asked.

"That's part of it, of course," Texas said. "Before I came here, I was in a convent for a while, same as you. I was safe there. But I hated it—dawn till dusk, all I did was knit scarves. I was terrible at it. They didn't even call me by my name there—I was Sister Catherine. I was nobody."

"And now?" I asked.

I saw her draw her small body up a little taller in the darkness.

"Well, now I'm the stable master for the Hole in the Wall Gang."

Later that week News and the Kid sold the cattle on to an unscrupulous rancher outside the Independent Town of Casper. In her reconnaissance at a nearby roadhouse, News heard about a wagon coming to Casper from Jackson, carrying a month's payroll for forty cowboys and ranch hands, all in gold and silver pieces, with only the driver and one guard to protect it.

"If we ride tomorrow morning we can hide out near Sutton's Gulch and jump them when they come past," News said. "Shouldn't take more than three of us—Tex, Elzy, and I can go."

"You and Texas deserve a rest," the Kid said. "I'll command this one—who else feels like stretching her legs a little?"

"I'll go," I said.

Everyone turned to look at me.

"What do you think, Lo?" asked the Kid, amused. "Is the good doctor ready?

"If it were up to me, I'd wait a few more weeks," Lo said. "But she understands the fundamentals."

"I think she's ready," Texas said.

I saw how the others heeded her, because she spoke up so rarely.

"Stand up," the Kid said. "Let me look at you."

I stood. Again all their eyes were on me, and I wondered what they saw: an interloper, a greenhorn, a little girl, and maybe, in at least one case, someone with enough wisdom to make something of herself. I lifted my chin and met the Kid's eyes. The Kid smiled.

"Agnes," the Kid said, "she'll need a trim before we go."

A few mornings later, Agnes Rose cut my hair. She sat on the top step to the bunkhouse and I sat on the bottom one, leaning against her knees. Her touch reminded me of my sisters, the way I used to let them pin my hair into ridiculous styles, ribbons every which way, giggling as their little fingers tickled my scalp.

The memory opened a pit of fear in my stomach. I told myself, again, that as long as Sheriff Branch was looking for me, my family would probably be safe. But I knew, too, that he might not search forever. And the longer I made myself hard to find, the more likely he would be to seek another outlet for my neighbors' anger. I felt my back muscles harden against Agnes Rose's legs.

"Are you nervous about tomorrow?" she asked.

She unwound my hair from its braid and began to snip. The hair fell in skeins, light brown in the red dirt.

"A little," I said.

The truth was I could not imagine what I was about to do. I knew what I wanted—to return to Hole in the Wall with the same triumph in my heart that I'd seen on the faces of News and Texas as they rode among the cattle. But of what it would take to hold up a wagon at gunpoint, I did not understand enough to be afraid.

"I suppose I don't know what to expect," I added.

"I didn't either, the first time," Agnes Rose said.

I felt my hair at my shoulders now, a strange new lightness at my back where the braid was missing.

"What was it like," I asked, "your first job?"

I felt her fingers at my ear and then the breeze at my neck where she'd cut the hair away.

"It was a disaster," she said. "I was intended to steal a horse. We were going to sell him on to a trader I know, make enough money to provision ourselves for the winter.

"The stable hand was a drunk, News said I could walk right in and take the stallion, easy as shaking hands. I put on a cowboy hat and a binder and I set out. 'Simple,' News said. 'A child could do it.'

"I was actually excited. I thought I'd make us a boatload of money, and the Kid and everybody else would praise me."

"So what happened?" I asked.

Another snip, and the back of my neck was bare.

"The stable hand took a temperance pledge," Agnes Rose said. "When I got there he was sitting out front of the barn with a shotgun, bloodshot eyes the size of dinner plates. I had to shoot him."

Snip. Meadow air on both ears, goosebumps on my neck.

"The rancher heard the shot," she went on. "He came out in his nightcap with a poker in his fist."

Agnes Rose was cutting close to my head now. I could feel the scissor blades on my scalp.

"The horse spooked and threw me off. The rancher was on me before I knew it. He wrestled me to the ground and knocked the gun out of my hand."

I clenched my jaw. I could only imagine what would happen to a woman alone, dressed in men's clothing, caught trying to steal a horse from someone else's ranch.

"How did you get away?" I asked.

I heard a smile in her voice.

"A trick I learned at Miss Meacham's, for when the men got fresh," she said. "You bite the inside of your lip until you taste blood, then you cough it into your hand. This time I smeared it right on the rancher's nightshirt. I wheezed and sputtered and I told him I was only stealing horses to pay for a sanitorium."

"That worked?" I asked. "He let you go?"

The smile disappeared.

"Of course not," she said. "But he lost his bearings for a minute. Long enough for me to find my gun and shoot him in the gut."

"Mother Mary," I said quietly.

"She wasn't there," Agnes Rose said, "I can tell you that. Two days later I staggered back into Hole in the Wall empty-handed. Cassie wanted to get rid of me. I think she still does."

"But you're here," I said.

"The Kid knows how to spot the usefulness in people, even if it doesn't present itself immediately. Maybe especially if it doesn't. After that job I never tried to steal a horse again. Now I focus on subtler work. I've made enough money for us to buy a dozen horses, with some left over for saddles."

She tousled what was left of my hair and blew on the back of my neck. A few stray clippings fell in the dirt.

"Come on," she said, leading me to Lo's shed.

In the cracked mirror I looked wholly different—ugly was my first thought, all the softness gone from my face now that my hair no longer hung around it. But Agnes Rose told me to straighten my back and lift my chin, and I could see something dimly then, a new way of looking and being.

"Handsome," she said. "Don't worry. Just listen to your gut. You know more than you think you do."

CHAPTER 4

Sutton's Gulch was southwest of the valley, but on the morning we set out, the Kid led us due south instead.

"Where are we going?" I asked.

"To the wall," the Kid said cheerily. "I want you to see the view."

The morning was gray and cool and I could smell the sage under the horses' hooves. But as we rode south the sun burned through the clouds, then shone so bright it seemed to bleach the landscape of its color. Dust caught in my throat and sweat soaked my shirt; coming from everywhere at once was the sound of locusts sawing.

At the base of the red wall the horse path narrowed to a footpath. A little way's up, maybe a half hour's hard hiking, I saw the notch, the Hole in the Wall. The Kid dismounted and tied Grace to a hitching post, its wood gone silvery with weather. Elzy and I tied our horses too. We climbed on foot up the rocky path until my thigh muscles screamed, and then we climbed some more. The path switched back on itself again and again. It was far longer than it had seemed from the ground, and far harder going, and I began to think the Hole in the Wall was a kind of illusion or mirage, and we would never reach it, and that the Kid would simply march us ever skyward as some kind of test or punishment, until our legs gave out and we dropped to the dust, begging for mercy. Then we rounded a bend and scrambled up a pebbled scree, and there we were in the cool darkness of it, the two rock faces slanting inward on either side of us, cradling us like hands with interlacing fingers. We sat in the dirt, wiping our faces and panting.

"Take a look, Doc," said the Kid, with a sweep of the hand. "Take it all in."

Down below, the valley shocked me with its glory. The grass shone silver-green in the sunlight, deepening to aquamarine where the creeks ran, parching out to gray in the dry flats where the red dirt peeked through. I saw stands of birch and aspen quivering in the breeze, and a herd of pronghorn drinking from the heart-shaped pond. We were so high that I could see the coal-black backs of buzzards circling.

"Do you know why we came here, Doctor?" the Kid asked.

"Because we can see in every direction," I said, childishly happy to have the right answer.

Indeed I could see the firepit far in the distance, a pock in the silver grass, and beside it the bunkhouse, the barn, and the pasture. Above them were the pass and the road north, where I had come from.

"That's one reason," the Kid said. "But it's not the only one. Look again."

I wanted badly to understand what the Kid meant, and I searched the landscape for secret meanings. I saw the cowboy shack in the creek's glittering elbow, and the cracked expanse of dry earth where coyotes and hawks hunted prairie dogs. Directly below us, so far down it made my head swim to look at them, were a row of red rocks shaped into tall columns by wind and weather, standing like sentries guarding the wall.

"There are a lot of good hiding places—" I began.

The Kid's voice changed, taking on the soaring quality I remembered from the first night I'd come to Hole in the Wall.

"The Lord made a covenant with Abram, saying, 'Unto thy seed have I given this land,'" the Kid said, "'from the river of Egypt unto the great river, the river Euphrates: the Kenites, and the Kenizzites, and the Kadmonites, and the Hittites, and the Perizzites, and the Rephaims, and the Amorites, and the Canaanites, and the Girgashites, and the Jebusites.'"

I was lost, but the Kid's face held my attention, the Kid's eyes dancing with excitement.

"When I met Cassie, we had nothing and no one. We cleaved to one another as a husband to his wife. For three hundred and seventy-eight days we wandered the Powder River country, looking for a place where we could make a home, where we could live in freedom without fear. And on the three hundred and seventy-ninth day we came over the red wall and saw this valley spread out before us, the land between two rivers that God promised to Abram.

"'I will give unto thee, and to thy seed after thee, the land wherein thou art a stranger, all the land of Canaan, for an everlasting possession,' God said. And I knew that this land was to be ours, an everlasting possession for generations and generations."

I tasted the same stale bitterness in my mouth, like tea gone cold in the cup overnight, that I'd tasted every time the Mother Superior read us Psalm 127, and reminded us that even though we would never have children, we must honor and respect the greater holiness of those who could.

"I'm sorry," I said, "but what generations? Aren't all of us here the last of our lines?"

The Kid's eyes only glowed brighter at this.

"Don't you remember your catechism, Doctor? Abram and his wife Sarai were barren. But God promised Abram the land of Canaan, and he gave him a new name. 'Thy name shall be Abraham,' God said, 'for a father of many nations have I made thee. And I will make thee exceeding fruitful, and I will make nations of thee, and kings shall come out of thee.'"

"Amen," said Elzy quietly. She looked up at the Kid with reverence but also with familiarity, the way one might look at a beloved older sibling.

"We may be barren in body, dear Doctor, but we shall be fathers of many nations, fathers and mothers both. You see, when we found this land, I knew it was promised not just for us, but for the descendants of our minds and hearts, all those cast out of their homes and banished by their families, all those slandered and maligned, imprisoned and abused, for no crime but that God saw fit not to plant children in their wombs. I knew that we would build a nation of the dispossessed, where we would be not barren women, but kings."

The Kid's words were exciting, and I wanted to feel carried away by them. But I remembered the power I'd felt in my fingers when setting a particularly difficult break, or guiding a baby headfirst into the world. That power had been taken from me, and I didn't see how it could return.

"I don't mean to be impertinent," I said, "but if God really cared about us, why wouldn't He let us have children so we could stay in our homes, with our families?"

The Kid looked at me for a moment in silence, and I saw Elzy's shoulders tense. I wondered if I should be afraid.

But then the Kid smiled, and spoke to me with a sweetness and sympathy I hadn't heard since I left my mother's house.

"You think God has forsaken you, Ada, is that it?" the Kid asked.

"If there is a God," I said, "then yes, I do."

"Poor thing. We all felt this way when we first arrived. Elzy, didn't you?"

"I didn't believe in anything when I came here," Elzy said.

"Even I sometimes succumbed to despair," the Kid said. "But then I realized: we were told a lie about God and what He wants from us."

"What does He want from us?" I asked.

The Kid bent close to me then, until our foreheads were touching.

"He will make you father of many nations, Ada," the Kid said. "Watch and see."

We came to Sutton's Gulch a few hours after nightfall and camped at the bottom, watering the horses at the stream that trickled there. I was tired from the climb and the long ride but I slept badly, dreaming and waking, dreaming and waking. Every time I woke I saw that the Kid was awake too, reading the Bible or drinking whiskey or simply walking in a circle round the dead coals of our fire.

Morning came cool and cloudy. Elzy was heating beans with chunks of pemmican on a skillet over the fire.

"Where's the Kid?" I asked.

"Watching the road," Elzy said. "If News is right, the wagon should be along around midmorning. But we don't want to miss it if they're early."

She dipped a tin cup into the mixture and handed it to me.

"No forks," she said. "Let it cool a little and slurp it down."

Elzy and I sat in silence, blowing into our cups. I remembered the way she'd looked at the Kid the day before, the love and respect in her eyes. I wanted to feel what she felt, or at least to understand it.

"Do you believe baby Jesus promised this land to us?" I asked her.

Elzy shrugged. "I didn't grow up on baby Jesus, or God, or any of that. My daddy didn't go in for it. I believe in the Kid."

"But if you don't believe what the Kid's saying, about God and everything, then what's left?" I asked. "Isn't it all just words?"

Elzy put down her cup. She looked offended now.

"I didn't say I don't believe it," she said. "I just don't always take it literally. Like when the Kid talks about building our nation, do I think we're going to re-create the United States of America? No, of course not. I wouldn't want to even if we could."

"Then what does it mean?" I asked.

"It's a way of holding us up," Elzy said. "It's how the Kid reminds us who we are."

"And who are we?"

We heard hoofbeats in the distance.

The Kid appeared at the lip of the gulch then, nose and mouth already covered by a scarf of purple silk. Elzy smiled at me, then removed a checked bandanna from her pocket.

"Didn't you hear?" she asked. "We're kings."

A few minutes' ride to the south was an overlook from which we could see several miles of road. At first I saw nothing—then, in the distance, a spot.

As we waited, the spot grew, and when we could see two men seated in a wagon, one with a rifle as long as my arm, we drove our horses fast down the face of the overlook to the roadway. I registered things I would remember later: two pronghorns springing away as we rode past, a sunbeam cutting through the clouds to the northeast, the driver saying something to the guard, the guard laughing.

Then we had them in our sights and the Kid said, "Sir, kindly drop the rifle," and the robbery began.

The guard was middle-aged, broad and short, curly hair flecked with gray under his hat. He climbed down from the wagon seat and laid his rifle in the dirt, then nodded to the driver, who was younger, a little taller, handsome, with black hair curling into his eyes. The Kid took the guard's rifle and handed it to me; my job was to go around to the back of the wagon and look for the money. Elzy and the Kid covered the two men.

From behind the wagon I stole a glance at the pair. Both had their hands up. The driver was frozen to the spot. But the older man, the guard, was angry and antic, shifting from foot to foot, kicking the dirt.

"How do you live with yourselves," he asked, looking at the Kid and me, "stealing from honest Christians who never did a thing to you? You're filthy parasites is what you are."

Elzy and the Kid did not seem to react. I couldn't read their eyes. In the back of the wagon were burlap bags, neatly stacked and labeled in blue ink with the name of a ranch, the N Bar G. Each was so heavy I could barely lift it. I began loading up the horses.

"He has children, you know," the guard said, pointing to the driver. "Two little boys and a girl, three, five, and nine. You want to explain to them why their daddy didn't get paid this month? Why he lost his job?"

"Easy," said the driver.

The guard ignored him. He took a step closer to Elzy and the Kid. Sweat sprouted under my arms. The guard did not seem afraid of them, and I did not know what he would do. My job was to handle the gold and silver, nothing more—the Kid had been clear on that point. But the Kid had not told me what to do if the others were in danger. I tried to listen to my gut, but my gut had no training for such a situation, and was silent.

"If your mothers could see you right now, I bet they'd weep from shame," the guard said. "I bet they'd curse the day they birthed you."

"Come on, easy," the driver said, pleading now. Something was between them, something that gave the guard all the power.

I had given two of the horses all they could carry and was working on Amity. The guard took another step toward Elzy. The Kid stood perfectly still, watching. My heart was pounding, my mouth was tinder-dry.

"Stay back," Elzy said.

The guard laughed.

"Stay back," he said in a high and mocking voice. "Or what? You'll shoot me, gelding? That I'd like to see."

"Don't test us, old man," the Kid said. I thought the Kid looked at me then, but I wasn't sure.

"Two geldings," the guard said. "I'm pissing in my pants! I'm shivering in my shoes!"

The guard was just a few yards from Elzy now. I was not a fast shot. If he rushed her now, he might be able to get her gun before I could aim and fire. If only I'd had another day, I kept thinking—another day or two of training with Lo, then I would understand what to do now, whether to stand silent and calm or shout back or fire my gun right into the old man's back and end the standoff now.

I did none of those things.

"Back up," I said. Even I heard the fear in my voice.

The guard wheeled around to look at me. I panicked. I squeezed the trigger and shot him in the thigh.

What happened next happened fast, but I've played it so many times in my mind that the memory is slow, like dancing. The driver reached into his boot and drew a six-shooter none of us had seen. He fired a single shot. Then Elzy shot him square in the chest. I saw his face as he fell: pure shock, he could not believe his life would end this way. The guard howled, a high chilling cry like storm wind, I will never forget it. He crouched over the driver. Their two heads pressed together, I saw now—perhaps had seen before—that they were father and son. We mounted the horses. We rode.

We were less than a mile away when Elzy began to list in the saddle.

"I'm fine," she told the Kid, but when my horse came up close to hers I saw the dark blood leaking down her sleeve.

She was limp as a doll as we lifted her onto the Kid's horse, and the Kid had to hold her upright all the way back to Hole in the Wall.

It was long past midnight when we got back, but the sound of the horses roused the others. The moon was bright and full and I could see their faces as they came out of the bunkhouse: News and Lo and Texas and Agnes Rose, all happy and hopeful and then afraid. Cassie came out last of all. News had helped the Kid lift Elzy down from the horse; Cassie went straight to her and pressed her forehead to Elzy's forehead, whispered something I couldn't hear. Then, to me, "What did you do?"

I couldn't even bring myself to say I was sorry, it seemed so worthless. Cassie turned to the Kid.

"I told you this would happen. You take in strays, and now—"

Elzy's knees gave out. News tried to hold her up but her head flopped forward, her whole body limp. Blood dripped from her sleeve into the dirt.

I thought of the worst wound I'd seen with Mama, a gash in Luella Mason's left thigh ten inches long, where a saw had slipped and bitten into her flesh. I remembered all the supplies I'd gathered from Mama's storeroom then, how I'd packed them carefully so the bottles didn't break.

"We need some iodine," I said, "and at least three feet of thin, clean cotton. And some tweezers, for the bullet."

"We don't have iodine," Texas said. "And we definitely don't have tweezers."

"Whiskey then, or whatever strong drink you have, and clean water, and something to mix them in, and the smallest knife you have."

Texas and Lo went to gather what I'd asked for. News and I carried Elzy into the bunkhouse; Cassie and the Kid followed behind. For a moment everyone followed my lead, and even I forgot that it was my fault that Elzy was hurt and the wagon driver was dead. The moment lasted until I unbuttoned Elzy's shirt and saw the wound in her bicep, small but raw and welling black blood at the center.

I was not afraid of blood. I had seen it enough times—blood from a cut, blood from a nose, blood from a birth, bloody sheets and towels, legs and vulvas, babies taking their first breaths, covered in blood. I was not afraid of pain—I'd been the one a woman clung to as she screamed her way into motherhood. I was not even afraid of death—I'd washed an old woman's body on the night after her last night, I'd dressed a stillborn baby in his shroud. But now I was the cause of someone's pain, and I was the only one who could stop it, and that made me afraid.

Texas brought me a bottle of whiskey, a jug of water, a soup pot and a ladle. Lo brought me a white nightdress with pale blue flowers. I added half the bottle and the whole jug, stirred, then tore off a length of the nightdress, soaked it, and wiped my hands down. I did the same with the knife. It was the first thing Mama taught me when I started going to births with her: Everything that touches the patient has to be clean.

Someone had lit all the kerosene lanterns in the bunkhouse, but I couldn't see anything at the center of Elzy's wound. I tore another handful of cloth and dunked it in the whiskey water. Then I gave Elzy a sip from the bottle.

"This is going to sting," I said, and began to wipe the old blood from the wound.

Elzy cried out, high and loud, that animal sound that comes from hurting bodies, but the wound was clean and I could see the lead glinting in the flesh. I knew an artery ran from the shoulder down to the elbow; if the knife slid wrong I would cut it open and she would die. Slowly I pressed the very tip against the metal. I could feel the bullet begin to shift, but Elzy screamed again and jerked away, and the knife sliced a new cut across the flesh of her upper arm. I waited for a moment without breathing, but the cut only trickled blood; the artery was safe.

"Hold her still," I said to whoever would help me, and Agnes Rose stepped in to hold Elzy's arm.

I washed the wound again, and again tried to pry the bullet loose. Again Elzy screamed, but Agnes Rose held her fast. I felt the bullet give but not give way, and when I pressed harder, the knife point slid off into the flesh. I felt Elzy's howl at the bottom of my gut.

I handed the knife to Agnes Rose and wiped my hands again with whiskey water.

"I'm going to try to get it out with my fingers," I said more to myself than to anyone else.

My hands were shaking. I knew I was almost as likely to kill Elzy as to save her. Then I would have two deaths on my conscience in a single day. I swallowed hard. I knew what Mama would have done.

I imagined the wagon driver standing in front of me. I imagined a bloodstain at the center of his chest and his eyes still open, full of sorrow and fear. I nodded. Then I took hold of the bullet and began to pull.

The bullet slid under my fingers. It slid and then it held. Elzy cried and her blood covered my hand.

In my head I recited what Sister Rose had whispered every night before we slept: "Mother Mary, shelter us, love us more than we deserve."

I pulled again and now I felt a new movement, and then the flesh gave up the lead with a wet sound and new bright blood filled the wound. It pooled but did not pulse; vein blood. I washed it away.

Elzy was still screaming, but with the bullet gone I felt a wave of power carrying me forward. Someone had already torn me a length of cotton. I washed the wound once more and wrapped it tight with many layers. Elzy's face was wet with tears but I could feel relief buzzing in the room, almost like joy. It would last until I lay down in my bunk to sleep and remembered the way the driver's father had cradled his body, just as he must have done the day he was born.

CHAPTER 5

After my failure at Sutton's Gulch, the others were cold or outright hostile to me. At night, I heard Cassie trying to convince the Kid to send me away, but Elzy's wound required my care. We were lucky—with daily applications of witch hazel and clean dressings the wound began to close, and the red border of infection I'd been anticipating with dread failed to materialize. Elzy wouldn't look at me when I examined her, and only spoke if something hurt.

On the morning of the seventh day after I got Elzy shot, Agnes Rose came to visit me in the orchard. I'd taken to spending most of my time there since the others had made it clear I wasn't welcome at the firepit, or in the bunkhouse, except to sleep or check on Elzy. When Agnes Rose came up the path I was rereading Mrs. Schaeffer's book, the part about stillbirths and their possible causes.

"What do you know about sleeping tonics?" Agnes Rose asked.

The question made me nervous. I didn't want to betray the Kid's confidence.

"Are you having trouble sleeping?" I asked.

Agnes Rose rolled her eyes.

"It's for a job," she said. "When you came here, you said you could mix something to put a man to sleep. Was that just talk?"

The person who had spoken so confidently that night about her own abilities felt like a stranger to me now. But I still remembered what she knew.

"I can do it," I said. "I just need some laudanum."

The trading post was two days' ride northwest of Hole in the Wall, on Lourdes Creek in the grasslands. Since it was Arapaho hunting ground there were no roadhouses, and when we stopped for the night near a small stream we saw the remains of other camps: eggshells, the charred leavings of a fire, human shit poorly covered in dirt.

Agnes Rose did not wear men's clothing—"It's not for me," she said—so we traveled as husband and wife, brass wedding rings greening our fingers. But she didn't need the pretense with the trader, who seemed to know her well. She greeted him in Arapaho.

"Your accent is improving," he replied in English.

"I know you're lying, but thank you for flattering me," she said. "News sends her regards, she's sorry she couldn't make it. But I'd like you to meet Doc, our newest recruit. She's a trained midwife."

The trader looked at me with curiosity. He was slight, older than me but younger than Mama, with thick eyeglasses and a sky-blue bead in each ear. On walls and shelves around and behind him were valuables that people had brought to pawn or trade—a gold-plated pocketknife, a revolver, a buckskin war shirt with beads and fringe, a lady's hat decorated with ostrich feathers, a mahogany grandfather clock with gilt numbers on its face. The head of a mountain lion, frozen in a roar.

"What made you join up with these ne'er-do-wells?" the trader asked me, pointing at Agnes Rose. "I thought the Americans took good care of their midwives."

"Not barren ones," I said.

He shook his head and said something in Arapaho. Mrs. Spencer at school had said that the Indians did not value children the way Christian people did. Thinking about it now, far from the schoolhouse, I realized it was likely Mrs. Spencer had never spoken to an Indian person. I myself had done so only a handful of times, when women came from Lakota country for my mother's services. I did not know what they thought about barren women, or what the trader thought, but I realized now that he might not feel the same way as the Fairchild ladies did, that perhaps barren wives were not hanged for witches everywhere.

"We're looking to buy some laudanum," Agnes Rose said. "How much do we need, Doc?"

"A hundred drops should do it," I said, "if it's strong."

The trader raised an eyebrow at Agnes Rose.

"And how are you paying for this, exactly?"

From her handbag, Agnes Rose produced a small sack of what I assumed was gold.

"We've had a good summer," she said. "This should cover it."

The trader looked inside the sack and hefted it in his hand.

"Agnes," he asked, "do you know where laudanum comes from?"

She looked at me, but I was no help. I knew laudanum was scarce and expensive—Mama got it from Dr. Carlisle, and only for very special cases, like cutting out a breast tumor or an ovarian cyst. I had no idea where Dr. Carlisle got it.

"It comes from China," the trader said. "The few merchants who still cross the Pacific sell it to traders in San Francisco or the Dalles, and they sell it on to traders who carry it across hundreds of miles of hard country until finally, weeks or months later, some of it makes its way to me. So while I'm prepared to give you a discount from my usual rate, Agnes—we've worked together a long time—I'm going to need about double what's in here."

"Come on, Nótkon," Agnes Rose said. "You and I both know it's not worth that. I can throw in twenty silver liberties."

I could hear anxiety in her voice. She hadn't been prepared for this. Nótkon shook his head.

"I'd be losing money," he said. "Now if you had some valuables from your last job to sweeten the deal—that necklace you brought last time paid for my son's wedding."

"We might be able to throw in some hatpins," Agnes Rose said, but I could tell she was stalling, and Nótkon was unimpressed. I looked around at his wares, the glint of the ruby in the hat, the sheen on a pair of snakeskin boots. A leather-bound Bible from before the Flu with gilt-edged pages and a scarlet ribbon to mark your place. I had an idea.

"I have something you might like," I said. "It's a medical manual."

Nótkon looked amused.

"No offense," he said, "but I don't have much use for American medicine. I seem to remember something about a Flu."

"This is new medicine," I said. "Mrs. Alice Schaeffer has a surgery down in Rocky Mountain country where she sees hundreds of women a year. She can cure things that killed women and babies in my town. She knows how to cut a baby from its mother's womb and sew the mother back up so both survive."

Nótkon tried not to show it, but I could tell he was intrigued. I took the book out of my satchel and laid it on the counter before him, open to the diagram of the woman sliced open to reveal the baby inside. He recoiled, then leaned closer. He began flipping pages. The minute hand of the grandfather clock ticked once, then twice.

Agnes Rose took the book away.

"Can't let you read all the secrets until you pay for it," she said.

Nótkon looked at me, then at Agnes Rose, then back at me again.

All the way back to Hole in the Wall, the tiny bottle of laudanum light in my satchel where the book had been, I repeated Mrs. Schaeffer's treatments to myself so I wouldn't forget them.

Fiddleback Ranch was the biggest cattle operation between Casper and the Bighorns. It was so big that a town had grown up around it, where all the cowboys and ranch hands lived in bungalows and rooming houses and bought coffee and sugar at the general store and drank in the evenings at the saloon and roadhouse, Veronica's. The owner of the ranch was a man named Roger McBride, the youngest son of a poor farmer from out east in corn country. McBride had come to the Powder River Valley with nothing but a horse and a knack for business, and now he owned not just the ranch but the mayor of the Independent Town of Fiddleback (who was widely rumored to be on his payroll), the sheriff (same rumors), half the houses in town (his agent collected rent on the first Saturday of the month, and was harsh in evicting those who couldn't pay), and a roving crew of bounty hunters who chased down cattle rustlers and generally protected his interests in Powder country and beyond (their numbers were said to be in the dozens).

News had been watching and listening at Fiddleback Ranch for a month, posing as a journeyman cowboy on a temporary job. She had learned that McBride sent one of his most trusted men to the bank in town—the Farmers' and Merchants' Bank of

Fiddleback, owned by the only man in town as rich as McBride, a Swede named Karl Nystrom—every Friday to deposit the ranch's income from cattle sales, stud, and other operations, and withdraw enough in small coin to pay his many employees. It would be nearly impossible to rob the man at gunpoint—throughout his short journey he was surrounded by people loyal to McBride. But with a little guile and expertise, it might be possible to waylay him.

Agnes Rose had been spending time in Fiddleback too. She'd been flirting with and flattering the bagman, one Alexander Bixby, for a matter of weeks. She had convinced him that she was a virginal young woman from a poor family who had been jilted by her fiancé after he got another woman pregnant. Punished for her virtue—her mama had taught her not to sleep with a man before her wedding night—and far from home, she was forced to take in piecework and live at a ladies' boarding-house near Crooked Creek, coming to Fiddleback only to sell her quilts and doilies. Bixby was taken with her sad story and her habit of telling him how impressed she was with the importance of his work. He liked to visit Veronica's for a single drink on his way back from the bank, and this time Agnes Rose had given him to understand that if he wanted to take her upstairs, she might be willing to forget her mama's lesson for the duration of an afternoon.

All we needed to do was get enough laudanum into Bixby's drink that he fell fast asleep once he got to the bedroom. Then Agnes Rose would take his satchel, climb out the back window, and we'd be half a day's ride away before he woke up.

The morning we set out, the first frost of fall was on the pasture. Agnes Rose wore a blonde wig with side curls, a long cloth coat with patches at the elbows (Lo had sewn them on at the last minute to add to Agnes's air of poverty and resourcefulness), and a threadbare pink traveling dress with a low neckline. News and I wore false mustaches that Lo had affixed to our upper lips with spirit gum—she had chatted easily with News while gluing hers in place, but tended to mine in silence. There had been some discussion around the firepit of whether I should be allowed to go on the job at all, but Agnes Rose argued that I would be needed to advise her on the timing of the laudanum, and to help administer additional drops should the first dose fail to take effect. The Kid was convinced, under one condition: I surrendered my gun before we set out. I'd be going in my capacity as a doctor, not an outlaw.

Fiddleback was a little more than a day's ride south, on the wide floodplain of the Powder. Our journey took us through flat country, the grass gone tawny in the cooling air. As we rode, the sky changed more than the land did, banks of cloud rolling fast across the blue, spattering us with rain before massing in the east in tall gray towers. The rain tamped the dust down and filled the air with the smell of sage—even though I felt alone and alien still in Powder country, that smell was becoming as familiar as the scent of my mother's cornbread or my sisters' hair.

When the sun was high in the sky and the air was warm enough I could almost pretend it was summer still, I heard a rumble in the distance. At first I thought it was thunder—the foothills to the east were gray with rain—but instead of dissipating it got louder, and then I felt the ground begin to shake under Amity's hooves.

"Shit," News said.

"What do we do?" Agnes Rose asked.

"Find the highest ground we can."

"What's happening?" I asked, but they both ignored me.

News led us northwest, back in the direction we'd come from, toward a serviceberry tree on a gentle hillock a few feet above the flatland.

"This is going to have to do," she said.

"What's happening?" I asked again.

Then I saw a dark patch growing in the northeast. My first thought was locusts, but soon I could see individual forms within the darkness, woolly and huge—buffalo.

"Keep a tight hold on Amity," said News, "or she'll spook and they'll trample you both."

I choked up on the reins. Amity's ears shivered back and forth like leaves.

"There, baby," I said, patting her neck, trying to keep my fingers from shaking.

When I looked up the herd was almost on top of us. In a cloud of red dust I saw the enormous heads of the buffalo. I had never seen something so heavy move so fast. They were like the giants in the stories Mama used to tell. They were like something from an older world.

Then they were all around us. The dust made me choke. The herd was its own weather. I saw News open her mouth but the hoofbeats drowned out her voice. Then Agnes Rose's horse, Prudence, began to twist and buck beneath her. Even through the dust I could see the fear on Agnes's face, I could see she had let her body go frozen. Prudence reared up on her hind legs, the whole bright black length of her rising above the herd. Agnes Rose clung to her back and hung on, but barely. The buffalo were so close to us that if Agnes lost her grip on Prudence she would be trampled for sure. They streamed around us with no sign of stopping, their hoofbeats rattling the teeth in my jaw. Only one thing was steady: underneath me I felt Amity's calm like a human hand in mine. I remembered what Texas had told me—the horse knew the country better than I did. Maybe, I thought, she knew what to do now.

I loosened my grip on the reins just enough to give her freedom of movement. She paced very slowly until she was neck and neck with Prudence. The horse's eyes were wild and her muzzle foamy, and I knew she could knock me or Amity unconscious with one kick, but Amity didn't stumble or shy. Instead she began to nuzzle Prudence along her snout and neck in a gesture so tender it made me miss my sisters, the way they would lean in to butterfly-kiss my cheeks with their eyelashes. Following Amity's lead, I reached over to Agnes Rose and put my hand on her shoulder. I tried to press all the steadying weight of Amity and me down into her body.

I felt the change in Agnes Rose before I saw it, the shoulders falling from the ears, the muscles working where once they'd quivered. She choked up on the reins, lifting Prudence's head so she couldn't buck. The horse huffed and twitched and began to quiet.

As quickly as it had reached us, the stampede left us behind. The herd thinned out—I could see red dirt between the animals again; then a few straggling beasts, thinner and more pallid than the rest; then nothing. News looked back at me and Agnes Rose. Already her face was clear of worry.

"Shall we?" she asked, and we rode away.

We camped overnight by a small lake about a mile outside of Fiddleback. News watered the horses while Agnes Rose and I went to gather firewood.

"Thanks for your help back there," Agnes Rose said. "You're a good rider."

The compliment washed over me like warm water. It had been days since anyone had said a kind word to me.

"How come you're helping me?" I asked. "You didn't have to push for me to come along. Why did you do that?"

"Like I told the Kid," Agnes Rose said, "we need you to handle the laudanum."

"I could have measured it out for you," I said. "It would have been easy enough."

We were scavenging in a stand of cottonwood trees half-burnt by lightning some time ago. Agnes Rose picked up a blackened branch, decided it was too burnt, and let it fall.

"You know what I did before Hole in the Wall?"

"I heard you were in jail," I said.

She smiled. "Only for a little while. I got married at fifteen and my husband's family threw me out on my seventeenth birthday. I ended up at a brothel in Telluride, but the work was hard and the madam took most of my money, and after two years I struck out on my own."

"How?" I asked. I had never heard of a barren woman doing much of anything on her own.

"You find a man to cover you," she said. "Sometimes he's your ally, sometimes he's your mark. If you're smart, and you don't stay with the same man or in the same town for too long, you can survive. You can even do well. I was a wealthy woman when I got arrested."

"What did you get arrested for?" I asked.

Agnes Rose hefted a last branch, fire-scarred but still bearing a few leaves, onto her pile.

"Bigamy," she said. "But that's another story. The point is, you live like I did, you start being able to spot what makes some people sink and other people swim. There's a quality, I don't even know how to describe it—sometimes it looks like luck and some-times it looks like skill and sometimes it doesn't look like either one. But you have it, I saw it when I met you. You've made a lot of mistakes, but you're a good bet. You'll swim."

The town of Fiddleback emerged slowly from the grassy flats. First came the ranchlands, marked off with barbed wire and, every mile, a post bearing McBride's fiddleback brand. The cows grazed in placid clusters—roan, black, and dusty white—and every mile or two a solitary bull loomed hulking and heavy-shouldered, presiding over his herd. Then came the cornfields, stalks tall for the harvest, the silk on the ears turning brown in the autumn sun. Then the modest clapboard homes of the shop-keepers and ranch hands, and the boardinghouses where the cowboys lived on their way to somewhere else, arranged around a carefully watered green. Then, on a small rise above the flats, the homes of the town's wealthiest residents, built with fluted columns or else with peaked roofs and gabled windows, in the style of mansions from before the Flu. And then, below the rise, the town's main street, with a bank and a butcher shop, a few shops selling men's and women's clothing, a general store, and at its eastern end, the large roadhouse known as Veronica's.

Inside, Veronica's was full of spills and smells and jostling, the most crowded place I'd been in more than a year. To get to the bar we had to push past more cowboys than I could count, and three women dressed like Agnes Rose but more provocatively, their breasts pushed up into the necklines of their dresses. The room was large but the ceilings were low; some of the taller men had to stoop to stand at the bar.

Agnes Rose ordered her drink first, then took a seat at the bar to wait for her man. After a few moments News followed. I went last, but when I pushed my way through the crush of men to rest my elbows on the bar's sticky wood, News was still waiting.

"What can I get for you?" Veronica asked me immediately.

She was an imposing woman of mysterious age, wearing a foot-tall chestnut wig and thick pancake makeup. Her eyes and her mouth moved separately as she looked me up and down while smiling.

I ordered a whiskey in what I hoped was a passable man's voice, and Veronica poured it and set it in front of me. Only then, and only after searching the bar for other men to serve, did Veronica turn to News, as though seeing her for the first time, and without the smile she'd put on for me. At first I was confused. Then I looked around the room and saw that nearly everyone in the bar—the other cowboys, the women giggling at their jokes, and Veronica herself—was white.

News and I took our drinks to a table in the middle of the room with a decent view of the bar.

"Sorry about that," I said.

"About what?" she asked, and her voice, though light, held a warning.

As we drank, I watched the cowboys. Most looked ordinary, like men I might have known back in Fairchild if I'd stayed there long enough to move among grown people. A few wore ostentatious hats or spurs or giant belt buckles, and one had a long, full beard as bright as an orange that he stroked theatrically as he talked. No one held my attention until I saw, at a table two away from ours, a very beautiful man. He had a long smooth face and heavy eyebrows and his lips were full in a way that made him look solemn, even when he laughed. I had not seen a man I found beautiful since I left my husband's house, and this man's mere presence in the room heated the skin on my face and between my legs. I was almost angry at him for being there, at a time when

I could not afford to find anyone or anything lovely, and I turned my back to him as I sat, even though I had to twist my body slightly and was not sure how to do so in a manly way.

Bixby was late. We had gotten to Veronica's a half hour before he usually arrived, but the half hour passed and then another quarter. I could tell that News was nervous even though she kept up a steady patter about the horses we were going to buy, and I could see that Agnes Rose was worried even though she was laughing and flirting with the other men at the bar. I thought again, as I had for weeks, that I should have stayed in the convent where I could have done useful work, learned what I could from the library, and harmed no one.

As I turned over my regrets in my mind, the man whose face I'd been avoiding stood up from his table. I couldn't help but watch him. He was tall but he didn't move with the ease of a tall, handsome man. There was something tentative about him. When he and a friend—short and broad, with a wide smile but a searching eye—brought their beers to our table, I felt both joy and panic.

Several men, I noticed, refused to stand aside for them as they came, and one seemed intentionally to jostle the shorter man, who was brown-skinned like News, so that some of his beer sloshed on the floor. His face clouded for an instant, but brightened again as he saw News and clapped her on the shoulder like an old friend.

"Nate," he said. "Good to see you. Who's the new kid?"

"This is Adam," News said. "He's working with me up north this season. I'm trying to teach him how to drink."

"You couldn't have a better teacher," the cowboy said, extending his hand. "I'm Henry, this is Lark. Pleased to meet you."

Henry's handshake was firm and friendly, Lark's almost harsh, a quick clasp and then release. I had not touched a man since my husband and I had forgotten the size of their hands, the way their calluses scratched against your skin.

"Lark," News said. "Your mama give you that name?"

The man's smile was embarrassed, a little weary.

"I got it working out in Idaho country when I was younger," he said. "I've always been an early riser. The boys used to give me a hard time for being out working when everyone else was still in bed. 'Up with the meadowlarks,' they'd say."

He looked at me instead of News when he answered, like he was curious about me. I knew to be afraid of curiosity—my act was not good enough to withstand much scrutiny. And yet I met his eyes, just for a moment. They were very light brown, almost yellow, like a cat's, with a burst of green at the center.

"It's good you brought your friend here," Henry said, taking a seat. "I have a proposition for the both of you."

"What is it?" I asked. I realized I knew almost nothing about the lives of cowboys, the people I was supposed to be imitating.

"The clerks from the Farmers' and Merchants' Bank over on Main Street like to come here for their whiskey," Henry said. "There are eight of them, and ordinarily, they work four to a watch—three in the front, and one in back to guard the vault. But their boss, the bank president, just left to visit his baby grandson in Wichita, and he doesn't return until June. So the men from the Farmers' and Merchants' have instituted their own version of bankers' hours—two of them man the front of the bank, while the other six drink or loaf or do whatever they like. Four enterprising souls—five to be safe—could take everything in the till if they visit between now and midsummer."

I wondered what News had told Henry about herself. Clearly he was aware News was a thief, or at least ready to become so if the opportunity struck.

"What he's not saying," said Lark, a wry smile on his face, "is that the sheriff in Fiddleback is as well known for his marksmanship as he is for his habit of dropping by the bank unannounced to chat with the clerks."

"No risk, no reward," said Henry. "The tills at the Farmers' and Merchants' hold at least ten thousand gold eagles. Split five ways, that's still enough to feed a man in high style for a year, or in moderate style for three. Adam, you interested?"

"Oh no," said News, "don't get him involved in this. He's just starting out. He needs to be making honest money, not thieving with you degenerates."

"You're right, you're right," Henry said. "What he needs is another drink. I'll get this round."

As Henry rose, a skinny, well-groomed man with a scowl on his face made his way to the bar, and broke out in a smile when he saw Agnes Rose. She stood to greet him, her manner different from what I'd seen at Hole in the Wall; here she was light and girlish in her movements, bobbing up and down on the balls of her feet. The man set down a heavy-looking oxblood leather satchel and gave her a courtly kiss on the cheek. I looked at News and she gave me an almost imperceptible nod.

"So why did you leave Dakota?" Lark asked me.

My heart kicked. At first I was sure I'd been found out, that he worked for Sheriff Branch or my husband's family, that he had tracked me all the way here. But when I glanced at News she didn't look overly concerned, just arched an eyebrow at me, waiting for me to respond.

"How do you know I'm from Dakota?" I asked, trying to sound like News—calm, comfortable, faintly teasing.

"I can hear it in your voice," he said. "I'm from Mobridge, on the Missouri."

I felt exposed. If he could hear Fairchild in my voice, what else could he hear? At the same time, the thought of him listening that closely to me, the intimacy of it, made me blush. I lifted my empty whiskey glass to my lips to hide my face and give myself time to think.

"Why'd you leave Mobridge?" I asked.

He was looking at me very directly, but I found I could only meet his gaze for a few seconds at a time before looking down into my whiskey again. I had not been like this with my husband, but then I'd known my husband all my life. When we began courting I was excited by the prospect of sex and romance between us, but as a person he was utterly familiar to me; I could tease him about the time Andy Nichols pulled his pants down in first form, or the time he hid from his baby brother just after the birth, because he was so afraid of the umbilical cord dangling from his belly like a tail. Sitting across from me was a man I knew nothing about.

"It was time for me to marry," he said, "and I didn't want to. So the only thing I could think to do was leave."

At first I didn't understand him. I had never asked myself whether I wanted to marry. I simply knew that it was what I had to do.

"Why didn't you want to get married?" I asked.

News rotated away from us slightly in her chair just then, pretending to watch Henry try to get the bartender's attention, but really watching Bixby and Agnes Rose. Either she hadn't given him the laudanum yet or I had missed it. The latter wouldn't be a bad thing; if I could see her spike Bixby's drink from across the room, so could other people. But it would mean I'd have no way of knowing when to expect Bixby to start to falter, or when to step in if things went wrong.

"I was in love with someone," Lark said, and as he said it my attention snapped back to him even though I knew I should be watching the bar. "She was older, and she was married already, with four children. Her husband was an important man from a big family. I knew I could never have her. But once I'd fallen for her, I couldn't bring myself to court any of the girls from town. They didn't interest me. So I saved until I could buy a horse, and then I took off."

I tried to picture what it would be like to leave home because you wanted to, not because you had to—to be able to simply choose a different life. It was beyond my imagining. I felt the heat in my body cool toward Lark a little, a distance open up. At the bar, Agnes Rose was stroking Bixby's arm, seductive as a mistress and tender as a mother. He looked quite drunk now, gesturing broadly with his free hand, drooping in close to Agnes and then straightening with a hiccup. Unless he had downed three whiskeys in a matter of minutes, the laudanum was starting to work.

I looked back at Lark with more curiosity now, more control. I wanted to understand what it was like to be someone like him.

"How did you know where to go?" I asked.

"I didn't," he said. "I just headed southwest because I heard that's where the big towns were. When I hit Medicine Bow, I thought I was in Telluride."

I smiled. Even I knew Telluride was two weeks' ride south of Medicine Bow and ten times as big.

"What about you?" Lark asked. "You look like someone who's far from home."

I saw News shift in her seat and followed her gaze. Bixby had gotten unsteadily to his feet. Agnes Rose was laughing and putting her arm around him, subtly supporting his weight. She led him away from the bar and through the door to the rooms upstairs.

News took a battered pocket watch out of her dungarees.

"We'd better get back soon, right Adam?"

I thought about Bixby's swaying walk and the number of drops Agnes Rose had given him, and tried to guess how long before he was sleeping.

"In ten minutes," I said. "No need to abandon your beer."

I turned back to Lark.

"I'm on my way to Pagosa Springs," I said. "I'm going to study with a famous doctor there. I'm just cowboying till I can afford the trip."

News gave me a warning look, but I didn't care. I felt stronger than I had in weeks. Lark smiled with half his mouth. Then Henry came back with our drinks.

"Veronica's got lead in her veins today," he said.

He and News exchanged a glance.

"Unfortunately, we have to be going," News said.

She took a slug of the beer Henry had bought.

"Drinks on us the next time we meet," she said. Then she lifted her glass: "To the Farmers' and Merchants' Bank of Fiddleback."

"To the Farmers' and Merchants'," Henry said. "May it make us rich, and you jealous."

Lark lifted his glass last.

"To Pagosa Springs," he said, looking me in the eye.

At first the door to the bedroom was locked. I could see worry cross News's face. The longer we stood in the hallway, the more we risked running into lovers taking rooms for the afternoon, who would wonder why two cowboys were loitering there instead of drinking in the bar below. And the longer the door stayed locked, the more likely it was that the laudanum hadn't worked, Agnes Rose would have to sleep with Bixby and we'd all ride home in defeat.

As I waited for News to tell me what to do, I heard heavy footsteps on the stairs, rattling the dusty etchings of milkmaids and shepherdesses on the walls. News pointed down the hallway, and I ran to one of the other doors, pretending to fumble with the knob.

"I'm not drunk," I heard a man slur in a drunk voice. "I'm just going to lie down for five minutes, and then I'll challenge any one of you——"

He reached the top of the stairs, a tall man with a big belly and a red face. He passed News, still standing at Bixby and Agnes Rose's door, then listed against the wall and dragged himself along it until he got to where I stood.

"That's my room," the man bellowed into my face, his breath stinking of stale beer. "You trying to break into my room?"

"I'm sorry," I said, "I must have gone to the wrong one."

I tried to get past him but he planted a meaty hand on each wall, blocking my path.

"Everybody thinks they can just take advantage of me," he said. "'Oh, Porter's drunk, you can steal his silver, you can flirt with his woman, you can lie down in his goddamn bed.' I'm onto all of your tricks and your jokes——"

"It was an honest mistake," I said, trying to keep my voice calm. "I'll just go to my room, and I won't bother you again."

Over his massive shoulder I saw the door at the end of the hallway open. News beckoned to me.

"You're all snakes," the man shouted. "Ronnie! Ronnie! Come up here. There's a snake in my room."

It was loud in the bar below, but only a matter of time before Veronica heard the drunk man shouting. Lo had taught me a little of how to fight a man, but nothing about how to handle one who was drunk and belligerent and standing in my way. I thought of the guard cradling the wagon driver in his arms. When I acted without knowledge, I knew, I was only too likely to do the wrong thing. I gave News a look full of panic and pleading. I saw her roll her eyes.

"Good sir," she called, coming down the hallway to meet us. "Why would my poor friend here try to break into your room? Look at you. You could beat him to a pulp. Everyone here is afraid of you."

"They should be," he said. "They should be scared of me, but they think, they think—"

"Trust me," News said. "When we walked in here today, three different people told us to watch out for you. 'That man there could kick you into the next county,' they said, and I took one look at you and I knew they were right."

"That's right," he said. "That's right. I could take any man down there right now."

He mimed throwing a punch and lurched against the right wall, freeing up half the hallway. Immediately I slid past him.

"Hey," he called, "I'm talking to you!"

But News and I dashed down the hall and in through Agnes Rose's door.

Bixby lay on top of the gingham bedspread, eyes closed, mouth open, shirt partly unbuttoned to reveal sparse black chest hair. His satchel sat next to the bed.

Agnes Rose was trying to open the window.

"That guy out there is going to have Veronica up here any second," I said, whispering so as not to wake Bixby.

"All right," said News. "Get ready."

News lifted the maple-wood chair from the side of the bed and, in a single motion, smashed out the bottom pane of the window. Agnes Rose grabbed the satchel with one hand, wrapped her coat around the other, punched out the remaining spikes of broken glass, and crawled through the empty window frame onto the roof outside.

"It's not such a bad drop," she said.

Then her head disappeared from view.

"You go next," News said. "I don't want you chickening out."

Despite what Agnes Rose had done, the window frame still glistened with tiny shards of glass. The roof beyond it slanted precipitously toward the ground below—I couldn't tell how far down, but certainly farther than I wanted to jump. I looked for a drainpipe, something Agnes Rose might have used to ease her descent, but I saw only wooden shingles, cracked and bleached by wind, sun, and snow.

"Hurry up," hissed News behind me.

I felt a wave of dizziness wash over me. I took a breath, bent through the window, and managed to get my hand and my right foot planted on the roof. When I tried to swing my left foot out, though, I lost purchase with my right, and then I was rolling, then falling, then landing on my back in a pile of horse-feed sacks.

"Get up," said Agnes Rose, extending a hand. "You're fine."

We rode until near sundown just to make sure no one was trailing us. I was breathless, sore, excited by what we had done. News and Agnes Rose seemed excited, too, and we talked and laughed as soon as we were out of earshot in empty red-rock country.

"Where did you find the feed sacks?" I asked Agnes Rose.

"Just lying around by the horse troughs," she said. "Ronnie's stable boy is sloppy. But you would've been all right without them. You saw the ceiling in there—that drop wasn't more than six feet."

The evening was clear and unseasonably warm. In the distance a pair of mottled hawks were hunting prairie dogs, the whole colony squealing in distress as the birds circled and dove.

"I'll miss Ronnie's," Agnes Rose said. "I was starting to like it there."

"I wasn't," News said. "Doc made a friend, though."

I blushed, caught off guard. Of course, I realized, News had been paying attention to me and Lark even when she was watching Agnes Rose and Bixby.

"I wouldn't say 'a friend,'" I said.

"Maybe more than a friend," News said, teasing.

I rolled my eyes, still blushing,

"I doubt I'll be charming many men dressed as a cowboy," I said.

News and Agnes looked at each other like I'd said something funny.

"That's the best way to charm some men," Agnes said. "Do you like men, Doc?"

I had not given the question any thought. Watching Cassie and Elzy had made me wonder if I might at some point come to like a woman, but since I felt no stirrings of attraction toward any of the women at Hole in the Wall—and understood that they would not be welcomed if I did—I had spent only a small amount of time considering the matter. Whether or not I liked men seemed unworthy even of that small consideration, since not liking men had never been presented to me as an option.

Still, I could remember craving my husband at the beginning of our marriage; I could remember wanting him so badly I felt a pain between my legs. And I could remember boys in school—and, if I was honest, Lark too—from whom I could not look away, whose faces or backs or muscled legs I saw when I closed my eyes.

"I suppose so," I said, staring at Amity's back.

"It's too bad," News said. "Girls are much safer."

The sky was purpling at its edges and the scrub thickening around the horses' hooves. A jackrabbit startled from our path, leggy but sleek from eating summer grass.

"The safest way to meet a man," Agnes Rose explained, "is to get dolled up and pretend to be a young lady with no family on the hunt for a husband. Couple times a year we usually go down to either Telluride or Casper. The bars down there are a little more congenial than Ronnie's, and you can usually meet someone and have some fun.

"Of course, News likes to live dangerously," she added, guiding Prudence away from a dry streambed.

"I just prefer not to play dress up," News said. "And you should talk. When was the last time you put on a pair of dungarees?"

Agnes Rose shook her head, smiling.

"Plenty of cowboys like other cowboys," News said. "But this is serious, Doc—if you let them know you're really a girl, you don't know what they'll do. My advice: you do whatever you want to them, but your clothes stay on. And sometime while you're drinking together, you mention a horrible accident you were in a while back. Gored by a bull, whatever. That explains anything they feel or don't feel on your body."

"The good news is, most men are pretty stupid," Agnes Rose said. "And pretty gullible. They want to believe what you tell them."

At sundown we camped in a gully with a trickle of water for the horses. Nightjars were calling overhead, and bats came out to feed, their bodies clumsy in the dusk. We got a fire going, and gathered round the satchel like it was a holy crèche.

"Doc should do it," Agnes said. "She's the one who knocked Bixby out."

"I just measured the laudanum," I said.

But I reached for the satchel anyway. I was proud after weeks of shame—finally I had done something right. I remembered with gratitude the lessons my mother had given me with an eye dropper, the lists of dosages she had made me memorize.

The leather was heavy in my hands and faintly sweet smelling; it made me think of expensive clothes and fine furnishings, of the mayor's house in Fairchild or the back room at the bank where the rich ranchers made their deals. I opened the buckle.

At first I thought the gold must be under the bottles. They were packed carefully, each wrapped in oilcloth, so as not to shatter with hard riding. The whiskey inside the one I opened smelled rank and weak—Bixby, it appeared, had a sideline in delivery for a mediocre bootlegger. And he had been carrying no coin at all: I even turned the satchel upside down to make sure. All that fell out was a slim paper envelope, sealed with wax. I slid my finger under the seal.

"'On the twenty-first day of September, eighteen hundred and ninety-four,'" I read aloud, "'two hundred golden eagles are added to the debt owed by Roger McBride of Fiddleback Ranch to the Farmers' and Merchants' Bank of Fiddleback. The total amount of the debt stands at fifty-six thousand eagles, or two hundred and twenty-four thousand in silver. The Farmers' and Merchants' Bank continues to hold the deed to Fiddleback Ranch and its assets and surrounding properties as collateral on the debt, and reserves the right to sell at any time.'"

For a moment we all sat frozen to our seats. Then Agnes Rose threw one of the whiskey bottles against the side of the gully, where it shattered into hundreds of pieces that reflected the firelight. The horses whinnied. The bats scattered. News looked up at the stars, then back at me.

"I don't know, Doc," she said. "Maybe you're a curse."

CHAPTER 6

Winter hit us hard at Hole in the Wall. One day the after-noon wind was warm in the orchard, and the next the firepit was hidden under a foot-thick carpet of snow. We were out of money; the Kid and Cassie had been counting on the contents of Bixby's satchel, and had spent much of what we'd stolen in the wagon raid on new shoes and saddles for the horses. So Cassie had to start us on strict rations—a ladleful of corn grits for break-fast, beans for dinner, and bacon fat only on Sundays. I thought about food constantly. When I couldn't sleep, I lay in my cot picturing butter melting into bread.

Worst of all, Elzy couldn't shoot. I saw her in the frozen-over orchard one morning, firing at snowballs with her left hand and missing half the time. After that I watched her carefully—she ate and drank and brushed her horse with her left hand, and though she still gestured with her right when she talked, I saw how clum-sily it gripped the leather when she pulled on her boots. I couldn't bring myself to ask to examine her, but I could tell what had happened. I remembered one of the books I'd read in Sister Tom's library, the diagrams of the nerves running through the body like threads. I knew the bullet had ripped through those fragile fibers, and now Elzy couldn't feel her hand.

Elzy wasn't just our best sharpshooter; she was also our best hunter. Cassie and Texas and the Kid went out to try to supplement our rations, but none of them could bring down the valley's skittish pronghorn like Elzy could—all they managed to shoot were a couple of turkeys, already scrawny from winter starving. Their stringy flesh barely flavored that night's watery stew. When we ate it, I could feel everyone's eyes on me.

At first I tried to come up with plans.

"The horse market in Sweetwater," I said to News one below-freezing morning, when we all huddled around the woodstove in the kitchen cabin, the cold only sharpening our hunger. "There must be a lot of money changing hands there. We could find someone flush from a sale and rob him on his way out of town."

Texas and Lo and Cassie rolled their eyes. News sighed. It was the third idea I'd floated that morning.

"Go saddle up Amity," News said. "I need to show you something."

I pulled a fur hat down low over my forehead and a wool scarf over my face; outside in the white day, the slice of skin between them burned. The snow was so cold it squeaked under our boots. The horses snuffled in the freezing air but were willing, their coats long and dense for the winter. The sun shone weak and yellow behind a flat layer of cloud, like it was going out.

We rode south in silence, up the path out of the valley. The horses' hooves left a crisp trail in the fresh snow. We'd been riding only a few minutes when I saw what News wanted to show me: ahead of us, the road was not just snowed over, it was gone. Where once we had been able to ride between two hills, now a single, smooth snowfield stretched unbroken from hilltop to hilltop, many times higher than the roof of the bunkhouse.

"Can we ride over it?" I asked.

"Sure," said News, "if you want Amity to get stuck in the snow and die."

I reached down to rub Amity's neck with my gloved hand, chastened.

"It'll be like this through March at least, maybe April," News said. "No raids till then."

In the dead of winter only the Kid was happy. While the others slept or drank fennel tea to keep their hunger pangs at bay—my only contribution to the winter so far, made with crushed fennel seeds from Cassie's pantry—the Kid sat in a corner of the bunk-house surrounded by maps and papers, getting up only to pace around the great room and stare out at the snow. One morning we woke at dawn to the Kid banging on a saucepan with a spoon, shouting, "Wake up, my beauties, my heroes, wake up!"

As we sat all together in the great room, wrapped in parkas and bedclothes and dishtowels and rags, I saw how much we'd lost since winter began, the hollows in our cheeks and the stains around our eyes. I knew the course of malnutrition—soon our teeth would loosen from our spongy gums, and the beds of our fingernails begin to bleed.

"Before I explain why I've gathered us all here this morning," the Kid began, "I want to give thanks to each of you, for all that you have given of yourselves. Elzy, of course, you have given the strength of your right hand. We are all humbled by your sacrifice."

Elzy looked out the window, grim-faced.

"News and Agnes, you went out among strangers for weeks upon weeks without the rest of us to help you. I know how living under a false name depletes the storehouse of the heart; I know what you gave for us and I am grateful."

Agnes smiled; News didn't, but she looked at the Kid with a devotion I'd never seen before.

"And Doc—I know some of you are still angry with her. But remember Matthew: 'If ye forgive not men their trespasses, neither will your Father forgive your trespasses.'"

"The Father will just have to stay mad at me," Cassie said.

"Think," the Kid went on, ignoring her, "without our doctor, we wouldn't have been able to do the Fiddleback job at all."

"And?" Cassie asked. "I mean no disrespect to News and Agnes, but Fiddleback was supposed to hold us for the winter. Now we've got nothing until the pass opens up."

"Not nothing," the Kid said. "We have this."

I recognized the envelope from Bixby's satchel. The Kid opened it and read the letter aloud.

"We've all seen that," Cassie said. "So McBride's in debt. If we'd known that, we wouldn't have tried to rob him in the first place."

"That's right," said the Kid. "We wouldn't have tried to rob McBride."

"So I fail to see why—" Cassie began.

"McBride doesn't own Fiddleback," the Kid said. "The bank does."

Agnes Rose caught on first. "We're going to rob the Farmers' and Merchants' Bank?" she asked.

The Kid smiled. "We're going to buy it."

The Kid's plan had many steps. First, we would, in fact, have to rob the bank. Thanks to Henry, we knew we'd only have to get past two men instead of the usual four. But it wouldn't be enough just to clean out the tills—we'd have to empty the bank's reserves, which meant robbing the vault. That would take time, not just to get the vault open but also to unload the heavy gold inside. The horses alone wouldn't be able to carry it in their saddlebags; we'd have to get a wagon. All of that meant we'd need a distraction, so before we even went into the bank, we'd set fire to one of the buildings next door—either a butcher shop or a store that sold ladies' necessaries, according to the Kid's maps.

Amid the noise and commotion caused by the fire, we'd break into the bank from the back and dynamite open the vault—faster and surer, the Kid said, than forcing someone at gunpoint to unlock it for us. Then, as we loaded the gold into the wagon, a few of us would hold up the clerks and steal whatever was in the tills at the front of the bank. When we'd scoured the premises for every note, coin, and gold bar, we'd ride away and wait seven days.

During that week, the Kid said, the ranchers in Casper wouldn't be able to pay their cowboys. The shop owners wouldn't be able to take out money to buy cotton or shovels or sugar. Every grandmother who tried to withdraw from her life savings would find out there was nothing left. Panic would set in.

Then, when the owners of the bank were afraid to show their faces to their neighbors, when they were holed up in the bank with revolvers to protect not their money but themselves, one of us would show up in the guise of a wealthy landowner from Chicago. This rich man would offer to buy the bank, and all its remaining assets, including its deeds to any lands and properties in Powder River country, for a sum around half of what had been stolen. He would be prepared to haggle—even three-quarters would be acceptable—but in their desperation, the owners were sure to accept eventually. The Farmers' and Merchants' Bank of Fiddleback would be ours.

"And then we'll own the town of Fiddleback," the Kid finished, "down to the grain in the silos and the cattle in the fields. It will be ours, as God gave Canaan to Abraham, and we will use it to build our nation."

In the silence that followed I could hear the snow ticking against the windows. Lo looked confused. News and Agnes Rose looked intrigued. Elzy turned to Cassie and opened her mouth, then shut it again.

Her small body bundled in a pinwheel quilt, Texas was the first to speak.

"I thought this was Canaan," she said.

The Kid's voice went cold. "What did you say?"

Texas held the Kid's gaze, her gray eyes steady.

"You heard me," she said. "I thought this was Canaan, Kid. Our promised land. Now you're talking about Fiddleback?"

The Kid paused, as though considering, then smiled.

"Canaan was large, sweet Texas. Remember what the Lord told Moses: 'The border shall fetch a compass from Azmon unto the river of Egypt, and the goings out of it shall be at the sea.'"

"I don't remember what the Lord told Moses," Texas said. "All I know is this plan sounds liable to get us killed. And for what, I don't understand."

"How long have we lived in this valley?" the Kid asked.

Texas looked confused.

"I've been here seven years," she said. "I understand that you and Cassie were here a good five years before that. So thirteen years, give or take."

"And in those thirteen years," the Kid asked, "how much have we profited from thieving?"

Texas turned to Lo, who shrugged. News and Agnes Rose were whispering to one another.

"Well," Texas said, "we have ten horses—I assume you started with one or two. We have the bunkhouse and the sheds, and the barn I built, and our pots and pans and other effects—"

"You see," said the Kid, addressing all of us again. "We've been raiding and robbing more than a dozen years, and our profit is ten horses and the roof over our heads, nothing more. If we go along as we have been, we'll never be able to shelter many more than we have now—and even what we have, we struggle to maintain. We must set our sights higher. We must reach out and claim our due."

"Even if we survive the robbery," Elzy cut in, "and we're somehow able to con the bankers into selling, do you think the good people of Fiddleback are going to welcome us with open arms? Are they going to rejoice that their new landlords are a gang of barren women?"

"You're right," the Kid said. "Buying the bank will be only the beginning."

The Kid said this as though it was exciting, eyes ablaze with nervous energy.

"The bank in Hannibal took half my daddy's wages every single month," Lo said. "Then they took all of it. Then they took our house. Are we going to do that?"

News spoke up before the Kid could. "In my town ordinary people ran the bank," she said. "There was a board and every year we had elections. One year my daddy served. That year everyone in town got a dividend. We spent ours on new storm shutters."

Lo rolled her eyes. "I'm sure they were very nice," she said. "I hope they kept you dry while my family was begging on the Blackwater River Road."

"You know what happened to my family, Lois Ann," News shot back. "Don't pretend you're the only one who knows about suffering."

The Kid's voice cut through their argument. "Cassie, I want to hear what you think."

Cassie squeezed Elzy's hand, and let it go. She took a breath.

"You know I never liked this idea in the first place, trying to bring more people in. But I listened to you, I looked at your maps,

I fed everyone while you made your plans. I did it out of respect, and I did it out of love. And now this—"

She paused, choosing her words. Elzy watched her.

"These thirteen years, when I've fallen into despair, your spirit has sustained me. You saw this place when I couldn't. You built it in your mind, and now we live here. But this, Kid, it's a castle in the air—there's no foundation to it."

The Kid nodded curtly. "Very well, you've registered your opposition. Is everyone else so unwilling to take a chance?"

Then Agnes Rose was talking over Elzy and Lo was yelling at News and Texas was trying to calm Lo but then yelling at News too.

"Doc," the Kid said through the chatter. "You've been keeping your own counsel. Will you join us as we take the land that was promised to us?"

"Oh no," said Cassie. Her voice had been calm before but now I could hear the rage rumbling underneath it. "Don't you call on her to help you now."

"The doctor is an equal member of our company," the Kid said evenly.

Cassie shook her head. "I'm starting to see why you wanted more people here in the first place," she said.

I was ashamed—even now Elzy was worrying at her bad hand with her good hand, moving the thumb back and forth as though she could wake up the nerves. And I knew that no one here owed me any particular kindness. But also I was angry. For months, I'd been accepting the smallest bowl of grits and the sludgy dregs of the coffee; I'd been silent when Cassie passed Lo the whiskey right across me at the firepit, when Texas piled other horses' shit into Amity's stall for me to clean. I'd done nothing but try to make up for what I'd done, and I'd asked for nothing, not even respect or consideration, in return. I was tired of asking for nothing.

"Do you want me to leave, Cassie?" I asked. "If you want me to go, you should say so."

Cassie didn't even look at me. She kept talking to the Kid.

"I think perhaps you just want people you can easily control," she said.

"Friend of my heart," said the Kid, "you shouldn't say things you can't take back."

"You're leading us astray, Kid," Cassie said quietly. There were tears in her eyes. "I think you know it."

The two stared at each other across the great room. For a moment the blaze behind the Kid's eyes faltered.

Then the Kid turned away from Cassie to look at me, Agnes Rose, and News. "Some among us may not want to share our haven with others," the Kid said. "Some of us believe that having secured a measure of comfort for ourselves, we should turn a blind eye to the suffering of others."

"Kid, that's not—" Cassie began.

The Kid talked over her.

"But surely there are enough of us with the generosity of spirit to do better. Surely some of us want to aid others who suffer the way we have suffered. And surely some of us know that though we may fail in our attempt, we at least have the obligation to try."

Cassie stood up from her cot.

"I'm going to make some grits so we can all eat," she said. "Go ahead and decide without me. You clearly don't care what I think anyway."

She left the door swinging on its hinges so that Lo had to jump up to close it, and by then a half inch of snow had settled over the floor.

Cassie's words rang in my ears. Looking around at the others who remained in the great room, I could almost see them begin to pull apart from one another and from the Kid. I felt fear rise in my throat—if the gang were to split in some sort of mutiny, what would become of me?

"Perhaps we could all use some time to reflect," the Kid said. "Let's pause in our deliberations and resume after breakfast."

After that a lassitude descended over the bunkhouse. Lo pulled the covers up over her chin and went back to sleep. Agnes Rose picked at a stray thread in her sock until the whole thing began to unravel. Elzy squeezed her bad hand into a fist again and again and again; it made me sick to watch her.

The snow whited-out the windows. The minutes stretched and sagged. Texas got up to check on Cassie, but Elzy shook her head. "Give her some time," she said.

Hunger dug a hole inside me. Lo reached under her bed, pulled out her bell-trimmed buckskin jacket, and began sucking on the fringe. Everyone politely ignored her. I was a little jealous. I put a finger in my mouth just to taste the salt of my skin.

Finally Elzy got out of bed and started putting on her boots.

"Tell her—" the Kid began.

"I'll decide what to tell her," Elzy said.

Elzy left; the day wore on. Almost immediately it was hard to tell how long she'd been gone—five minutes, ten, an hour. After the wind howled particularly loudly, Texas got up and looked outside. Then I did. The air was so thick with snow I couldn't see the kitchen cabin.

"I'll go after them," Texas said, pulling on her boots.

By the feathers of ice on the windows and the bitterness of the wind coming in around the door, I could tell it wasn't much above zero outside. If Cassie or Elzy had somehow failed to make it to the kitchen cabin or back, if they'd gotten stuck in the snow, then they didn't have long. I had never treated someone with hypothermia before, but I was sure I knew more about it than anyone else there.

"You stay here," I told Texas. "I'll go."

The snow was piled so high I could barely get out the door. I followed in what must have been Elzy's tracks, but already they were softened over by several inches of fresh powder. I guessed the temperature at around five degrees—any colder than that and it would have been too cold to snow. Every time the wind gusted, it burned my face and stole my breath from my throat. I could see less than two feet ahead of me. I only made it to the kitchen cabin by following Elzy's trail.

Inside it was terribly cold, barely warmer than out in the snow. The cabin was dark, and at first I thought it was empty. Then I saw Elzy and Cassie huddled together in a corner. Elzy was crying. She looked up at me, and I saw whoever she had been before she came to Hole in the Wall, someone frightened and alone.

"I didn't know what to do," she said. "I didn't want to leave her."

I knelt in front of them. Cassie's head was slumped forward. I lifted her chin; her skin was cold and her neck was limp. But when I worked my fingers under her scarf and pressed them against her throat, I felt the weakest of pulses there.

"No," I said. "She's alive."

I shut my eyes as I'd seen Mama do when she needed to make a plan. Between the two of us, we could carry Cassie back to the bunkhouse where it was already warm. But that would take time and a trip back through the snow and wind, during which Cassie's body temperature would drop even further.

"You need to get a fire going," I said to Elzy.

The stove's iron belly was empty—Cassie hadn't even tried to make grits. Probably she had come to the cabin to sulk and then the cold had caught her by surprise.

Mama had explained to us one especially cold winter how freezing could sneak up on you—how after a while you would stop shivering and feel almost warm, then calm, like someone had wrapped you in a blanket. "But that's when you're in the most danger," Mama said.

If we were out playing and one of my sisters stopped shivering, or if her lips turned blue or she didn't make sense when she talked, I was supposed to bring her home immediately. But if we were too far, then Mama said I should find any warm place—a neighbor's house, even a horse barn would do. Then I would strip my sister down, naked or close to it, and myself also, and then get someone else to wrap us tight together, swaddling us like a baby so that the heat of my body could enter her body and warm her from the outside in.

I unwound the scarf from Cassie's neck. I felt a tiny, weak warming across my wrist, which I realized was her breath. I began to undo the buttons of her parka.

"What are you doing?" Elzy shouted, turning away from the stove. She had lit the kindling; it crackled but I couldn't yet feel the heat.

"She needs warmth right against her skin," I said. "I have to get her undressed."

"You can't undress her," Elzy said. "Then she'll freeze for sure. Are you trying to kill her?"

I remembered how Mama had explained it to me, how the body freezes and shuts down.

"Cassie's body is out of heat," I told Elzy, "and we need to put it back. Until then, all her warm clothes won't do any good."

Elzy shook her head.

"You should go," she said. "I'll take care of her myself. I don't need you."

Cassie's lips had turned a bruisy purplish color. I felt a chill down my spine that I recognized from really bad births—the feeling of death not just in the room but close by, ready.

I looked up at Elzy.

"I know you don't trust me," I said. "I know it's my fault you got hurt, and I'm sorry. But if I leave now, Cassie's going to die." Then I made the kind of promise Mama had told me never to make.

"If I stay," I said, "she'll live."

Elzy stared into my face. I saw the fear in her. I saw that what I'd said had worked.

"Here," I said, softer now. "I'll finish the fire. You strip down, as much as you can stand. Then I'm going to wrap you up together. You're going to be her warmth."

Elzy nodded. She began undoing the buttons of her parka with her left hand. I piled fresh wood on top of the kindling in the stove. Thin flames licked up around the logs.

When Elzy was undressed down to a pair of homespun under-drawers—her winter skin pale as a tooth, the scar at her shoulder livid against it—I helped her take off Cassie's parka and sweater and pants. Each layer was cold, cold, cold. I let Elzy remove Cassie's undershirt, which she did so tenderly, even with just one good hand, that I felt a stab of loneliness in my chest.

I spread Cassie's parka on the ground and together we rolled Cassie onto it. Then Elzy lay beside her and wound her long body around Cassie's body. Cassie was stout and sturdy but today she looked small. I laid Elzy's parka on top of them both, then wrapped them as best I could, adding sweaters on top for extra warmth. Elzy nestled Cassie's head against her chest, then shut her eyes.

I don't know how long they lay like that, the room slowly warming. Outside the wind died down but the snow kept falling; everything was soft and muffled and white. I was afraid Cassie would die and my promise would be broken, and my fear continued without worsening or abating, seeming to stretch back and forward across my life, infinite. Memories began to play in my mind vividly, as though they were still happening. In particular I remembered a day in the winter of Bee's first year, when Mama was still so sick she never got out of bed. Ulla's mama and the other town ladies sometimes came to help me with Bee, but that day snow had been falling thickly for hours and no one wanted to venture out. Janie and Jessamine both had the flu and were bundled in their beds, sleeping off their fevers. Bee was six months old—out of her dreamy newborn days and awake to the full horror of living.

That morning as I tried to give her a bottle, she opened her eyes wide, stared at me, and screamed without end. Nothing would quiet her, she spat out the bottle's nipple, she screamed as I walked her back and forth, bounced her, sang, and recited the names of all the major bones in the human body, all things that had calmed her in the past. In time I became used to her screaming, it seemed like the new condition of my life, I would always be holding her, she would always be screaming, no one was coming to help us, we would be alone forever. I felt desolate but also peaceful. Eventually she quieted, she took the bottle, the snow stopped and spring came and Mama got out of bed and I grew up and got married and was driven away. But in the cabin with the snow falling outside, it was as though I had never left that room, that time of fear and calm together, that child who needed me but whom I could not soothe.

What brought me back was a change in the quality of the silence. Mama said the stories the old ladies told about the evil eye were ignorant, and I know she was right. I don't believe you can feel a person's gaze, but I believe you can hear it. When sleeping people open their eyes, their breathing changes, and so do the tiny movements of their bodies, even if they are very sick or tired and can barely move at all. It was this change that I heard in the cabin that day, and so I knew before Elzy, maybe even before Cassie herself, that Cassie was awake.

For the next few days, no one talked about the plan the Kid had proposed. All of us were occupied with caring for Cassie. Texas took over cooking and spoon-fed her warm grits. Lo combed her hair and wrapped her in blankets. Elzy held her hand, and the Kid kept circling and fretting over her, with an anxiety I'd never seen, asking me repeatedly if she was going to be all right.

"She'll be fine," I said.

Cassie was fully conscious and speaking, and while her toes were frostbitten, I did not think she would lose any of them. I made a footbath of warm water and feverfew to ease the stinging as her blood came back into her snow-burnt skin, and then I wrapped her feet loosely in lengths of clean cotton. She didn't talk to me as I cared for her, only responding yes or no when I asked if something hurt, and even then she refused to meet my eyes. The others, however, especially Texas and the Kid, treated me with a new gravity, asking my opinion on what was best to feed Cassie or whether we should use up more of our limited firewood to give the bunkhouse extra warmth. I tried not to think about what would've happened if Cassie had died in Elzy's arms in the kitchen cabin, if I'd promised to save her and had failed.

On the fourth day of Cassie's convalescence she could walk a little, and the sun came out over the valley. We shoveled a path from the bunkhouse to the kitchen cabin and the horse barn. I visited Amity and stroked her watchful face, and Texas let me feed her a wizened carrot she'd been saving. A little joy crept in around the edges of that day—Cassie laughed at something the Kid told her, too quiet for anyone else to hear; News got out her fiddle for the first time in weeks and played "My Pretty Jane" and "Shinbone Alley"; while we were shoveling, Texas and Lo threw snowballs at each other and then, as though deciding something, at me.

That night, after a dinner of beans lightly burned by Texas, the Kid stood and faced Cassie.

"Cass, friend of my heart, for many years it was just the two of us at Hole in the Wall. Those were blessed years; everything we reap now was sown then. And even as we began to grow, we grew slowly—News, you came to us, and then Elzy, then Texas, then Lo, then Agnes Rose. And then the good doctor, who I think has earned an apology for the skepticism with which we initially treated her."

News began to clap, and the others joined in. I felt a surprising warmth in my chest; it had been so long since I had been surrounded by people who cared for me. Only Cassie did not clap. Instead she looked down at her bandaged feet.

"When we were few, we rarely disagreed," the Kid went on. News and Agnes Rose exchanged an amused glance.

"But as we become many, we will encounter more differences of opinion. And so I propose this course of action for the consideration of my plan regarding the Farmers' and Merchants' Bank of Fiddleback, and all such matters in future, should they prove controversial:

"Take three days. Speak among yourselves. I promise not to try to sway you any more than I've already done. If at the end of that time the better part of you disapprove of my proposal, I'll accept your decision and I won't seek to change it. But if a majority supports the proposition, then we'll start the preparations right away. And I'll endeavor to make sure you never regret putting your trust in me."

The next day we ran out of beans, so News and I butchered a pair of leather riding pants. I laid them out flat on a clean sheet, and News cut along the seams until the legs came apart, then sliced each one into thin strips.

"I'm not cooking that," Cassie said, so we carried the pile of leather to the kitchen cabin ourselves and set a pot to boiling.

Hunger made us crazed and giddy.

"Should we add turpentine?" News asked. "Or look, here are some roofing nails."

"If we wait long enough," I said, "we might catch some mice to put in."

"You think you're joking," said News, stirring the strips into the water. "We ate mice in eighty-nine. Lo didn't want to, she said they spread diseases. So the Kid ate one first. Nothing happened, so we all ate them, and we survived that winter."

A smell of sweat came wafting up from the pot. It was disgusting, but it still made me hungry.

"What do you think of the Kid's plan?" I asked.

News laughed. "It's ridiculous," she said. She rummaged through the packets and jars on Cassie's spice shelf, found some oregano, and dumped it in the boiling water.

"Then again, if it works, think of it. A whole town. The Kid could be the mayor. Maybe I'd be the sheriff. We could live out in the open, no more hiding, no more running away."

"I don't know," I said. "My town wasn't so kind to me. I'm not sure I'm eager to go back to one."

"I wish I could go back to Elmyra," News said. "I miss it every day."

"Even though they ran you out?" I asked.

News examined a cloudy jar of dried mushrooms. "Who says they ran me out?" she asked. "Our sheriff used to come over for dinner every second Sunday. He knew I was barren, everybody did. Nobody cared. I helped take care of my sister-in-law's children. We were happy."

I took the jar from News, sniffed the contents, and put it back on the shelf. "Don't use that," I said. "So what happened?"

Her voice took on a hard edge.

"Dr. Lively happened."

I remembered the book I'd seen in the convent library, about the mixing of bloodlines.

"He came to your town?" I asked.

"He didn't have to. The mayor became a devotee. Black and white people lived together in Elmyra, they had for generations. Abolitionists founded our town, before the Flu—those were our ancestors. Then Mayor Miller got it into his head that racial mixing caused barrenness. Next thing we knew he had annulled a dozen marriages. The sheriff showed up at my parents' house at night and made my mama move out. And of course, as a barren woman and the child of a mixed marriage, I was the mayor's new favorite science experiment. He wanted to bring me with him to different towns to help him convince other mayors to adopt Lively's ideas."

News added a liberal shaking of pepper to the pot.

"For a long time after I left I thought, maybe when Mayor Miller dies I can go home. Then I heard his son took over, so I gave that up. But now—" She tasted the leather soup, made a face, and added more oregano. "I know it's crazy," she said. "We'll be killed for sure. But on the off chance that we survive, I keep thinking, maybe it could be like home."

"Do you remember what you told me up at Hole in the Wall?" I asked Elzy.

She was sitting cross-legged on her cot on the bunkhouse's upper level, cleaning and oiling all the hunting rifles. I saw she had developed a system, gripping the barrel with her right hand and operating the brush and cloth with her left. Unless you knew what to look for—the way she turned to watch her right hand every time she moved it, the way she occasionally used her left hand to readjust the fingers—you would not have known she had ever been injured.

"Remind me," Elzy said. "I've had a lot on my mind since then."

"You told me the Kid didn't mean it literally, all that about the promised land. You said it was a way of holding us together."

Elzy didn't look up from her work. "That sounds like me," she said.

I knelt by the gun parts laid out on clean cotton. "What do you say now?"

Elzy put the barrel down on the cloth. She moved to run her good hand through her hair, noticed the oil on it, and wrapped both arms around her knees. Sitting like that, she looked sweet and scrawny, like a boy in ninth or tenth form, before manhood has fully descended upon him.

"Maybe I was wrong," Elzy said. "Maybe the Kid was always serious and I just wasn't paying attention. Or maybe something's different now. I don't know."

Elzy shook her head and went back to oiling a barrel. "But you know, I was right about one thing. It did hold us together for a long time, all that high-flown talk. That dream about who we could be. Even if we didn't believe it."

"And now?" I asked.

"Well, now it might get us killed."

After a day and a half I had a good idea of where most of the gang stood: Agnes Rose and News in favor of the plan despite their reservations; Cassie, Elzy, and Lo against. Texas was the only one I wasn't sure about. When she rode out the day before the vote to gather birch bark, I volunteered to go along.

The day was overcast, white on white. The land was muffled. We crossed the grasslands where pronghorn jumped and meadowlarks sang in the summertime; now our horses were the only things that moved.

We found a stand of birch and tied up Faith and Amity. Texas approached a trunk and plunged her knife in deep, past the outer layer of bark to the pale starch beneath that we could chew to sate our hunger. Then, with the deftness of an expert, she sliced away a footlong narrow strip, rolled it up, and put it in the pocket of her parka.

"Did you learn this on the farm?" I asked her.

She looked at me like I was very stupid.

"My daddy was the biggest horse breeder between Abilene and Cheyenne country. We never had to live on birchbark."

"I'm sorry," I said. "I just wondered how you learned to harvest it so well."

"I was on my own for a winter before I found the convent," Texas said. "I wasn't used to fending for myself, but I had to learn real quick."

I stabbed the nearest tree and tried to slice away a strip, but I was clumsy with my gloves and soon dropped the knife into the deep snow.

"Do you think Cassie's right?" I asked as I searched.

"That the Kid's gone wrong in the head? I don't know," Texas said, "but it doesn't matter. Wrong or right, the Kid's dreaming bigger than this place now, and it's going to end in war."

"So you're voting no?" I asked. I found the knife and lifted it to the tree, then dropped it again.

"I'm voting yes," she said.

I had not figured Texas for someone with a death wish.

"Why?" I asked.

She pulled free another slick strip of bark, her third in the time I'd been trying to cut one.

"The sheriff who hanged my family—" she said, "I promised myself one day I'd come back and kill him. But I can't do it alone. I need someone to ride down to Amarillo with me and keep lookout, back me up if anything goes wrong."

Texas reached into the snow, fished out my knife, and put it in her pocket. I looked at my boots, chastened.

"I told the Kid I'd back the Fiddleback plan. If it works, the Kid will help me with the sheriff."

"And if it doesn't work?"

"I'll try something else."

She sounded utterly calm.

"Elzy thinks we'll all get killed," I said.

"Well, I don't plan to get killed," she said. "But if I do, so be it. At least I'll have done my best."

The next day a warm chinook wind came up from the south, and the temperature climbed—it might have been twenty-five degrees, but it felt like spring to us after so many days at zero or below, and we forgot even our hunger, piling outside to play like puppies in the snowdrifts. The Kid joined in for a while, making an angel in the smooth snow in front of the bunkhouse, but then peeled off toward the horse pasture, hands in pockets. I followed.

"We're out of valerian," the Kid said, turning around.

I was caught off guard.

"I'm sorry," I said. "We can get some more as soon as the pass is open."

"Is there anything else that works the same?"

"Chamomile," I said. "It's not as good, but it's something. I think Cassie has some dried in the kitchen cabin."

The Kid nodded, then turned away from me, looking out across the pasture at the red wall now white with snow.

"The man your Mama treated," the Kid said after a moment, "the one who couldn't sleep. Was he troubled by terrors?"

"I'm sorry," I said, "I'm not sure what you mean."

The Kid sounded impatient. "Did he have night terrors? Fears he couldn't name? Did he see shapes out of the corner of his eye, phantoms that disappeared when he turned to look at them?"

"No," I said. "He never described anything like that."

The Kid began walking away from me across the pasture. Even in the warm wind it looked desolate—horseless and trackless, flat snow sweeping down to the fences and then beyond into the valley. So recently a confident leader, the Kid was a lonely figure now, shoulders tensed up to the ears, eyes on the ground. I thought again of what Elzy had said, but it was too late now— I'd made my decision. I caught up with the Kid.

"There's something else," I said. "The laudanum I used on Bixby. I still have some left in the trunk under my bed. A single drop will help you sleep. More is dangerous. And you should only take a drop if you really need it—too many nights in a row and you'll start to need more and more. You'll—a person can become dependent."

"Should anyone require such a remedy," the Kid said, "I'll be sure to dispense it carefully."

Part of me felt guilty making my next request, but another part knew now was the time, when the Kid was already beholden to me for my discretion.

"There's something I need to do," I said. "I've been planning it ever since I joined the sisters. There's a master midwife down in Pagosa Springs, and she knows more than anyone I've ever heard of about barrenness and childbirth, and I need to go and work with her. I think I can help her."

I had never said the last part before, and I was surprised to find I believed it.

"Each one among us joined our number freely," the Kid said, "and each is free to depart. You know that."

"I can't get there on my own," I said. "I need a horse, and money, and someone to ride down with me so I don't get killed. And I think—" I paused, unused to such brazenness. "I think you need my vote or you'll lose the Fiddleback plan."

The Kid's smile had no joy in it.

"You've been talking to Texas."

I didn't say anything.

"Well, fair enough. What you want will be easily accomplished when we've taken possession of Fiddleback. But you have to swear your loyalty until then. Can you promise to fight for our nation, no matter what comes?"

"I promise," I said.

The Kid reached out a hand and we shook. Through our thick gloves the gesture felt strange, like the Kid was far away.

"Thank you," I said.

"I'll accept your gratitude one day," the Kid said. "But I haven't earned it yet."

We voted that night. News and Texas and I had gone out to look at the stars. News and I knew the simple constellations—the dippers and Orion—but Texas could point out fish and crabs and women in the sky, and even showed us stars that shone red or blue instead of white. She was tracing Gemini with her index finger when Lo called us back to the bunkhouse. Inside, the Kid was already speaking.

"My friends," the Kid said, "I won't insult you by repeating myself. I will only remind you that 'Faith, if it hath not works, is dead, being alone.' Now is the time for our good works, my beauties, my heroes. Now is the time for justice on Earth."

Everyone was quiet for a moment and I thought of Holy Child, the Mother Superior holding us all in silence with her Sunday sermon.

"All in favor of buying the Farmers' and Merchants' Bank of Fiddleback, raise a hand."

News and Agnes voted right away. Texas waited a moment, then joined them. Lo stared straight ahead, hands in her pockets. Elzy and Cassie clasped hands and didn't move. I looked at the Kid for some kind of confirmation of our agreement, but the Kid was now totally unlike the Kid earlier that day—shoulders back, head high, voice full of strength and bravado. I lifted my hand. I was going to have to take my chances.

CHAPTER 7

It was early April when Agnes Rose and I rode out of the valley. The snow was melting; if you listened you could hear it, running back into the earth. The smell of wet soil was sweet after so many sterile months, and the scrawny pronghorns and jackrabbits looked surprised by the sunlight, as if they'd forgotten it existed.

Our first stop was Nótkon's trading post, but he did not have what we wanted.

"Who would buy dynamite from me?" he asked, pushing our pile of bullets and spices—the last valuables we had left after the long winter—back across the counter. "Only someone crazy. I never took you for crazy, Agnes Rose."

"Maybe one of your suppliers could find some?" Agnes asked. "We could come back in two weeks or a month, with some gold—"

Nótkon shook his head.

"If I sell you a gun, and you shoot somebody, no one's going to trace that back to me, because everyone sells guns. But nobody sells dynamite. So if I manage to find you some, and you blow something up, the sheriff's posse is going to come straight to my door—after they've taken care of you, that is."

"We understand," said Agnes Rose, gathering up our motley offerings. "Thanks anyway."

But I was not finished. "What if I wanted to make some dynamite?" I asked. "Could I do that?"

Nótkon looked at me the same way he had when I told him about Mrs. Alice Schaeffer, like he was impressed and maybe a little disturbed.

"Dynamite? No," he said. "But you can make an explosive that will do the trick."

"What do I need?" I asked.

"That's outside my purview, I'm afraid," Nótkon said. "But you seem like a resourceful sort. I'm sure you'll get the information you're looking for."

We met the bookseller at a roadhouse a day's ride west of the valley, in pine country. The place made Veronica's look like a palace. It was the remnant of an old house, probably built before the Flu and torn nearly apart for firewood in the years after, when so many houses stood empty. Now only the kitchen and a single bedroom remained. The proprietor, a drained-looking woman named Wilma, had set up the bar on the old sideboard next to the stove, and the whiskey she poured us was warm from the burning wood.

The bookseller looked nervous, as always. Over the winter he had grown a sandy-colored mustache, and he took quick careful sips of whiskey from beneath it, eyes darting over the room. Ten or twelve men sat with us at the long wooden table, once handsome, now riven with cracks from its abandoned years and stained with liquor and tallow from its renaissance. At least ten more men drank standing up, leaning against the walls. This was an older, harder clientele than at Veronica's—trappers and traders, men from forest country who went weeks at a time without seeing another human being. Now brought together, some were silent still as though they'd forgotten how to speak, or perhaps ordered their lives specifically to avoid it. But a few had been released from solitude into jolliness or belligerence, and they were loud enough to make up for everyone else, to cover our voices as we talked.

"I have what you need," the bookseller said. "The field manual of the St. Louis Militia. Has everything you need to know about homemade explosives, plus combat drills, camouflage, and how to survive in the wilderness for up to thirty days with no food or fresh water. I can give it to you for fifty silver liberties."

I rolled my eyes.

"Come on," I said. "You think I've forgotten what books cost? We'll give you a box of good bullets, and I think Agnes Rose has some jewelry she can throw in."

Agnes Rose opened her leather travel pouch to show him the brooches and earrings we were selling.

"All of that plus the pouch it comes in," the bookseller said. "And I'll have to give you the cheaper copy, without the diagrams."

I looked at Agnes Rose. She nodded.

"We don't need diagrams," I said, raising my glass. "Deal."

The bookseller clinked his glass with mine, avoiding eye contact, then finished his warm drink and pushed back his chair.

"Before you go," I said, trying to get myself ready for the answer, "have you heard any news of Sheriff Branch recently?"

He shook his head.

"I knew you were lying to me. I should charge you more just for putting me in danger. If he'd found me with you in my wagon—"

"But he didn't," I said. "Look, he doesn't know where I am now, I'm sure of that." (I was sure of no such thing.) "I'm only curious if he's still on the lookout."

"There's still a price on your head, if that's what you mean," said the bookseller. "I've had two different bounty hunters ask

me about you this year. Apparently you're wanted in Fairchild
for deceiving a young man into marriage, as well as for the still-
birth of a neighbor's baby and for giving another baby a cleft lip
by sharing a bottle of wine with the mother."

Agnes Rose pushed her drink away. "You don't believe that
kind of garbage, do you?" she asked. "An educated man like you?"

The bookseller shrugged. "Doesn't matter what I believe. But
I'll tell you this." He leaned over the table and lowered his voice.
"I met Branch a couple of months ago. In Rapid City, before the
winter. He was out there helping a family with their cattle drive,
because the father was taken ill. He was a kind man, intelligent.
It made me think, probably this Ada person could have reasoned
with him. Probably if they just sat down together, they could
have come to an understanding. And sitting here with you now,
talking about explosives—sometimes I think you women up in
the valley like making trouble, that's all."

I saw Agnes Rose reach for the false pocket in her dress that
led to her gun. I reached for mine, too, holstered on my belt.

"Don't worry," the bookseller went on. "I didn't tell him
anything. I've known the Kid for years, and you were right, the
money's good. But maybe you should try breaking bread with
people from time to time instead of fighting them. It's a good
deal safer."

Ten minutes later, as the bookseller searched in his wagon for
the un-illustrated version of the St. Louis Militia field manual,
Agnes Rose whispered that we should kill him.

"I don't know how we can trust him now," she said.

"Everyone here saw us with him," I whispered back. "If we
kill him here, they'll know it was us."

"Maybe we can ask him to give us a lift somewhere," Agnes
said. "Pretend our horse lost a shoe."

"Both of our horses?" I asked. "He'll see through it."

The truth was, I didn't want to kill the bookseller in cold blood. I still saw the face of the young wagon driver when I tried to sleep at night. And he had been a total stranger to me. I'd spent days with the bookseller—I knew the way he hummed a tuneless song to himself when he thought no one was listening, the way he chewed his cuticles down to blood, the left hand and then the right. I did not like him, and Agnes was right, I did not trust him, but I was not sure I could bring myself to end his life.

"I have another idea," I said.

I raised my voice just loud enough for the bookseller to hear inside the wagon.

"We'll have to test it first," I said. "We don't want to get all the way to Casper with dud explosives."

"Casper?" asked Agnes Rose.

I gave her a look, and she caught on.

"We should buy whatever we need down south and test it at Badger Hollow," Agnes said. "That way, we won't have to ride all the way from the valley to Casper with explosives in our saddlebags."

The bookseller climbed out of the wagon with the book in his hands.

"You won't need to buy much," he said. "From what I remember, the main ingredient is horseshit."

The bookseller was right. Frederick Blunt, the secretary of the St. Louis Militia in the year 1857, when the field manual was published, recommended five pounds of horse manure, a half pound of saltpeter, and a long fuse.

"These materials, if properly assembled, will make a bomb sufficient to destroy a small wagon or outbuilding," Blunt wrote. "Two bombs will flatten a full-size wooden house. With four bombs, the militia was able to destroy a fort occupied by the Vinegar Boys, thus strengthening our position at the junction of the Illinois and Missouri Rivers, where we hope to establish a seat of government."

I started with a single bomb—what I hoped was five pounds of shit from the barn, mixed in a feed bag with saltpeter and lit with a bootlace. I tested it far from the bunkhouse, near a snow-melt stream in case it started a fire. Marsh marigolds were just beginning to open their white blooms, and the place smelled earthy and vegetal. I thought of Mama's garden; her calendulas and coneflowers would be blooming soon.

The bookseller was right that in his way, Sheriff Branch was kind and intelligent. I kept telling myself that he would never harm my family, that he would be satisfied with searching for me. Perhaps it would protect them, I thought, that they truly did not know where I was. No one did—no one who had known me in Fairchild knew that I was an outlaw now, that I was kneeling before a makeshift bomb with a lit match, hoping to rob a bank and buy a town. It was a lonely but exhilarating feeling.

The bomb was a disappointment. The flame ran obediently up the bootlace and caught the feed bag, which crackled merrily on the damp earth, but produced nothing you could call an explosion. We waited a minute, two minutes, five.

"Does the manual say how long it takes?" Agnes asked.

"No," I said, "but it's not much good if it's this slow. Some-body's going to notice if there's a bunch of burning shit in the bank vault."

The next time I spread the manure out first to dry all day in the sun. When it was baked hard and had attracted a black crust of flies, I scooped it into a new feed bag and tried again. This time Lo joined News and Agnes to watch the experi-ment. This time, again, the experiment failed.

"If we can't get the bombs to work," Lo said, trying to sound casual, "we'll have to abandon the plan."

"They'll work," I said, though I did not know how.

I tried more saltpeter and less saltpeter, more manure and less. I tried longer fuses and shorter fuses, leaving the bag open to the air and tying it tight. Once I got desperate and lit the mouth of the bag without even tying a fuse on. Luckily that attempt failed like all the others.

I stopped telling people when I was testing bombs, but they found out anyway, and by the time of my fuseless test everyone but Cassie and the Kid was coming out to watch. The rivalry between the ones who wanted the tests to succeed and the ones who wanted them to fail was obvious, lighthearted on its surface but serious at its core. After I stamped out the bomb and the crowd dispersed, Elzy approached me.

"How much longer are you going to do this?" she asked.

"Until it works," I said, though I had no ideas left.

"It doesn't look like you're getting any closer," she said. "Why not tell the Kid it can't be done?"

"Because it can," I said.

Elzy sighed and wiped sweat from her brow with her good hand. It was nearly May and warm in the sun, though the shade still held the memory of winter.

"I'm sure you have your reasons for wanting to try the Kid's plan," she said. "I'm sure you think they're good ones. But you and I both know how dangerous it is. Maybe this is a chance for you to reconsider your vote. If you tell the Kid the explosives don't work, the Kid will have to call everything off."

"Think about it," she said, this time running her bad hand through her hair, a gesture whose clumsiness seemed intentional. "You could still save all of our lives."

For a moment I said nothing. Since the vote I had begun to feel like part of the gang in ways I had not expected. In the mornings, I had started helping Texas feed and water the horses, and though we spoke little I felt a calm with her that I hadn't felt since I walked to school with Susie, before we picked up Ulla and the day filled up with her jokes and gossip. In the evenings, Lo was continuing my fighting lessons, and in return I was teaching her about medicines and poisons, what we had to buy from traders and what we could gather around the bunkhouse, which herbs we could dry and suspend in tea or oil to cure coughs and fevers and clean infected skin.

I saw how the valley, now blooming into beauty after the long winter, could feel like home. What I had planned instead was so amorphous and uncertain. Mrs. Alice Schaeffer might want nothing to do with me. She might have closed her surgery. She might have died.

But if I stayed in the valley, I would learn no more about myself or people like me than I had known when I left the convent. I would die without knowing what made me the way I was.

"The Kid won't give up that easily," I told Elzy. "If this doesn't work, we'll find something that does."

That night, while the rest of the gang bickered and played dominoes and drifted off to bed, the Kid sat brooding over maps and papers, eyes unfocused and bloodshot. I stayed up as the others went to sleep, and once Cassie began to breathe rhythmically in her cot, the Kid motioned me outside.

The spring moon was bright and high, the shadows of the rock walls sharp on the valley floor. An owl hooted, close and loud. The fine gray fabric of the Kid's coat and hat took on a soft sheen in the moonlight.

"Have you been sleeping?" I asked.

The Kid looked at the moon and shrugged.

"What about the—" I paused, trying to find the most respectful way to ask about night terrors and fears with no names. "What about the other symptoms?" I finished.

"Have you ever been responsible for other people, Doctor? Have you held their lives in your hands?"

"You know I have," I said.

The Kid nodded.

"My daddy was a pastor," the Kid said. "Our town had a mayor, but really he was in charge. He baptized every single baby. He married a new couple nearly every Sunday. And when a wife was being beaten by her husband, when a widower broke down and thought about joining his dead wife, when a child was sick or missing or a grandfather was entering his second childhood and losing his mind, my daddy was there with counsel, day and night, and sometimes with food or money or a bed, whatever was needed, because every person in the congregation was like part of him and when they suffered, he suffered."

"He sounds like a great man," I said.

"He was very strong," the Kid said. "Three hundred and sixty days a year, he held everyone up. And then for a week, he fell apart. He didn't sleep. He saw things and heard voices. He accused us of things we didn't do. He never hit us, but he would break things—once he smashed every dish in the kitchen, and we ate cold bread and cheese off of napkins until we saved up enough to replace them."

"Are you worried that's going to happen to you?" I asked. "That you're going to have an attack like he did?"

"I was supposed to take over the church," the Kid said. "Not my older brother or my younger brother—me. I started preaching before the congregation when I was eleven years old and I was more popular than the assistant pastor. I knew how to listen to people—when my daddy was busy visiting someone else, the parishioners started pouring out their hearts to me. Everyone said I was just like my daddy."

The Kid sighed and smiled. "I should've known I'd get the bad part too."

"What helped your daddy?" I asked. "If there's a medicine, I can make it or we can get it from Nótkon, I'm sure of it."

"Nothing helped. In the beginning the doctor or the midwife would come to look at him, but the only thing that ever worked was waiting. Mama would tell the church elders Daddy was very sick, and arrange for the assistant pastor to give the Sunday sermon. Then she'd draw all the curtains and keep everyone away from Daddy, visitor or family, until he was himself again."

The owl called again, farther away this time. Clouds were massing around the moon. The Kid turned away from me to face the red wall, now harsh black and white in the moonlight.

"I still have my wits about me," the Kid said. "The laudanum helps. I'm being judicious with it, as you said. But if I forget myself, if I behave as though I'm not a mortal human, but a god on earth, and no man or woman can harm me, then you must take me to the cowboy shack down by the creek. I'll stay there until the sickness passes."

"I can do that," I said, "but shouldn't you be talking to Cassie about all this?"

"Cassie suspects," the Kid said. "But she doesn't know how ill I could become. If she knew—"

The Kid took off the gray hat, passed an elegant hand over a close-cropped scalp. Bareheaded beneath the night sky, the Kid looked older and more weary than I'd ever seen.

"Our friends in there"—the Kid said, gesturing at the bunkhouse—"they may not always like me or agree with me, but they rely on me. I've begun to falter, I know they see it. But I'm still myself, for now."

The Kid put the hat back on.

"If I have to go away," the Kid said, "tell them I've been taken with fever, tell them whatever you can think of. Just don't tell them the truth."

I was afraid then—not of the Kid or whatever had ailed the Kid's father, but of what would happen if I was responsible for holding the whole gang together. I was afraid, too, of what would happen if I couldn't make a working bomb soon; every day we didn't make progress on the Kid's plan, I sensed, meant another sleepless night. But I knew it would do no good to let the Kid know I was scared.

"You can count on me," I said.

"Good," said the Kid. "Come on, time for bed. The night air's been good for me. I should take these constitutionals more often."

The Kid began walking back to the bunkhouse, and I hurried to catch up. I had so many questions, and I didn't want to let the moment pass without asking at least one.

"Why didn't you take over your father's church?" I asked. "What happened?"

The Kid gave me a smile and a shake of the head at the same time.

"Another day," the Kid said. "I'm tired."

I spent the next day with the field manual, looking for clues. I had read the section on bombs hundreds of times, but I had not read the whole book cover to cover. Much of it was not, strictly speaking, a manual at all, but instead a record of the accomplishments of Frederick Blunt himself. Through his negotiation skills,

Blunt had apparently helped form the militia, bringing together the fighting-age men of three extended families who had fled northwest when the Flu came to the old city of St. Louis. Thanks to his cunning and military acumen, the men had been able to defeat or contract with several other bands of white settlers who had escaped the dying city, resulting in control of significant territory in Missouri River country, as well as the loyalty of nearly five hundred people. Blunt was then instrumental in establishing a town seat in the place they called Meeting of the Waters, and defending it against attacks by rival bands of refugees while simultaneously sending scouts west to treat with Osage leaders and to create satellite settlements against the day—soon, Blunt was sure—when the population of Meeting of the Waters would overwhelm its location on a peninsula between the rivers and necessitate a move.

Amid all this, Blunt apparently remained secretary of the militia, never ascending to the rank of captain or becoming mayor of Meeting of the Waters, which suggested to me that many of the triumphs he attributed to himself had in fact been achieved by other people, or perhaps not achieved at all. Still, his account was very detailed, down to the number of bullets, musket balls and other ammunition the militia kept in their stockpile, the time it took to build a town hall out of lumber salvaged from nearby abandoned homes, and the type of grain the militiamen and their families fed their horses. It was this last that caught my eye.

"The foals born in the spring of 1853 did not thrive as their elders had," Blunt wrote, "suffering from broken bones and a number of other ailments. Andrew Langhorne, an experienced farmer who served as our farrier, speculated that since coming to Meeting of the Waters we had come to rely too heavily on oats and corn in the horse feed and not enough on pasture grass.

Indeed, foals set to pasture the next spring and given oats and corn only as supplements were stronger, and this has been our practice ever since."

At Hole in the Wall the horses ate pasture grass in the summer and dry alfalfa and hay in the winter; most had never even tasted oats or corn. Luckily such feed was not expensive, and I was able to get several bags from Nótkon in exchange for one of our older guns and some of the herbal tinctures I'd put up in the fall.

I was all but certain the experiment would be worthless, and so I didn't even tell Texas what I was doing. I said I was supplementing Amity's feed because she had seemed colicky lately, and when it came time to clean the barn I secretly stored her shit separately from the rest. When I had enough dried and bagged, I crept out of the bunkhouse early in the morning while everyone else slept, when the sky was just beginning to blue with sunlight.

As I lit the fuse I was thinking about what I would do next, how I would tell the Kid that I could not make us any bombs. The Kid had been sleeping when I left—upright in a chair with hat and boots still on, but sleeping nonetheless. The day before, I had checked the laudanum in the trunk, and while it had certainly dwindled, the Kid had clearly used it sparingly. Probably the Kid was doing better, I told myself. You had to be very strong, after all, to pull together a gang from nothing and lead it for years through danger and privation, keeping eight people together in the face of all that could pull them apart.

Without bombs, I knew, we'd have to get someone from the bank to open the vault for us. That would take time, in which the sheriff's posse might arrive, or the rest of the bank employees might band together to rush us. The plan would become more dangerous—the Kid might need to call another vote, or at the very least convince Elzy and Cassie and Lo that the risks were not so great. Still, I told myself as the flame slid up the bootlace, the

Kid could handle it. Surely the ability to make provisions for future sickness meant that the sickness was, at present, not so advanced.

I heard a sound behind me then, something moving in the tall grass. I turned, thinking snake, thinking mountain lion, and so when the bomb went off with the sound of earth tearing open, I was looking right into the eyes of the Kid, who had not been sleeping at all.

CHAPTER 8

The Easter Market in Casper was like nothing I'd ever seen. At the center of the town fairgrounds was a canvas tent big enough to hold everyone in Fairchild. Inside, women in white bonnets and yellow dresses were getting ready for the Sunday service, hanging tapestries of baby Jesus leaving the tomb in the arms of Mary Magdalene; baby Jesus appearing before the disciples; baby Jesus ascending to Heaven, flanked by angels. Around the tent, merchants and traders from up and down the Powder sold their wares from the backs of their wagons: hollowed-out duck and chicken eggs painted with flowers or resurrection scenes; Babies' Tears made of gelatin and sugar and flavored with berry juices or brandy; beaded moccasins and bags trimmed with porcupine quills; flower crowns; sweet pies with rhubarb and savory pies with lamb; fine Mexican silver; and last-minute costumes for Mothering Monday, baggy bright dresses for men and hats and mustaches for women, along with gray wigs to turn children into old grannies.

At the center of the fairgrounds were the livestock stalls, loud with the complaints of animals and noisome with their mingled smells. There I saw a hog the size of a steer and a steer the size of the kitchen cabin at Hole in the Wall; I saw a snow-white chicken with a long feathered tail like the train of a wedding gown, and a tame black bear that stood on its hind legs and wore a hat like a man.

We met Henry and Lark among the horses. Henry was examining a beautiful roan mare, who held her head high as he walked around her stall, as though she knew her own worth. Lark was occupied with a smaller horse, dappled gray like river stones with wild, mistrustful eyes. He clucked to it softly with his tongue and it hesitated, then went to him and ate a sugar cube from his flat palm.

When News had suggested to the Kid that Henry and Lark could help us steal a wagon to the carry the gold away from Fiddleback, I'd been too embarrassed to endorse the idea. Cassie, predictably, didn't like it—we'd never needed outside help with a job before, she said. But News pointed out that wasn't quite true—Henry and Lark and many others had given her tips and information in the past. And in any case, the biggest thing we'd ever stolen in the past was a horse. Henry and Lark had done a wagon job before, and knew how to manage a hitch and a team of new, scared horses. The Kid had agreed quickly, and it made sense for me to go with News. I already knew the two men, and by now News and I worked together well enough to make up, largely, for my lack of experience. When we walked among the horses as Nate and Adam, I felt, if not comfortable in my man's stride, then at least hidden by it—no one who looked at me would guess I was a barren woman, a discarded wife, an outlaw wanted for cursing women's wombs even though I had helped coax dozens of babies into the world.

But as soon as I saw Lark, I felt exposed, as though anyone who saw me would be able to tell what I was thinking. He carried himself with more confidence than I remembered; what I had taken for unease in Fiddleback seemed now more like caution, as he held his body still while the shy horse licked his hand. When he turned to face me, I turned away as if I didn't see him, and turned back only when Henry joined him and News greeted them both, clapping them on their backs and shaking their hands.

"Should we find somewhere we can talk?" News asked.

Henry shook his head.

"Look around you," he said. I did—I saw children chasing each other and jostling to pet the ponies; women in sensible bonnets or colorful fascinators haggling and flirting, laughing and whispering, a few selling cheap glass beaded jewelry right off their own plump arms; and men in Sunday suits and dungarees and buckskins and every combination thereof, measuring the horses' backs and scrutinizing their hooves, waving notes and bags of coin in the air, arguing, shoving each other both in jest and in provocation, and generally conducting what seemed to be a combination of business, friendship, and war.

"I guarantee you one in ten men here right now is a horse thief, and one in twenty women. There's no place safer for us to talk; we blend right in."

We strolled down the line of horse stalls, Henry and News in front, Lark and I in the rear.

"Tomorrow is Mothering Monday," Henry said. "Everybody will be feasting and drinking and carrying on. We wait till the party's in full swing, then we find an unattended wagon, hitch up our horses, and ride off with it."

"What do we do about the sheriff's posse?" News asked. "Surely they'll be on patrol."

"Of course," said Henry, "but I've been to this Market before. At least in my experience, the men in the posse like to take a drink on Mothering Monday as much as anyone. And since everyone will be dressed up, they'll be all turned around—odds are they won't know we aren't the ones who drove the wagon in on Good Friday in the first place. Lark and Adam will look like fine, upstanding young merchants, don't you think? Especially in their Monday best."

We looped back around to the costume stalls.

"I saw a pink housedress here with your name on it," Henry said to News, pointing to the cheapest of the stalls, where a hand-lettered sign advertised a dress and hat together for a bargain price of five silver liberties.

"Please," said News, fingering a parrot-green ensemble. "You know pink isn't my color."

I selected a blue dress with small white polka dots. It was pretty, like something I might have worn in Fairchild, and it made me think of dances before I was married, when Ulla and Susie and I would stand against the wall looking at boys and then looking away until they came up to ask us to dance.

News took one look at it and put it back on the rack, picking out instead an ugly yellow one printed with huge pink roses, plus some garish red greasepaint.

"You're not supposed to look pretty," she whispered as Henry and Lark browsed a nearby rack. "You're supposed to look ridiculous."

The woman who took our money and wrapped our purchases in brown paper was very striking, with large green eyes and a determined jut to her chin. She kept her eyes locked on News's face as she counted out our change, a gaze I thought was rude until I understood its meaning.

"Will I see you at the dance tomorrow?" News asked as she pocketed the coins.

"You'll see me," the woman said.

"Tomorrow, then," said News, tipping the brim of her hat.

Henry smiled as we left the stall, shaking his head.

"Swift work as always," he said to News.

"Just being friendly," News replied.

Our path next led us back to the tent, where a man was beginning to address the crowd. News and Henry took up a position behind a tentpole festooned with ribbon; I had to look around it in order to see. The man who spoke was short and slight, with a round, bald head and horn-rimmed glasses, but he had a loud, confident voice and a way of moving around the stage that made him seem to occupy a space bigger than his physical form.

"Now some foals are strong and hardy and others are weak and sickly," the preacher said. "Some grow up fast and sure-footed, and others are slow and clumsy, barely good for pulling a plow. Some weather every season and others succumb to fever their very first winter."

"Come on," said Henry to News, his voice softer now. "Let's go get a drink. They're selling double whiskeys for five coppers over by the Babies' Tears."

News shook her head. "You go if you want," she said. "I want to hear this."

"Any good rancher knows that nine times out of ten, a strong horse comes from strong stock," the preacher said. "A weak horse comes from weak stock. That's just the way it is.

"And we know that human beings are the same way. A fertile woman usually comes from a big family. A mother with a cleft lip or a clubfoot, like as not, will have children with the same ailment."

The man's words were familiar to me, but I struggled to place them.

"Now," he went on, "I have something to show you that I believe will drive home my point."

A pleasant-faced young woman in a yellow dress and bonnet led onto the stage two goats, a brown nanny goat with short hair and a shaggy black billy goat with a long beard. Both were plump and vigorous, tugging on their leads, making the woman giggle as she tried to contain them.

"This fine animal," said the man, gesturing at the billy goat, "is of Colorado stock, a champion mountain climber. And this lass by his side is a lowland breed, called an Arizona red. The two come from entirely different climates and conditions, and under ordinary circumstances, they would never cross paths. But in the spirit of scientific inquiry, I have induced them to breed with one another."

The woman led them away, and came back with a miserable-looking animal, scrawny and pink-eyed, its hips twisted and gait painful to watch. On its head were not two but four horns, inter-twined like the branches of a sticker bush. As soon as I saw it, I realized I must be watching Dr. Edward Lively.

"Now this unfortunate beast," the doctor said, "is the product of two vibrant, beautiful animals, as you just saw. Bred with their own kind, both have produced many perfectly healthy kids. But bred, as you might say, *against* their kind, they have engendered this poor creature, who suffers a total of thirteen types of deformity, those you can see from where you sit being only the most obvious."

The crowd began to murmur with interest and approval. I saw something I had not noticed when I first entered the tent: while I had seen black buyers and sellers at the market, and heard Arapaho and other languages I didn't recognize, almost everyone gathered to watch Dr. Lively was white.

"Tell me now," the doctor said, "if these animals, who are relatively simple in their bodily structure, revert to such monstrosity when bred against their nature, how much worse must it be when man, the most complex creature of all, takes up with a mate who is of different stock?"

The murmur grew louder. Then a woman stood up, blonde and pink-cheeked, a little younger than my mother.

"My son's wife still hasn't given him a child, and it's been nearly two years," she called out to Dr. Lively. "I suspect there's mixed blood in her family. Could that be the reason?"

"It could indeed, madam," Dr. Lively said. "According to my research, nearly half of all cases of barrenness are caused by some form of racial mixing or another, sometimes quite far back in the family tree. And of course this is far from the only ailment—"

"Nate," Henry said.

This time News nodded, and Lark and I followed them out of the tent.

For a long time no one said anything. We bought moonshine from a wagon stall. News's hand shook around the glass. The stall also sold patent medicines, bright blue and red and green, with labels that said things like "Pleasant Dreams" and "Vim and Virility." Traveling salesmen had come through Fairchild with bottles like these from time to time; I knew they were colored water at best.

Lark was the first of us to speak. "That man is nobody," he said. "The main event today is the Reverend Delano, from Laramie. He won't preach until long after nightfall. The crowd will be five times the size."

"Lark—" said Henry, a warning. I wondered how much he knew of News's past.

"No, Lark's right," News said. "He's nobody."

She was smiling, but her eyes glittered with rage. She drained her glass.

"Adam," she said, "why don't you get us another round?"

As I stood, a young woman approached the stall. Her stride was purposeful but when she reached the makeshift counter where the owner stood, she hesitated as though nervous. "Do you have anything for fertility?" she asked finally, lowering her voice on the last word.

"Absolutely," the stall owner said. "You'll want our Fruitful Womb tonic. I've sold all the bottles, but we have more in the back. I'll just bottle some up for you now."

He came out from behind the counter—no more than a pine board balanced on sawhorses—and disappeared around the back of his wagon.

"I'd save your money if I were you," I said to the woman when he was gone.

She was short and strong-bodied, with a raspberry-colored birthmark at her throat. When I spoke, she looked frightened, and I remembered that to her I was a strange man, interrupting what must be, for her, a sensitive transaction.

"I don't mean to intrude," I said. "It's just that I'm a doctor. And these tonics are a waste of money. How long have you been married?"

The woman still looked suspicious, but she answered, "Nine months."

"Give it a year," I said. "If you're not pregnant by then, there's no medicine can help you. The safest thing is to get away. There's a convent, the Sisters of the Holy Child—"

The stall owner came back with two large glass bottles, one full of blue liquid and one full of green. "Either one of these is effective on its own," he told the woman, "but for the quickest results, I'd advise you to take two tablespoons of the Fruitful Womb every morning"—he held up the blue bottle—"and then a tablespoon of this one, the Mother's Friend, before you go to sleep."

He tapped on the green bottle with his index finger. "They work together, you see, to regulate the feminine fluids."

The woman looked at me as she opened her pocketbook.

"I'll take both," she said.

That night the four of us pitched a tent alongside dozens of others on the outskirts of the fairgrounds by the banks of the river. While Lark and Henry looked for a spot, News spoke to me under her breath.

"We'll sleep in our clothes tonight," she said. "Henry's camped with me before—he won't say anything. If Lark does, you get cold easy. Let him rib you a little bit if he wants to. If you're easygoing about it he'll forget it soon enough."

Lark and Henry looked like they had settled on a place. Henry removed mallet, pegs, and thick canvas from his horse's saddlebags.

"If you need to piss," News went on, "go to the outhouse by the big tent. Don't go down by the river or into the trees— someone might see you. It's not your period, is it?"

I shook my head.

"Good. It's mine. If yours starts, I have some clean rags."

Later that night I waited for one of the outhouses. The others in the long line kept looking at me with curiosity, even suspicion. Whenever I'd been among people in my men's clothes before, I'd always been afraid of being found out. Now that I was clearly taken for someone I wasn't, I felt a wave of something uncanny pass through me, almost but not quite dizziness. I thought of a feeling Ulla used to talk about, a shivering strangeness that would come on her without warning, the sense that she was outside her body looking in. "Somebody walking over your grave," she used to say.

I took News's advice and tried to seem calm and loose, holding my head high, absently kicking an eggshell with my boot. The feeling ebbed but didn't pass, hanging on in the corner of my mind, a low but insistent buzz.

Up ahead the outhouse door swung open. I felt the attention of the waiting women turn away from me, and I followed the line of their gaze. Lark met my eyes when I looked at him, and, for a moment before he nodded curtly and walked on back to the tents, I saw in his face what I knew he saw in mine: the recognition that both of us must have something to hide.

By the time we got to the big tent around three o'clock the next afternoon, the day was already wild. A short woman wearing a man's shirt unbuttoned to show the tops of her round breasts pulled me in to dance with her. News grinned and gave me a thumbs-up; I rolled my eyes. We'd all agreed we'd spend an hour at the dance to blend in with the crowd and so we were convincingly sweaty and boozy and flushed when it came time to drive a wagon out. News had succeeded in making me look ridiculous in my yellow dress, the greasepaint giving my lips and cheeks a cartoonish brightness.

And yet she managed to look dashing in the green frock she threw over her dungarees, her hat adorned with feathers and cloth flowers. In the crowd I saw the young woman from the costume stall, now dressed as a handsome boy in a slim dark suit, with a mustache drawn in kohl above her lips. News approached her quickly, as though merely walking past, then paused and tipped her hat again, slowly this time. As she raised the brim I saw her smile below it. Then she turned and walked out of the tent. I saw the woman in the dark suit wait a moment, then follow.

I had never danced a man's part before but it didn't seem to matter—the tent was too crowded and the people too drunk to do much beyond the clumsiest reel. My dance partner pressed her breasts against my stomach and looked up at me, inviting—when I took a step away from her she shrugged, released my hands, and moved on to the man next to me, who had a bonnet and a black beard and a dotted Swiss apron straining over his belly.

A young woman wearing a gray mustache and eyeglasses without lenses carried a tray full of sloshing golden beers—I bought one and drank deep. On the stage where Dr. Lively had been preaching the day before, now two fiddlers and a short man with a tall bass guitar were playing at furious speed.

Looking around at the other dancers, I saw Lark—almost elegant in his purple-checked housedress—dancing close with a redheaded woman who threw back her head and laughed at something he said. My jealousy was no weaker for being pointless. The night before we'd slept next to each other as two men. He'd said nothing when I crawled into my bedroll fully dressed. He, meanwhile, had unbuttoned his shirt while I tried not to look. Only when he turned his long back away from me to sleep did I let myself glance, and then the image stayed with me as I shut my eyes. I was no closer to knowing what he had to conceal, but I knew it was not what I was hiding.

Another woman—this one older, an expert dancer—took my free hand in hers. With her I found my feet and began to lead, or at least collaborate. The beer entered my blood and my hips and shoulders relaxed. I knew that none of these people were my friends—I was going to steal from them, and if they knew what I was, some would have me hanged for a witch, while others would have my family expelled from town, or worse, in order to keep the poison of me from spreading to other bloodlines. And yet the woman who danced with me smelled like apples and wine. The fiddlers were laughing to each other as they played. Someone refilled my beer glass without asking for money. The woman and I parted and another took her place, and then the music changed and we joined a circle with other dancers, all of us holding hands, all of us moving in toward the center and back out again, singing and shouting.

I dropped the hand of the man next to me—chest hair, the low-necked red gown of a barmaid—to clap along with the music, and when I tried to take it again I felt a squeeze, a familiar firmness. I turned to see Lark, his cheeks flushed, his eyes shining. I squeezed back, then regretted it—a single squeeze could be a friendly greeting, but surely a second was too much, surely I'd given myself away. I dropped his hand and turned away from him.

I had never been so aware of anyone as I was for the next few minutes as Lark danced next to me. The band kept playing and the crowd kept clapping and I kept moving along with them, but all my mind was consumed with the circumstances of his body, where it was in relation to mine. I did not look back at him. I thought it safest to pretend to ignore him until he got tired of my rudeness and found another woman to dance with.

Then the music changed again. The crowd whooped. Our circle began moving, three steps left, three steps right. On the second set I could see out of the corner of my eye that Lark was dropping out of the circle to pass behind me; I was both relieved and bereft to see him go. Then, as he passed by, he placed a hand on the small of my back and left it there. It was a gesture that would seem like nothing from the outside, if anyone bothered to look—one man pushing past another on a crowded dance floor. But to me its meaning was so clear that my body pushed right past my mind's surprise; I leaned back into him, pressing the full length of my back into his chest. I felt his breath on my neck. Then he was gone.

A fat man wearing nothing but a baby blanket and an enormous cloth diaper took the stage.

"Mothers and fathers, boys and girls, cowboys and . . . ladies of the evening, gather round," he shouted. "Quit your dancing and carrying on for a moment and listen to me. It's time for the most important part of our day's festivities. It's time to crown the Mother of the Year!"

This was our cue. As the man-baby called men in elaborate costumes up to the stage ("Mrs. Winifred Higginbotham" had five baby dolls strapped to him, including one, for some reason, on his left forearm), I squeezed through the crowd to the edge of the tent and out into the evening air.

News and Henry and Lark were already at our meeting place, a stall that had once sold brightly colored eggs and now provided a modicum of privacy for four separate couples, one in each corner, the women's hands catching in the folds of the men's dresses, the men struggling with the buttons on the women's pants.

I stole a glance at Lark but he was laughing with Henry about something, seemingly oblivious to my presence. I must have misinterpreted his touch in the tent, I thought. He'd meant it as a friendly gesture, man to man, and I'd put myself in danger by responding in a way he'd never intended. After all, I'd seen him laughing and flirting with the redheaded woman. There was no reason to think he'd be interested in what I appeared to be: a nervous young man in an ugly dress.

"Ready?" News asked.

We fetched the horses and walked the lines of wagons. As Henry had predicted, all of them were unguarded, save a few selling valuable wares—icons of baby Jesus trimmed in gold leaf, cardamom and cinnamon and perfumes that hung in the cooling air. We chose a modest wagon near the edge of the fairgrounds— from the flour dusting the seats in front, it seemed the owner was a baker. Under the canvas canopy I could still smell hot cross buns.

I was trying to buckle Amity into the wagon traces when the women came strolling by. One was tall, pretty, with long caramel-colored hair down her back. Her broadcloth shirt was modestly buttoned, but her trousers were tight, revealing more of her body than a dress ever would.

The other woman was shorter and softer, with dark hair pinned up in braids under a man's black hat. She had wide brown eyes and a round, childlike face. Both women were young, not much older than me.

The round-faced woman became captivated by Amity, stroking her gray flank and looking into her dark eyes. Amity regarded her with a mix of tolerance and caution. Meanwhile, the loose-haired woman approached me.

"Shouldn't you be dancing?" she asked.

Her voice was teasing and playful. I tried to respond in kind.

"I could ask you the same question," I said.

"Audrey and I are married women," she said, holding up her left hand to show me her gold ring. "We don't dance with strange men."

"Well," I said, thinking quickly, "I guess we have the same excuse. I'm engaged."

"Congratulations," the woman cooed, drawing closer to me. I could smell her sweat and her perfume—men's clothing notwithstanding, she was wearing paintbrush flower oil, the kind Ulla's mama used to make in the springtime and mix into women's paints and powders. The smell was sweet but with a darkness to it, and I felt drawn to the woman in a way that surprised me. I imagined leaning close to her and inhaling the scent of her hair.

"So who's the lucky woman?" she asked.

"Her name is Ada," I said. "She's studying to be a midwife back in Fairchild, where I'm from."

It made me smile to think of myself as a wife to myself—the woman I could've been and the man I was pretending to be, both of them luckier in life than the person I really was.

"Does she come from a good family?" asked the woman called Audrey, turning from Amity to me. She spoke softly, but her voice had a kind of urgency behind it.

"Of course," I said. "She's one of four children and her mother is the best midwife in all of Dakota country."

"But"—Audrey glanced at Henry and News and then leaned close to me, almost whispering—"is her bloodline pure?"

From what I had learned about deceiving strangers, I knew I should say yes, so I could maintain whatever rosy image they had of me. But I also knew that no one learns anything without being taught. I had failed with the woman with the birthmark, but I had gotten off on the wrong foot with her. These women seemed to like and feel at ease with me; perhaps they would be easier to sway.

"I don't go in for that nonsense," I said. "Some babies are sickly, some babies are healthy. It's got nothing to do with whether the parents are black or white."

"Not just the parents," Audrey said in her ardent whisper. "It's like Dr. Lively was saying about horses. Your horse here, she must come from good stock all the way back. Just one ancestor with a lame foot or a weak back is enough to ruin the blood."

"Our husbands are traders," said the loose-haired woman, pride making her voice go stiff and proper. "We've been all up and down this country from the Bighorns to the Rockies. We know what bad blood can do."

"That's ridiculous," I said. "My fiancée has attended over fifty births. She could tell you—babies from mixed families are just as healthy as babies with a pure bloodline, or whatever you call it. There's no difference."

News gave me a warning look.

"You're wrong," Audrey said. "Dr. Lively has seen hundreds of babies deformed by the mixing of blood. He once saw a doctor in Laramie poison a cat by feeding it the blood of a black woman and a white man mixed together."

"If Dr. Lively believes that," I said, "he's stupider than he looks."

"Dr. Lively learned to read and write before he could walk," Audrey said. "He's a prodigy. Maybe you don't like what he has to say because of the company you keep."

She looked at Henry and News and back at me again.

"If you don't like my associates," I said, "you're free to leave us alone."

"We will," said the loose-haired woman. "And we'll tell our friends to stay away from your stall too. What are you selling, anyway? I don't remember you from last year."

"Hot cross buns," I said quickly, the first thing that came to mind. "But we're sold out."

"Lucky for you," said the loose-haired woman. "My advice? Don't come back here next year. We don't have any use for ignorant people here."

As she spoke, I saw her peer past me into the back of the wagon, which I only now saw was full of farm implements—hoes and scythes and plow blades, each one clearly marked with a price.

No one said anything as we drove the wagon toward the outskirts of the fairgrounds. News held the reins and I sat up front with her; Henry and Lark rode behind with the farm equipment. News drove the horses as fast as she could without exciting suspicion.

Evening was shading into night and the shadows were long on the campground as we rode past, attenuated shapes of men in women's clothes and women in men's clothes, embracing in tents and against trees and on the cooling ground. No one looked up to take notice of us, and we passed out of the fairgrounds and onto the road to town without incident, the only sound the jingling of the wagon hitches and the occasional huff of one of the horses as they pulled us out of danger.

"I'm sorry," I said to News. "I should've looked in the back of the wagon right away."

"You should've kept your mouth shut," News said. "What was that? Your fiancée? Haven't you learned anything about how to talk to people?"

"I thought maybe I could change their minds," I said. "I thought if they heard it from a midwife, maybe they'd listen."

"To them you're not a midwife," News said. "You're just a strange man who insulted their precious doctor. You must be pretty convinced of your powers of persuasion if you thought that was going to work."

Her tone was snide and cynical; I'd never heard her speak like that before.

"I just wanted to help," I said. "I thought you'd appreciate it."

"Oh, I see," said News. "You wanted to help. You figured that if only someone with a bit of education explained things clearly to these Lively people, they'd stop looking at me like I was a deformed goat and start treating me like a person. Do I have that right?"

"That's not—" I began.

"And if only somebody'd had the presence of mind to explain things to the mayor back home in Elmyra, perhaps I'd be with my family right now. It's just too bad no one with your intelligence and education was around to help us. What a relief that you're here now!"

"I'm sorry for trying to stand up for you," I said, angry now. "I won't make that mistake again."

"I don't need anyone to stand up for me, Doctor. Certainly not you."

The road from the fairgrounds into the town of Casper was narrow and paved with gravel; our teeth chattered as the horses pulled us over it. All along the roadsides lay refuse from the market: empty bags that had once held Babies' Tears or fruit tarts or other sweets; eggshells; chicken bones; discarded Easter bonnets and men's hats and even a false beard, lying in the road like an animal. After what felt like miles of silence while I chewed over my anger at News—could I really be in the wrong when I had done what I thought was the braver thing to do?—we rounded a bend in the road and came upon a gate meant to keep cows from wandering from the fairgrounds into town. The gate had been open when we arrived at the market the day before, but now it was latched, and anyone who wanted to pass through would have to dismount and pull it open by hand.

News brought the wagon to a stop and without speaking, I got out to unlatch the gate. It was crude—lengths of barbed wire stretched between two heavy wooden posts, one of which fit through a metal ring at the bottom to form the latch. The wire was pulled so tight that I had trouble sliding the post out of the ring. Lark jumped down from the back of the wagon to help me, and we had just pulled the post free, allowing the wagon to pass through, when three men on fast horses came around the bend with guns drawn.

Lark didn't hesitate.

"Go!" he shouted to News.

News gave him a single nod, then cracked the reins and set the horses galloping, leaving us behind in a cloud of gravel and garbage and dust.

The sheriff's deputy searched me. He was a big man with meaty, careless hands, and at first I thought he might miss what I was hiding. He felt my ankles, knees, hips, waist, and found nothing amiss there, but then his hands slid under my arms and found the thick fabric I had used to bind my breasts.

"What's this?" he asked.

"I was wounded in a barfight," I said. "I just have a bandage there, that's all."

"Show me," the deputy said.

I unbuttoned the first two buttons of my ridiculous flowered dress to reveal the very top of the binder.

"I have to wear it for a few more weeks," I said, "until the wound heals."

We caught the attention of the sheriff then, a skinny man with pockmarked skin and a dark red cowboy hat who had been searching Lark.

"Show us the whole thing," he said.

My heart was pounding in my ears as I unbuttoned the dress and laid the binder bare.

"That's not like any bandage I've ever seen," the deputy said.

"It's no bandage," the sheriff said, recognition and disgust mingling on his face. "Take it off."

The evening air was cold on my naked skin. The deputy looked confused.

"What's a woman doing thieving on the Powder River Road?" he asked the sheriff. "Is this some kind of Easter foolery?"

"She's no woman," the sheriff said. "I've seen this before, back in Colorado country. I knew a young man down there, very popular with the ladies. But when he seduced the mayor's wife we arrested him for adultery—and we found one of these 'bandages' under his clothes. He, or she, or it, whatever you like, had a woman's breasts, a woman's body. Turned out her real name was Caroline and she'd escaped from jail in Salida, where she'd been held on suspicion of witchcraft. She'd been posing as a man ever since, leading unsuspecting women into wickedness."

"What did you do with her?" the deputy asked, staring openly now at my breasts.

"We put her in the stocks for three days and three nights," the sheriff said. "After that, we would have released her, but she was already dead."

"We don't have stocks here," the deputy said, still staring.

"The judge will think of something," the sheriff said. "You know what surprised me? When people came to cast their stones and shoes and whatnot at Caroline, the women were twice as savage as the men. If it weren't for the women, she might have survived."

I had not thought of my mother-in-law in months, but I thought of her as I buttoned the dress over my naked chest. The way she looked at me on the kitchen the day she sent me away, the loathing in her eyes, and the satisfaction at being able to punish me—I saw both now in the faces of the sheriff and his deputy.

I had not hated my mother-in-law for kicking me out, my husband for failing to stop her, or Sheriff Branch for treating me like a contagion when he had known me all my life. I had been angry and afraid, but not hateful. Now my hatred reached back from the two men before me all the way to Fairchild, where I imagined my husband's family sitting down to dinner with their new daughter-in-law. I imagined my hate as a flame racing along the dirt road until it licked at their door.

I did not look at the sheriff or his deputy again as they cuffed our wrists and chained us to the deputy's horse. My fate was sealed; I did not care what they thought of me or what they said. Instead I watched Lark. He met my eyes with a look that was warm and steady and calm, as though nothing he had seen that day disturbed or even surprised him. The look confused me, but it also sustained me, keeping the worst of my fears from overwhelming me as the men marched us down the road and into town.

The jail was a long, low building arranged around a central corridor down which a twitch-eyed guard paced, carrying a kerosene lantern and stopping periodically to sip something from a copper mug. The first room on the left, the one to which we were brought, held two other prisoners, a man and a woman, lying on long wooden benches above a dirt floor. It was separated from the corridor by a padlocked door with a window—too small for a man to crawl through, but large enough for the guard to keep an eye on the prisoners, and for us to watch him. Night had fallen and the only light in the room came from his lamp, passing across our faces as he paced by, then leaving us in darkness.

"What did you do?" the woman asked when the sheriff and his deputy had left.

Her voice in the darkness sounded young, but when the lamplight tracked across her face I saw her skin was weathered, like a year-old apple gone puckered and wrinkly in the storeroom.

"We stole a wagon," Lark said, but the woman was looking at me.

My binder gone, the shape of my breasts was visible through my clothes. And I had stopped trying to walk and gesture like a man; no point in keeping up the deception now. I looked like what I was: a woman in an ugly dress, sitting in a jail awaiting her fate.

"Where's your Easter costume?" she asked, looking at Lark in his purple frock, wondering no doubt why I wasn't in dungarees.

I was wary of telling her anything about myself. Even here, it seemed like a mistake to reveal too much.

"What are you in here for?" I asked instead.

"Why," she said, "can't you tell? I'm a witch!"

When the light crossed her again she was sitting up and smiling at me. One of her front teeth was missing, giving her an impish appearance.

"Are you barren?" I asked.

"I have five sons, each one more good-for-nothing than the last," she said. "But my sisters-in-law, neither of them could have babies after I married their brother. So they pointed the finger and here I sit, twenty years next month."

I felt a kinship with her, so strong in that dark place that I had to fight the urge to reach out and take her hand.

"My mama is a midwife," I said. "She says there's not the slightest truth to what people say about witches making women barren. It's just a silly story told by silly people."

"And what, pray tell, does cause barrenness, Miss Daughter-of-a-Midwife?" the woman asked me.

"Nobody really knows," I said. "But one day, I aim to find out."

"Well, then you can tell the sheriff and I'm sure he'll have me released," the woman said, not unkindly. "Until then, I'm going to get some rest. You should do the same. The judge is off for

Easter week, so you have another day in here, maybe two, before you find out what's to become of you. You should make the most of it."

The woman curled up on her bench and shut her eyes. The man had not spoken a word; he seemed to be sleeping too. I waited until the woman's breathing went slow and even with sleep, and then I whispered to Lark.

"How did you know?" I asked.

His voice came closer than I'd thought in the flat dark.

"I didn't know," he said, "but I suspected. You're doing a good job—an ordinary person would never guess. But there's a lightness in the way you move, especially when you dance. Men are heavier in their bones than women, even when they're slim, and you can see it if you know how to look."

"And you know how to look?" I asked.

"I do."

The guard passed in front of the window and the lamplight gave Lark's face to me like a present. I searched it for clues—that pretty mouth, yes, but also a day's growth of beard on his cheeks and chin, a man's prominent brow. I decided there was no reason anymore not to ask.

"Are you a woman?"

The light left his face before I could see his reaction.

"No," he said.

"I saw you at the outhouse on the fairgrounds," I said. "You were the only man there."

"And?" he asked.

"And there must be something you don't want people to see."

For a moment he was quiet in the darkness and I thought maybe I'd offended him. Then the lamp passed by the window and I saw his face was amused, resigned.

"Fair enough," he said, "we can trade secrets. When we met I told you I left Mobridge because I was in love with a married woman, right? Well it wasn't a woman, it was a man. And I didn't leave of my own accord."

That explained why Lark had been so interested in me in Fiddleback. And presumably he wouldn't be interested in me now—even in the dark of the jail I found I cared about this. I tasted disappointment like metal in my mouth.

Back home I had known two boys who were rumored to like other boys. Both were married to women by the time I left, with children on the way. Neither had ever had to leave town.

"What happened?" I asked.

"The man I loved, he stopped sleeping with his wife. They only had one child. His wife's family found out about us and set the sheriff's posse on me. In Mobridge, the usual penalty for interfering in the conception of children was gelding."

"Gelding?" I asked. I thought I understood what he was saying, but I hoped I didn't.

"Sometimes they used a red-hot poker to do the job. I was lucky—on me they used ordinary castrating shears. Oh, and then they threw me in jail. That's where I got the name Lark."

The light passed across him, but I looked away; I could not match what I was learning with what I felt for him, the thrum of desire in my belly that persisted even now.

"Why 'Lark'?" I asked.

"Because eunuchs are supposed to be beautiful singers," he said, "with high clear voices like meadowlarks."

"Your voice isn't high," I said.

"They didn't take everything from me," he said. "A lot, but not everything."

I wanted to know exactly what they'd taken, and what was left; if he could still feel pleasure when he went to bed with someone; and what it felt like, to go through the world with such a wound. I didn't know how to ask any of those questions.

"How did you get out of jail?" I asked instead.

He laughed in the dark.

"Don't get excited," he said. "I don't have any special knack for escape. My parents got together the money to pay the sheriff to release me, on the condition that I leave town and never come back. Don't suppose you have any rich relatives around here."

"No one except News and the others," I said. "And I'm not sure they'll come back for me. I wasn't universally popular before today, and now—"

"Who are the others?" Lark asked. "Nate—News?—gave us the impression he worked solo. Even you were a surprise."

The guard's lamp washed over the room, catching the silent man for a moment clearly in its light. I saw now that his eyes were open but pointed blankly at empty space, nothing animating behind them. His mouth hung slack, moving slightly as he breathed. One of his hands trailed on the dirt floor; its nails curled all the way over the fingertips in filthy grayish claws. I understood clearly then that I could die in this jail, that it might in fact be better if I was hanged.

"There are eight of us," I told Lark. There seemed no sense in keeping secrets now. "All of us are barren. For now we hide out in the mountains, up at Hole in the Wall. But we're trying to make Fiddleback into a place where people like us can live in safety. The wagon was part of that—is part of that."

I realized for the first time that the Kid's plan had become my plan. I wanted it to succeed, not just because it would get me to Pagosa Springs but because I wanted the town the Kid imagined to exist in Powder country. I imagined treating a barren woman at the surgery in Pagosa Springs and telling her I knew of a place she could go and live without fear.

For a moment we sat in silence and darkness. Then Lark asked, "Is that why you left Dakota? Because you're barren?"

The light came across his face and I saw him watching me so closely I dropped my eyes in embarrassment.

"I was married," I said. "After a year I didn't get pregnant, so my husband's family threw me out. Now the sheriff in Fairchild wants me hanged for witchcraft. I can never go back there."

"Do you miss it?" Lark asked. "I can't say I miss Mobridge."

"I miss my family," I said. "Don't you miss yours?"

He paused in the soft dark.

"My mama used to take me with her to forage for morels and fiddleheads to sell at market," he said finally. "I had six brothers and sisters and I wasn't my mama's favorite—that was my sister Tilly. But my mama said I had the best eye for growing things. Every time I spotted a mushroom on the forest floor, her face would light up. She'd say, 'See, James? You have a gift.' "

"James," I said.

"That's right. It was my daddy's daddy's name. Nobody's called me that for a long time, though. I've gotten to like Lark. I'm not ashamed of what I did, or what happened to me. I used to be, but not anymore."

I thought about the winter dance the year before I got married, me and Ulla and Susie and the other girls from school running outside in our dresses in the freezing air just for the shock of it, then running back inside gasping and falling all over one another, the boys looking at us in what I knew was jealousy, wishing we loved them as much as we loved each other. I thought about Bee running in from the garden in springtime to tell me that the mourning dove eggs had hatched and the tiny pink babies were reaching up to their mother with open mouths.

I thought of the last birth I attended with my mother, a long labor, the baby faceup inside the birth canal, and how I was able to get the mother in position to push the baby out without my mama's help, and how she cried afterward, her baby on her naked chest, and kept saying "Thank you, thank you, thank you."

"I'll never see my mama or my sisters again," I said. "My littlest sister, Bee—I was like a second mama to her. Now she'll think I abandoned her. I don't even know if she's safe. How can I not hate what I am, if this is what it's brought me?"

I had never spoken such a thing aloud, but I felt it now as keenly as I'd felt it for the sheriff and his deputy on the Powder River Road. I hated my uselessness, the way my body had taken my family and my calling from me. I had thought the gang might give me a purpose, but here I was in a jail cell while the others, no doubt, readied themselves for the Fiddleback job without me. I had trained from childhood to heal sick people and bring babies and their mothers safely through birth, and now I would die, more likely than not, in a jail far from my home, and in more than a year I'd delivered no babies and healed just two people, one of them suffering from a wound I'd caused.

The light returned, and this time I looked Lark full in the face. It made me angry, even if we were both about to die, that he had come this far with no contempt for himself and no regret. It made me jealous.

"After I got out of Mobridge," he said as the dark fell on us again, "I wanted to kill myself. I got a job in a roadhouse and I cut my wrists with a bread knife."

I heard a rustle of fabric.

"Here," he said, "feel."

The scar was wide and slippery on the muscle of his forearm. Underneath it I could feel his pulse.

"Some part of me must not have been serious, because I didn't cut deep enough. The owner found me ruining his kitchen floor with my blood. He was kind, but I was a liability. When I was healed he sent me away. After that I didn't try again, but that didn't mean the desire wasn't there. For five years I thought about it every day."

"And then?" I asked.

"And then I got a job with a traveling veterinarian. He was getting old and needed someone strong to help him with the larger animals, the cows and horses. At first I hated him—he was mean and demanding and he scolded me over every little thing.

"But one day we were called to examine a horse with founder. The rancher had waited too long to call and the horse could barely walk—when the vet diagnosed her, the rancher was going to shoot her. So the vet took her himself. Over the next three months I saw him nurse her—he soaked her feet in ice baths, trimmed her hooves, and when she was ready, he rode her a little more every day until she was almost as good as new. He could never sell her—she'd be a little bit lame for the rest of her life—but he kept her on his own farm and fed her and cared for her along with his other horses. Once I asked him why he hadn't let the rancher euthanize her, and he looked at me like I was crazy.

" 'She's a living thing,' he said.

"Afterward I watched how he was with all the animals, from the most beautiful prize stallion to the scrawniest chicken, as though each was worthy of his utmost care and attention. On the rare occasions when he had to put an animal down, he did it quickly, and took care to calm the animal first, so it didn't die in fear and pain.

"In the whole time I worked for him, he never warmed up to me. In fact I think he hated me. But I knew if I ever tried anything like I'd done at the roadhouse, he'd do anything he had to do to save me—he'd consider my life worth any amount of effort, dislike me though he did. And so I never tried anything, and when I'd been working for him for a year, I discovered I didn't think about it anymore. Except for a few dark times, I haven't since."

When the light returned, Lark's face and the way he held his body made sense to me in a way they hadn't before. That combination of caution and confidence—I imagined the old veterinarian slowly training the sick horse to walk again, to trot, to canter, knowing where her weak points were but knowing, too, how she could become strong. I wished I could think of my own failed body with that kind of care. Instead I was full of shame and fear.

"We're going to die in here," I said.

"Maybe," Lark said. "But we're not dead yet."

We knew morning only by the changing of the guard, the new one tall and young, the kerosene lamp revealing a soft, hairless face. He had brought along a bag of hard-boiled eggs in bright colors, which he peeled and ate as he paced. I had been lying with my head on the bench and my eyes shut, but I had not been asleep. I had been turning plans over and over in my mind.

"If I throw myself against the window—" I said to Lark as he began to stir.

"Save your energy," the woman said. When the light crossed her, I saw her eyes remained shut, her body relaxed in its sleeping posture. And yet her voice was fully awake and alert. I wondered how long she'd been listening.

"There's no way out of here," she said. "That glass is double-paned, with metal wires in between. This might not be a big town but the sheriff comes up from Telluride. He's caught some of the worst outlaws west of the Mississippi. He made sure this jail was watertight."

"So that's it then?" I asked. "We're just going to rot in here?"

I regretted my words immediately. This woman had served twenty years for the misfortunes of her sisters-in-law, and here I was panicking after a single night. But when the light came back, she was smiling. With her missing tooth she reminded me of Ulla suddenly, that mischievous gap in her grin.

"There is one thing you can try," she said. "I'd do it myself, but I haven't found anybody willing. You can ask to get married."

"I'm not sure our young friend out there is going to be keen on marrying either of us," Lark said, "if that's what you mean."

"It's not," the woman said. "The sheriff here is very serious about the holiness of the family. If you request a marriage, he'll have you taken to a church for the ceremony. And then he'll give you a private place to consummate the union. If you can manage to conceive a child—well then you might just save both your lives."

"I can't have children," I told her. There seemed little risk in admitting it now.

"Even so," she said. "You'll have the trip to the church and the wedding ceremony to figure something out. You'll be under armed guard, of course, but our little church is a lot easier to bust out of than this jail."

The mirth in the woman's voice felt out of place in the dark and airless room.

"Why are you telling us this?" I asked, suspicious.

The woman sat up and stretched.

"I've had a lot of time to think about how much I hate the sheriff," she said. "Anything that hurts him is reward enough for me."

I could feel Lark's smile in the dark.

"What do you think, Ada?" he asked. "Will you marry me?"

"Don't be ridiculous," the sheriff said. "Of course I won't take you to the church. You're wanted for grand theft. And you," he said, looking at me—"I don't even know what crime the judge will want to charge you with. If it weren't Easter week, you'd be dead by now."

He held his own kerosene lamp as he spoke to us, illuminating the room with a flickering light. I could see the marks on the walls where other prisoners—probably now long dead—had scratched their names and prayers and curses with dirty fingernails.

"With all due respect, sir," said Lark, "our marriage won't be holy in the eyes of baby Jesus unless we consecrate it in a church."

"And the trip to church will give you plenty of chances to give my guards the slip," said the sheriff. "I know how your kind thinks. No, if you want to get married I won't stop you. But you'll be having the ceremony in here."

"And afterward?" Lark asked.

"Afterward, what?"

Lark took my hand. Before I knew what I was doing, I squeezed his palm, and he squeezed back. The memory of the dance under the tent came back to me.

"I don't mean to be indelicate," he said, "but my bride and I will need somewhere private to consummate our marriage."

The sheriff looked away from us with a prudish embarrassment that, under other circumstances, I might have found sweet.

"Yes, yes," he said. "We'll put you in the gentlemen's quarters."

*

The priest came the following morning—I knew it only because the night guard had come and gone and the young day guard had returned. By my figuring, we had another day left of Easter week, another day before we had to meet the judge.

The woman had shrugged when I asked what we should do now that we wouldn't be going to church.

"I learned long ago not to get my hopes up," she said. "At least you'll get to spend an afternoon in the nice part of this place. Usually it's only for folks who can pay."

Lark and I decided our best move was to wait until the guard took us to the gentlemen's quarters. Then Lark would try to knock the lamp out of his hand. While the guard scrambled to put out the flames, we'd try to make a run for it. It wasn't a particularly good plan, but it was the only one we had. And first we had to get married.

The priest was middle-aged, with a handsome, strong-jawed face and black hair going gray. He walked with two canes; in the lamplight I saw that though his shoulders and chest were powerful, his legs were as short and slender as a child's. He lowered himself onto the bench next to us, the guard shut the door behind him, and the dark, for the moment, erased us all.

"I'm Father Daniel," the priest said. "Ordinarily, when I meet with couples before their wedding day, my purpose is to make sure they understand the gravity of the marriage sacrament, and to prepare them for their lives together. In this case, unfortunately, I have another task: to ensure that both of you enter into this marriage with godly intentions, and not merely as a way of delaying whatever justice is due for your crimes. It's undignified, I'm sure you'll agree, for a man of God to play the role of investigator, but that is the situation in which we find ourselves."

At the convent, we had been instructed to show great deference to the priests who visited us occasionally to preach a sermon or conduct a special Mass. I had been unimpressed with them, as a general rule—old men who droned about the proper responsibilities of women. But this priest's manner—weary but good-humored, as though the marriage of two convicts was by no means the most unusual or unpleasant task he'd had to perform that week—endeared him to me.

"Thank you for visiting us, Father," I said.

"Don't thank me yet," he said. "Now, let's begin with the groom. Why don't you tell me how the two of you met?"

My whole body went tense. I did not know how the two of us would construct a love story that would satisfy this man, who was clearly no fool.

But Lark did not hesitate.

"It was in the town of Fiddleback, in Powder River country," he said. "My friend and I were passing through on our way to Crooked Creek to do some cattle rustling. Ada came through with an associate of hers, a man we'd done business with in the past. She was dressed as a man then, and she looked very handsome—a fine young cowboy with a straight back and an intelligent eye. We spoke a little, and she told me she was bent on traveling to Colorado to practice medicine. I'm a suspicious sort ordinarily, but I found myself taken with her. She had—I'd call it a vehemence about her that made me want to know her more. A few months later—"

"That's enough," Father Daniel said. "Now it's the bride's turn. Young lady, you can tell me how you fell in love."

The guard's light passed across us. The sly smile on Lark's face, and the empty-headed man moldering in the corner, and the probability of either my impending death or my slow, agonizing deterioration in this dark and airless room—all of these made me bold.

"The day we met," I said, "I thought he was the most beautiful man I'd ever seen. I had no mind to marry or have anything to do with a man, but after we came back from Fiddleback, my thoughts kept returning to him. So imagine my happiness when I found out that my associates wanted his help stealing a wagon at the Easter Market so we could sell it on and reap the profits.

"My associates and I are careful thieves," I went on. "We met with Lark many times before the market to plan and scheme. He and I found ourselves becoming fast friends. One night when Lark and I were sewing our disguises—the women's clothes we'd wear to pass ourselves off as revelers on Easter Monday—I decided I couldn't hide it anymore.

" 'I used to have a dress like that,' I said, pointing to the gingham frock he was stitching. And when he looked up from his work I saw he was not entirely surprised.

" 'You know me as Adam,' I said, 'but I was born Ada Magnusson, the eldest of four daughters. I'm an outlaw and a fugitive, and when I left my home I thought I'd left my woman's heart behind.'

" 'But now,' I said, 'I find it beats inside me still.' "

I looked at Lark, and waited for the guard's lamp to illuminate us so he could see me looking. He picked up where I had left off.

"I told her that I'd taken her at first for a resolute young man, his speech direct and his aim true, with a fine hand for horses and a proud set to his jaw. And I said that at some moment, I'd become aware that walking in her men's boots was a young woman, hiding a part of herself and yet showing quite clearly the strength and anger and consuming curiosity that animated her being. And at some other moment, I told her, I'd fallen in love. I couldn't say when each occurred, I told her, but now that neither of us was hiding from the other, I said my heart was hers if she would have it, and that if she was agreeable we ought to marry as soon as our thievery was completed and the wagon safely sold."

"And tell me," Father Daniel asked, "how had you determined to set up your household, had your theft come off as you had planned?"

"We planned to travel to Colorado country," I answered, "so I could apprentice with a master midwife there. Once I had learned all I could, my husband and I would travel all throughout the mountain and prairie towns. I would deliver babies and treat women with female ailments, and he would offer his services as a veterinarian, a trade for which he trained in his youth. We would leave the outlaw life and live quietly, and yet remain adventurers still, waking every week in a new bed, a new vista outside our windows."

The door opened and the guard peered in, his lamp making a cone of light with his fist at the apex.

"Get a move on," he said. "How long can it take to marry two thieves?"

"By all rights it should take longer to marry thieves than honest men and women," Father Daniel replied, "because the presiding priest must take more time to ensure they are responsible and upstanding enough to marry. But don't worry. I have just one question left before I determine whether I will perform the ceremony."

The guard rolled his eyes and shut the door.

"Sometimes I think a priest is only just above a thief himself in terms of the respect of his fellow man," Father Daniel said. "My last question, in any case, is this: In your adventuring life, how had you planned to bring up children?"

Before this question, my pulse had been quick with excitement. I was not naïve enough to think that Lark really felt all the things he said about me—I knew we were engaged in a game of make-believe. But I liked the game, despite the circumstances under which I had to play it, and I was reasonably sure Lark did too. In the blackness of the jail it was easy to imagine our flirtation over sewing implements, Lark's proposal, our life together delivering babies and tending to animals—easy to imagine all this in our future, rather than in an invented past. And yet when Father Daniel mentioned children I remembered that none of what we had spun was possible for us, and that I would probably never see the outside of a jail again, let alone the clear sky of mountain country out my window.

"We assumed we'd manage somehow," I said, unable to think of anything better.

"What my love means to say," Lark cut in, "is that we'd train our children in our trades, just as we had been trained by our elders. I would teach them to care for lame horses and sick dogs. And my wife, she would instruct them in the ways of midwifery, so that her knowledge would travel farther than she ever could, and live on long after her death."

"A quarter of an hour in a jail cell is hardly enough time or space to learn a person's real motives," the priest said. "The truth is, you may well be deceiving me as to your intentions toward one another. But I prefer to believe the best of people when I can, and I choose to believe the best of you: that if you were free now, you would indeed marry and lead a godly life together, not travel on separate paths to further thievery. I will perform the ceremony."

At my first wedding, I wore an eyelet lace gown and wild roses in my hair. At my second wedding, I wore a dress filthy with road dust and the sweat of several frightened days and nights. At my first wedding, everyone I had ever loved sat in pews at our church, smiling up at me as I spoke my vows. At my second wedding, the only guests were a catatonic man and a mysterious old woman, the latter of whom had agreed to act as a witness. At my first wedding, I believed my life was about to begin. At my second wedding, I was reasonably sure it had already ended.

And yet after my second husband kissed me for the first time, when our faces were still close together in the dark, the smell of his sweat and breath firing every nerve in me, I began to laugh—not because our wedding was funny, although the solemnity with which the priest read the vows and we said our "I do's" and the woman scrawled her mark on a marriage license the priest produced from his satchel were all funny in their way, but because even in that place, facing lifelong imprisonment and possible death, I felt that the two of us had gotten away with something.

As soon as the priest left, the guard returned.

"Ready for your wedding night?" he asked, not entirely unkindly.

In the lamplight, Lark and I locked eyes, getting ready for what we were about to do. The guard cuffed us both and chained us together, then motioned with his gun for us to walk ahead of him down the corridor. Lark acted quickly. As he passed in front of the guard he wheeled around and, with both cuffed wrists, knocked the lamp out of the guard's hand.

For a moment all was shattered glass and shouting. The oil blazed on the cell floor; the woman jumped onto a bench to avoid it. Lark ran; I ran with him, dragged by the chain between us. He looked back at me and on his face I saw what I felt—that improbable, unlooked-for exhilaration. Then I heard the shots.

A strange thing about pain is how slowly it travels. Here are all the things that happened after the guard's bullet hit me and before I crumpled to the ground: Lark and I ran two more paces down the corridor, toward the door to the outside world, which stood ajar slightly, as though the guard was so sure of his power that he needed no backup measures, not even the precaution of an additional lock; my heart lifted like a bird to see the open air in such close reach; in the sunlight streaming in through the door, Lark saw the blood streaming down my leg; I ran three paces, outstripping Lark; I had a memory, clearer and more vivid than the jail itself, of the day I broke my arm falling out of a tree just a few months after Mama got better and began caring for us again, how she scooped me up and held me to her chest, and how she fed me broth and barley candy and made much of me for weeks while I healed, and never reproached me even though I was clearly too big for the tree branch I'd been standing on, and old enough to know better; I wondered what had brought that memory to mind; I felt a wave of nausea; I called Lark's name.

By the time the pain overtook me, a terrible cold grinding, a feeling of great wrongness deep in the core of me, the guard was already dragging me and Lark down the corridor and back into the room where we'd been married.

When the haze of pain cleared enough for me to reason and perceive again, I heard Lark's voice in my ear.

"It's all right," Lark was saying. "Try to breathe. Breathe in and out as slowly as you can."

I breathed, and the pain did not lessen, but the breathing made some space inside my mind which I found was enough to allow for speech.

"Are you hurt?" I asked.

"Only a little," Lark said. "I'm fine, but you're not. I need you to tell me how to help you."

I touched my right pantleg and felt the blood soaking through the fabric. For a moment my mind went white with panic.

"Ada," Lark said. "You need to focus. You're the doctor. Tell me what to do."

With great effort I imagined myself out of my own body, tending to that body at a remove. A badly bleeding leg wound in a place with no water, no iodine, no needles and no thread—all a doctor could do in such a situation was bind the leg tightly and hope for the best.

"Tear me off a piece of your shirt," I said.

I heard the fabric rip.

"Now wrap it around my leg as tight as you can."

I saw white again.

"You're screaming."

"Good. That means it's tight enough. Now keep pressure on it."

A whiteness, and then a return to the intense, specific pain, broadened and deepened slightly by the weight of Lark's hands.

"Now what?" he asked.

"That's it," I said.

"You're still bleeding, I can feel it."

"There's nothing else to do," I said. "With any luck, the blood will start to clot before I lose too much."

"Luck?" Lark asked. "That's all we have to go on?"

I felt the warmth of his hands pressing into me, as though they could hold my body together.

"Agnes Rose says I'm lucky," I said.

"Who?" he asked, but I was drifting, floating somewhere beyond pain and hope, where future, present, and past melted together and I was forever opening my eyes on a Colorado morning, breathing Lark's breath into my mouth, gazing down at baby Bee as she smiled her first smile.

CHAPTER 9

My mama's house in Fairchild stood on a dirt road, on either side of which someone had planted flowering dogwood trees. Whenever I came back anxious or ill at ease—after a hard birth, or a difficult day at school, or a dance where no boys noticed me—the sight and smell of the dogwoods calmed me. As soon as I turned onto that road, I felt like I was home.

I had the same feeling on the Sunday after Easter, when Amity reached the top of the pass above Hole in the Wall and I saw the entire valley spread out below. The feeling was so strong and so wholly unexpected that I nearly wept.

"Thank you," I said to News, who rode behind me and held Amity's reins.

"Stop thanking me," News said. "What you did was stupid, and you deserved to suffer for it. But I wasn't going to let you hang, and neither was the Kid."

"Anyway," said Agnes Rose, "that guard was an easy mark. I never get tired of sweet-talking stupid men."

By now, I reasoned, the day guard had probably arrived to find the night guard sharing the jail cell with the catatonic man, and the rest of us long gone. The woman had bolted out the cell door with a speed that made me wonder again if she was much younger than she looked.

"No offense," Agnes Rose added to Lark.

"None taken," he said. "I'm not stupid."

"You're funny," Agnes Rose said. "Piece of advice: don't try to be funny with the others. Especially not Cassie. They're not going to like us bringing you home, and the quieter you are, the better."

Lark's wound was smaller than mine—a graze along his left thigh—but I could tell from his face that he was in pain. Texas, who rode ahead of us on Faith, had been against bringing Lark to Hole in the Wall, and had only been persuaded when News had vouched for him. Now Lark rode behind Agnes Rose on Prudence, bleeding into his boot, both of us awaiting the Kid's final decision on whether he should stay or go.

Through the fog of my injury—my wound had stopped bleeding, but the whiskey, water, and pemmican News had offered me had only partially restored my strength—I could tell that something was troubling Agnes Rose. Her voice was loud with artificial cheer, and her words increased in frequency and decreased in importance as we drew closer to Hole in the Wall, as though she was trying to fill the silence.

Finally, as we rounded the last bend in the road and the bunkhouse came into view, she said, "The Kid's been a little ill lately."

"Ill how?" I asked.

"Bloodshot eyes, never sleeping. And then—" She paused. "That's the main thing. Just not sleeping very much. Maybe you can help."

I didn't tell Agnes Rose I had already been helping the Kid sleep, or that her words made the back of my neck prickle with dread. I remembered the story of the Kid's father, shut away in the house with the curtains drawn until he could preach again.

"There's something else," I said.

"Last night," Agnes Rose said, "the Kid lit a suit on fire."

I wasn't sure I understood. "What suit?"

"Well," said Agnes Rose, "the Kid was wearing a fine woolen suit, and then the Kid lit that suit on fire."

"Mother Mary," I said.

"Everyone else had gone to bed, and the Kid started telling me about what we'd do when the job was done. It started out normal enough—like how we'd need to get the people in Fiddleback on our side. But then it got strange. The Kid was talking about how once we took Fiddleback, then we could take Casper, then Telluride, then Chicago. We'd remake America, the Kid said, but we'd do it right, and no Flu or fever would harm us, because we'd be protected by God."

I tried to be careful, so as not to give the Kid's secret away.

"That does sound strange," I said. "Did the Kid say how we were going to accomplish all that?"

"No," said Agnes Rose. "I asked, and the Kid accused me of doubting. Then the Kid said we'd accomplish it as we accomplished everything, through the power of the infant Lord Jesus. And that if I didn't believe, perhaps I needed a sign of His favor. And before I could do anything, the Kid simply dipped an arm into the fire.

"I think the point was to show that even flames were powerless against us. But of course, they aren't. And as soon as the sleeve caught it was like a spell was broken, and the Kid looked at me in absolute terror."

"What did you do?" I asked.

"Luckily I had a blanket about my shoulders. I leapt on the Kid and rolled the arm up until the fire went out. The Kid made me promise not to tell anyone. The burn isn't bad—I bandaged it myself, though you'll want to check it for infection. But the rest of it—I've seen the Kid do and say a lot of outlandish things, Ada. But I've never seen anything like this."

It was evening when we arrived, and the others were circled around the firepit eating tin cups of stew. As soon as we came into view with a stranger in our midst, Cassie and the Kid rose to meet the horses. Cassie, as Agnes Rose had predicted, looked angry and suspicious, but the Kid seemed strong and at ease, a bandage peeking out of a shirtsleeve the only sign that anything was amiss.

"This is Lark," I said. "He helped us steal the wagon, and he kept me from bleeding to death when we were in jail. He's hurt, and he needs rest. Can he stay here a few days with us?"

"Doing a job with him is one thing," Cassie said, "but bringing him here? News, what were you thinking? We've never had a man here before."

"What does that matter?" News asked. "Out in the world, I'm as much a man as he is. I don't see you kicking me out."

"News, you know what I mean," Cassie said.

"I don't," News said. "We needed help, I found someone trustworthy to help us. Now he needs our help, and you're going to turn him away?"

"Is he really trustworthy?" Cassie asked. "What reason does he have not to lead some sheriff or bounty hunter right to our doorstep as soon as it suits him?"

"You don't understand—" I said.

But before I could finish the Kid shouted, "Stop!" loudly enough that Lo and Elzy looked up startled from the firepit. I saw fear cross Cassie's face. But when the Kid spoke again, the words were measured and calm.

"Sir, I want to hear from you," the Kid said to Lark. "Surely you understand why some of us might have difficulty trusting you. What do you have to say for yourself?"

Lark paused. I gave him what I hoped was an encouraging look.

"Probably you shouldn't," Lark said finally. "But if you don't, wouldn't you rather have me here where you can keep an eye on me?"

"The man has a point, Cassie," the Kid said. "Now that he knows where we are, we either keep him or we kill him. And I'm not inclined to shoot someone who helped our doctor. Not yet, anyway."

I was lucky—the bullet had missed my shinbone, passing through the flesh and out the other side. Under my direction, Texas disinfected the wound with a rag dipped in a basin full of whiskey and hot water, then stitched and dressed it while I lay on my cot, biting down on a leather bridle to distract myself from the pain.

"Your turn," said Texas to Lark when it was done. "Let's get these off you."

She moved to unbutton Lark's bloodstained pants, but Lark took hold of his belt and shook his head.

"I'm all right," he said.

"You're not all right," said Texas. "You're bleeding onto the quilt."

"I think the bleeding's stopped."

Texas turned to me. "Tell your friend here he needs his wound dressed," she said. "Otherwise he'll get gangrene, and I'm not spending my days looking after a one-legged man."

"I'll do it, Texas," I said. "Now that mine's closed I feel better already."

"You look terrible," Texas said. "Your face is the color of mashed potatoes." She turned to Lark. "I wouldn't want her working on me in this state," she said.

"I'll take my chances," said Lark.

Texas shrugged. "Suit yourself. If she passes out while she's stitching you, I'm not coming to help."

"Why not tell them about what happened to you?" I asked Lark when Texas was gone. "It might make them trust you more."

"It's not their business," Lark said.

"You told me," I said. "Is it my business?"

Lark smiled. "Of course it is. You're my wife."

I dropped my eyes.

"Very funny," I said.

I was not sure where I stood with him. I believed he had meant at least some of what he said in the jail—he had not kissed me like someone merely playing a role. But I knew, too, that he was a thief who made much of his living fooling people. I thought of how Agnes Rose must have spoken to the jailhouse guard, and looked at him up from under her eyelashes—she must have made him believe that she found him interesting and handsome and that she wanted him. If Agnes Rose could do it then surely Lark could do it too.

"Texas is right," I said. "You need your wound cleaned. Is it okay if I take off your pants?"

"I'll do it," Lark said.

The wound was not deep but it had bled copiously, coating his thigh and soaking the right half of his underwear.

"I'm sorry," I said, pointing awkwardly. "You should probably take those off too."

He nodded, but instead began unbuttoning his shirt. His chest was long and lean, his skin the color of honey. A trail of black hair led from his navel under the waistband of his undershorts. He locked eyes with me, then removed them.

What I saw was ugly, there is no denying it. Lark's scrotum was intact, but above it was a tiny stump, puckered like a belly button. I could tell the wound had become badly infected after it was dealt, because it was surrounded by a starburst of scar tissue as big as a man's hand, still pinkish and shining as though it was fresh. What I saw was not just disfigurement; it was the record of terrible pain. I had the instinct to look away.

But I had been fighting that instinct all my life. I had not looked away when my mama had taken me to my first birth, when a woman groaned from deep down in her belly and a screaming, blood-covered head spurted out between her thighs. I had not looked away when another woman's flesh ripped from birth canal to anus so her baby could be born. I had not looked away when my neighbors brought us their broken bodies: their weeping sores, their crusted rashes, their breasts rock-hard and bright red with mastitis, their vaginas leaking clumpy yeast. I had not looked away when Mama washed and dressed and tended their most inflamed, infected parts, and I had not looked away when I was older and it became my job to tend them. I had not looked away when it came time to learn where God or Nature had strayed from the normal path to make my body; I was looking still. I dipped a rag in the basin of water. I let my eyes travel the length of his whole body, taking it all in.

"You're very beautiful," I told him.

In his face I saw relief.

"So are you," he said.

That day was the first time I had sex without the thought of conceiving a child. What we did, my first husband and I had never done—young as he was, I don't think he knew you could put your tongue between a woman's legs—and what I felt, I had never felt with my first husband. It was not only the feeling in my body that was different—all that wanting stirred up to fury and then released, my stomach dropping as though I was falling from a great height. It was also the feeling of doing something solely for its own sake, each moment not the beginning of the future, but its own, solitary now. Afterward I felt a stillness in my body I had never felt before, as though for a moment I was complete in myself, I was all that was needed.

We could lie together only for a short while, our wounded bodies pressed against each other, before I heard voices outside and knew that the others would be coming in soon. We began to struggle back into our clothes, remembering the pain we'd put aside.

Agnes Rose entered the bunkhouse as we were buttoning our shirts, a small smile on her face the only acknowledgement of what she'd seen. She held out a walking stick made of an oak branch.

"Come on, Doc," she said. "The Kid's calling a meeting."

Lark rose to help me up, but Agnes shook her head.

"I'll help her," she said. "You stay here. No offense, but this meeting's not for you."

The Kid looked powerful in a silver-gray silk suit jacket with a black shirt and black riding pants, all of it spotless even amid the red dust.

"Now is the time when all of our work comes to fruition," the Kid said. "Tomorrow, we ride for Fiddleback. We take what should be ours."

Cassie looked taken aback.

"We can't go tomorrow," she said. "Doc can't even walk. And we haven't found the right spot for the fire yet. We need at least another week."

"We don't have another week," the Kid said. "People are counting on us."

"Who's counting on us?" Cassie asked. "Nobody even knows we exist."

"Our nation is counting on us," the Kid said. "The barren women of this country, from the Mississippi to the Pacific Ocean. They're all counting on us, whether they know it or not. If we don't help them, no one will."

"The Pacific Ocean?" Cassie said. "I didn't like this plan when it was just Fiddleback, and now it's—well, I don't even know what you're saying. There are only eight of us, Kid."

The Kid crossed to where Cassie sat.

"Do you remember what Christ said to Martha?" the Kid asked.

"You always do this, Kid," Cassie said. "Don't do this."

"Christ said to Martha, 'I am the resurrection and the life. He who believes in me, though he may die, he shall live. And whoever lives and believes in me shall never die.' Do you understand, Cassie?"

"You know I'm not a good Christian, Kid," Cassie said. "You need rest."

"Christian?" the Kid shouted. "Christian? Cassie, Christ was only an example, a messenger if you will. He came to teach us that when we have righteousness within us, we can never be killed, because what is right can never die. You see, don't you, Agnes Rose? News? We are the resurrection and the life."

The Kid's speech was fast and breathless; the Kid's eyes made me think of a fire burning itself out. Lo and Texas looked at each other, and Elzy looked at Cassie, all their gazes crackling with unease. Finally Agnes Rose spoke.

"All those people counting on us," she said, "they need us to be smart. We can't rush off without a finished plan. Let's take two days. By then Doc might be healed enough to ride, and News can pick a placc for the fire. Just one extra day, Kid. I guarantee you won't regret it." As she finished, she gave me a pointed look.

"I agree," I said. "I feel the calling you're talking about, Kid. I've felt it since I got here. If you go tomorrow, I'll have to stay behind. I won't be able to do what I'm called to do."

The Kid walked around the firepit to stare down at me with violent eyes. I braced myself as though for a kick or punch.

"You're right," the Kid said. "It should be all of us. Two days. Two days, and then we ride to Fiddleback. Who's ready to remake the world?"

There was a split-second of silence, and then Agnes Rose led the circle in a half-hearted cheer.

When everyone else was asleep—Lark on a makeshift bed of feed sacks and horse blankets—I found the Kid in the orchard, sitting on the stump where I'd first learned to shoot. The pear trees were blooming, white blossoms in frothy clusters that shone in the moonlight. You'd never know the fruit was rock-hard and bitter as medicine. I sat next to the Kid in the cold grass.

"How long has it been since you slept?" I asked.

"I've been sleeping just fine," the Kid said. "I just came out here to do some thinking."

The Kid sounded so ordinary, I almost believed it.

"What are you thinking about?" I asked.

"Same as ever," the Kid said. "Fiddleback. What can go wrong. What will go wrong. How to remedy it when it does."

"You sounded a lot more confident earlier tonight," I said. "It sounded like you thought we couldn't possibly fail."

"Of course we can fail," the Kid said. "The fire might not catch, or the safe might be too sturdy for our bombs, or the wagon might lose a wheel, or the sheriff's posse might run us down and hang all of us. I'd wager we're far more likely to fail than to succeed."

"But back at the firepit, you said—"

"I know what I said!"

The Kid's voice was loud in the quiet night. Something took off from one of the pear trees and flapped away on dark wings.

"I just get a little carried away sometimes," the Kid said, a bit more quietly. "They all understand that. They know not to take what I say as gospel."

The Kid's face was indignant and defensive, but also weary and anxious. I could tell we were both worried about what I would say next.

"Do you remember what you told me before I left?" I asked. "About your father?"

The Kid stood up.

"Don't patronize me. Of course I remember. But you don't have to worry about that anymore. I thought I might be going that way, but it turns out I'm not. I'll be all right in the morning."

"Kid," I said slowly, "you said that if you began to speak as though you were not a mortal human, and no man or beast could harm you, I should take you to the cowboy shack and let you stay out there until you recovered your senses."

"How dare you?" The Kid's voice was a hiss. "You owe me everything. You'd be dangling from a gallows right now if not for me. And you presume to question my sanity?"

"I'm not questioning—"

The Kid drew a gun. It gleamed in the moonlight with an oily sheen like snakeskin.

"Get away from me," the Kid said.

I held up my hands and began backing away.

"I'm just saying you need some rest." I tried again.

The Kid fired the gun into the air. Night creatures fluttered and scurried away from the blast.

"Go!" the Kid shouted.

As best as I could on my injured leg, I ran.

Agnes Rose was sitting on the bunkhouse steps when I got back.

"Thank baby Jesus," she said when she saw me. "I thought I heard a shot."

"You did," I said. "It's all right. Well, it's not. The Kid is sick."

"Can you cure it?"

"It's not like that," I said. "We made a plan before I left. If this happened, the Kid wanted to go to the cowboy shack to recuperate in private. But now the Kid won't listen to me."

In the direction of the orchard I could still hear birds chattering and settling—the guttural complaints of ravens, the low ghost-call of an owl.

"Well, there's only one thing to do," she said. "We wait until the Kid finally sleeps, and we take the gun. Then we take the Kid out to the cowboy shack—by force if we have to—and we trade off standing guard until it passes."

I imagined it—holding the Kid at gunpoint, tying the Kid's wrists, hoisting the Kid up onto a horse. I knew we could do it. But every time I thought of binding the Kid's arms behind the Kid's back, I remembered the way the sheriff and his deputy had looked at me on the road out of Casper, like I was less than human, like I was rotten food. I would not treat the Kid the way they had treated me.

"No," I said. "It should be the Kid's choice."

Agnes Rose sighed. "All right," she said, "but how do we convince the Kid to choose wisely?"

"Who does the Kid listen to?" I asked.

"Before tonight," Agnes Rose said, "I would've said the Kid listens to you."

"Obviously not," I said. "Who else?"

Agnes Rose thought for a moment. The stars were going out, the sky over the mountains very slightly bluing.

"The Kid trusts Cassie," she said.

"But they're always fighting," I said.

"They don't agree on much," she said. "But Cassie's known the Kid longer than anyone. Maybe she'll know what to say."

I stood still for a long time in the dark next to Cassie's cot in the great room. I remembered the Kid's insinuation that something terrible would happen if Cassie and the others found out. It struck me that the Kid had not given Cassie enough credit. She must have known something was not right with the Kid; she had known the Kid too long and too well to miss it. I did not know why she had not confronted the Kid in front of the others, why she had not refused, flat-out, to continue with the Kid's plan. Probably if we successfully got the Kid to the cowboy shack, Cassie would scuttle it once and for all. Surely the Kid would never forgive me for that. And yet I could not think of another way.

Cassie woke with a jerk and a look of fear in her eyes so abject and primal that I, too, felt afraid. Quickly, though, it was replaced with annoyance.

"What time is it?" she demanded.

"It's the Kid," I said. "The Kid needs help."

It could not have been more than an hour that we waited outside the bunkhouse while Cassie went up to the orchard after the Kid.

In that time the sky went from blue-black to royal blue to aquamarine and then, in the sudden manner of the mountain regions, bright with streaks of gold and pink like the tails of gleaming horses. The meadowlarks awoke, with songs that, on another day, would have made me smile. Coyotes chuckled in the predawn and then went silent, shamed out of their scavenging by the light of day.

Agnes Rose and I sat on the steps, or she sat on the steps and I paced, or she paced and I sat on the steps, or both of us paced in circles that grew in size until they intersected only every few minutes, the two of us nodding at each other, making faces of mingled encouragement and worry. We didn't speak. I didn't know what Agnes Rose was hoping for as the morning waxed and warmed around us, as we drew closer to the inevitable time when the rest of the gang would wake and find the Kid gone.

I knew only what I was selfishly afraid of: that Cassie would fail, the gang would split, and the Fiddleback plan would wither and die; or that Cassie would succeed, she would take charge, and the Fiddleback plan would wither and die. Either way I would lose my chance to go to Pagosa Springs. Hole in the Wall might feel like home to me now, but I did not belong at home yet. I had work to do, and as I saw the possibility of doing it recede into the brightening distance, I grew ever more afraid that I would lose myself—not in the way the Kid had, but slowly, every day blanking out a piece of my heart and mind, until I faced some sheriff's gun or executioner's gallows with no fear or sorrow, because that which was worth protecting had already ebbed away.

When, finally, just as the sun crested the mountains and cast its lemony light across the bunkhouse steps, Cassie came down from the orchard with the Kid by her side, Agnes Rose and I rushed to greet them with questions and offers on our lips.

"Are you all right?" Agnes Rose asked. "Kid, you scared us."

"I'll get a horse ready," I said. "Kid, which one do you want to ride?"

"I'm all right, Agnes," the Kid said in a clear but quiet voice. "Doc, Cassie will get my horse ready. You have your own work to do."

"Tell the others the Kid and I went on a trail ride," Cassie said. "If they ask where, say you don't know. I'll explain everything when I get back."

If Cassie expected that this would satisfy the rest of the gang, she was mistaken. As soon as the others woke—first Texas, to look after the horses, then Elzy, startled to find Cassie's bunk empty, then Lo, and finally News—each wanted to know where the Kid was, and once they found no answers forthcoming, a general confusion bordering on panic settled over the bunkhouse, which Agnes Rose and I were powerless to defuse.

"I knew it," Texas said. "Is the Kid sick, Doc? Is it serious?"

"What about the job?" Lo asked. "We've been rushing it too much. If the Kid's not right, we should wait until the fall at least, maybe longer."

"We can't delay the job," News said. "Doc can help the Kid, right Doc?"

By the time Cassie returned at high noon, hollow-eyed with worry and lack of sleep, both Agnes Rose and I had invented tasks outdoors to avoid the increasingly insistent questioning of our compatriots. I was gathering mint when she rode up, and so when she called us all to the bunkhouse moments later, I still carried a basket full of fragrant, dew-flecked leaves.

"First," Cassie said to the assembled company, "the Kid is going to be all right. There's no immediate danger."

"What happened?" Lo interrupted. "Where is the Kid now?" Cassie held her hand up.

"Let me finish," she said. "The Kid is going to be all right, but the Kid is very ill right now. It's an ailment that, frankly, I don't pretend to understand, but it's something that the Kid anticipated and made a plan for, out of concern for all of us."

"What's the plan?" News asked.

"The only treatments for this illness are rest and time," Cassie said. "So the Kid will be resting somewhere safe until it passes."

"Where?" Elzy asked. "When can we visit?"

"The Kid has asked for complete solitude for the time being," Cassie said, "and so I've been instructed not to reveal the place. Rest assured that the Kid will have everything necessary for a swift recovery."

For a moment everyone talked at once. Only Lark was quiet, looking at me with confusion. I squeezed his hand, a promise of a future explanation.

It was Lo who finally broke through the din: "We should call off the job," she said. "Who knows how long until the Kid will be well again?"

Cassie nodded and took a slow breath.

"The Kid knew that some of you would be worried about the job, and asked me to pass along a message to everyone: the Kid has complete confidence in all of us, and knows that even without one of our number, we will succeed."

Again the bunkhouse grew loud with competing voices. Again Lo spoke over everyone.

Elzy had been looking out the window, avoiding Cassie's eyes, and when she spoke, her voice was quiet but hard. "Cass," she said, "your loyalty to the Kid isn't a good reason to put us all in danger. Why don't we just wait until the Kid recovers?"

"You know I'd like to," Cassie said, "but our time is running out. Remember, the bank president comes back in June, and then the vault will be guarded again."

Lo opened her mouth, shut it, then opened it again. "Cass," she said, "you know as well as I do this job never made any sense for us. We're not bankers, we're not landlords. We came here to get away from those kinds of people. Mother of God, running a town? I can't imagine anything worse. And now's our chance to reconsider. If we let the moment pass while the Kid recovers, the Kid could never blame us."

"We don't need to argue," News said. "Let's have a vote. The Kid would respect that, no matter what we decide."

"You're right," Cassie said. "All those in favor of sticking with the plan, raise a hand."

Cassie lifted her own hand, and News and Agnes Rose and I followed. Texas raised a hand too.

Lo shook her head.

"Good luck to you," she said. "I hope you don't get shot in the street in Fiddleback, or strung up in the town square. And if by some miracle you succeed, I hope you make Fiddleback into a paradise, I really do."

She pulled her rucksack from under her cot.

"Where are you going?" Texas asked.

Lo shrugged.

"I was on my own before I came here. I'll be on my own again. I'll be all right. Don't forget, I taught every single one of you how to hide."

Elzy followed Lo to the door.

"Lo, wait," she said. "You can't just leave."

"I can, El," said Lo, shouldering her rucksack. "And you can too. Maybe you should think about it."

And Lo shut the door behind her, leaving a stunned silence in the room. News and Agnes Rose looked at each other with worried eyes. Texas put her head in her hands. Only Lark, sitting cross-legged on his bunk, his long feet bare, looked unafraid.

"We can't do anything now," Elzy said to Cassie. "We're two down, and I'm not even half the shot I used to be. We have to start a fire, break into a vault, hold up who knows how many bank clerks—"

"Two," said News.

"Fine, two," Elzy went on. "Plus loading up a wagon with gold bars and driving it back up here. How are we going to do that with just six people? We'll be slaughtered."

Lark lifted his eyes to Elzy's face.

"Seven," he said.

That night I went to the kitchen cabin as Cassie was preparing dinner. Now that it was spring we had rabbits in our snares, fat with new grass. Cassie had laid out two pearly pink carcasses on a butcher block. A broth boiled on the stove, its smell green and spicy.

"If the Kid needs help with sleeping," I said, handing over the near-empty bottle of laudanum, "two drops in tea or water, no more. And don't leave it in the cowboy shack. The Kid shouldn't be alone with it just now."

"Thanks," Cassie said.

She slid a small sharp knife under the front legs of the first rabbit and sliced them away from the body. I lingered.

"You could've called the plan off," I said. "Why didn't you?"

Cassie carefully trimmed the fat from the inside of each front leg and set it aside in a yellowish-white pile. Then she sliced upward from the loin to rib cage and cut the meat away from the ribs. She worked for so long, and so silently, that I thought she might not have heard me. Then she said, "The day I met the Kid, my husband cut off all my hair. He said I wasn't a real woman, and I didn't deserve to look like one."

"That's awful," I said, not knowing what else to say.

She cut along the rabbit's pelvis, looking for the back-leg joint.

"I believed him," she said. "I believed everything he said about me. It was the Kid who didn't believe."

"So you owe the Kid?" I asked. "Is that it?"

Cassie shook her head. She reached inside the rabbit's leg flesh and popped the leg-joint open.

"The Kid was a ranch hand for my husband," she said. "We used to meet in the barn and plan our escape. At first I thought it was just for me. I thought the Kid was so selfless, a hero. Then my husband went on a cattle drive and I let the Kid stay the night in my bed. The Kid never slept."

She popped the second joint and cut each leg free.

"After that I started to notice things. The red threads in the Kid's eyes. The way the Kid always talked about the future whenever the past came up. I saw the Kid had some terrible pain to carry, and helping me was a way to carry it."

"The sickness," I said. "The one the Kid's father had."

"That was part of it, I think," Cassie said. "But I always thought there might be more. The Kid has always stood a little bit apart, even from me."

Cassie brought the flat of her knife down on the rabbit's spine with a force that made me jump.

"So when you ask, do I owe the Kid, the answer is yes, of course, the Kid gave me a life. But also the Kid needs to be a hero. The Kid needs to be the Kid. If I take that away—"

She bent the rabbit's pelvis backward away from the spine, then sliced it off and tossed it in the boiling water. "If I take that away, then I don't know what," she said.

She turned away from me and began to trim silvery skin from the outside of the loin.

I took a breath.

"What happened to the two of you?" I asked.

"What do you mean?"

"After you left your husband. Texas said something happened, and then you had to come here to be far away from everything. What happened?"

Cassie put down her knife.

"We moved to an integrated town near Arapaho land and called ourselves the McCartys: the Kid was the husband and I was the wife. Nearly a year we lived that way, perfectly happy. The Kid worked for a rancher and I took in sewing. We lived in rooms at first, and then when we had a little money we built a house on the edge of town. With our own hands we built it; I'd never seen the Kid sleep so well as when we'd spent all day sanding the doors to fit."

"And then?"

"There was an accident at the ranch. A horse kicked the Kid in the head. The Kid wasn't moving; everyone feared the worst. Before anyone could send for me, the doctor was there undressing the Kid to check for a heartbeat.

"The rancher was kind. He could have had the Kid thrown in jail, but instead he gave us the night to pack. 'If I see your face in town tomorrow, I'll have no choice but to call the sheriff,' he said.

"We were gathering what little we had when the men came. I don't think the rancher sent them. I think he was honest. But in the end it doesn't matter. First they shot our horses. Then they put a torch to our little house. We only escaped because the men were drunk, and because months of running had made us fast. For miles, the Kid kept looking back at the house we'd built, going up in flames."

"I'm so sorry," I said.

Cassie shrugged.

"Now you know," she said. "Go get me some purslanes. And not the ones the snails have been eating."

CHAPTER 10

On the thirtieth of May in the year of our Lord 1895, the Hole in the Wall gang rode for Fiddleback—minus its leader, plus one itinerant thief, cowboy, and veterinarian's assistant. The journey took a day, and we camped by the same lake where Agnes Rose and News and I had stopped a few weeks before. There we fed and watered the horses, and passed around a bottle of gin that Agnes Rose produced from Prudence's saddlebag. News had brought along her fiddle, and she began to play "Sweet Marie," first slowly and then faster, her eyes closing, a smile forming on her face. After a time Texas got up to dance. Cassie and Elzy quietly joined hands.

The night reminded me of my very first at Hole in the Wall, but missing from our circle now were Lo with her beautiful jacket covered in bells, and the Kid presiding over all of us, binding us together.

"You're quiet," Agnes Rose said to me, passing the bottle.

The herbs cooled my tongue; the alcohol warmed my throat.

"Do you think Lo will be okay on her own?"

I handed the bottle back and Agnes Rose took a long drink.

"She should be worrying about us," she said.

I looked around the circle in the falling light. Where that first night I had seen only wildness and joy in the gang's celebration, now I could sense a desperation in the way Texas jumped and somersaulted, the way we all swigged from the bottle. Cassie whispered something and Elzy gave a high, fevered laugh.

All this time I had been following Texas's lead, assuming that sticking to the Kid's plan was the best way for me to assure my passage to Pagosa Springs. But now I was afraid. In the last few days it had occurred to me that perhaps the Kid would not recover, and that when I returned from Fiddleback, the Kid might be unable to hold up the other end of the bargain—if I returned from Fiddleback at all.

"Why are you going through with this?" I asked Agnes Rose.

She was quiet a moment. She slid out the pins that held her hair in place, and the heavy auburn braids fell down past her shoulders.

"What do you mean?" she asked.

"I mean, I know why Cassie's doing it, and Texas. I have an idea, I think, about Elzy and News. But you clearly know how to fend for yourself. Why don't you leave? Why risk your life for the Kid's plan?"

Agnes Rose untied the ribbon from the end of one braid, then the other.

"I don't talk about this much," she said, "but I loved my first husband. We were very happy together. I wanted badly to have his children. We tried for years; he was patient with me. When he finally kicked me out, I knew how to keep from getting hanged, that's true enough. I knew how to make money. It's like I told you—I'm a swimmer. But my grief nearly dragged me under."

She began to unwind her left braid, the locks emerging in glossy curls.

"The year I met the Kid, I'd tried to kill myself twice. The second time I would've succeeded if one of the other girls hadn't been quick with the ipecac. The Kid couldn't promise me money or safety, but when the Kid talked about making a place in the world for people like us—well, for the first time since I'd left home, I saw my way to some kind of purpose in my life."

"I understand," I said.

She gave me a long look.

"Then you'll understand why I can't just strike out on my own again," she said.

She shook her hair out, a wild lion's mane, glowing in the firelight.

"Anyway," she said, "A plan is a good thing, but it's not the only thing. We've survived this long because the Kid knows how to improvise. Whatever happens in Fiddleback, the Kid will find a way to turn it to our advantage."

"If the Kid recovers," I said.

"The Kid is going to recover," Agnes Rose said.

She stood and held out both her hands. "Come on," she said, "dance with me."

We waited until the afternoon of the next day to ride into Fiddleback proper, so as to catch the clerks sleepy from their lunchtime ale. On the ranchlands, the spring calves had grown tall and leggy on their mothers' milk. In the cornfields, the plants were high as a five-year-old child, nearly ready for the harvest. We slowed down on a side street a few blocks from Main Street, and Agnes Rose and I climbed out.

In the weeks prior, News had mapped out the bank and the establishments that abutted it down to the cracks in the window glass. She'd found that while Madame Trumbull's lingerie store seemed like an ideal site for a fire—all that lace and tulle—in fact Madame was very diligent about securing her wares, and the back entrance was locked at all times with a sturdy dead bolt. The proprietor of Stewart's Meats, on the other hand, routinely left the back door unlocked, and was an assiduous but disorderly record keeper. His back storeroom was piled floor to ceiling with paper ledgers, some lightly stained with meat drippings, detailing every aspect of the operations of his business from the purchase of steers at market to complaints lodged by customers about rancid pork. It was there, amid the accumulated history of the butcher's entire career, that the robbery of the Farmers' and Merchants' Bank of Fiddleback began.

At that moment, Texas was driving the wagon in at a leisurely pace along the town's back streets, dressed in the cheap hat and waxed mustache of a traveling salesman. In case anyone stopped her, the back of the wagon was packed with an assortment of cheap cotton and cracked pottery purchased from Nótkon at a steep discount, which we'd jettison to make room for the gold.

Once the fire was set, Agnes Rose, News, Elzy, and I would enter the bank through the front door. We were dressed as young housewives in bonnets and cotton frocks. We would engage the clerks in complex financial transactions, augmented by flirtation, while Lark and Cassie simply strolled through the lobby of the bank into the side room where the vault sat, unguarded and ready to be blown wide open. As soon as we heard the sound, the four of us in the front of the bank would draw our pistols from our petticoats and instruct the clerks to empty the tills. We'd load up the wagon and, if all went well, drive the horses back to Hole in the Wall with all the liquid assets of the Farmers' and Merchants' on their backs, while the sheriff and his posse fought the fire and the clerks tried to understand what had just happened to them.

"I feel sorry for the butcher," I said, hesitating with the matchbook in my hands. "He never did anything to us."

"He'll smell the smoke long before he's in any danger," Agnes Rose said. "He won't get hurt."

"He'll lose his shop," I said.

"Think about it this way," Agnes Rose said. "If you were climbing the steps to the gallows in the town square right now, about to be hanged for a witch, do you think the butcher would raise a hand to help you? Or do you think he'd be cheering with all the rest?"

"Everybody cheers the hanging of a witch," I said.

Agnes Rose looked at her dainty watch.

"Everybody but us," she said, and she took the matches from me and set one of the ledgers alight.

The fire caught with shocking speed. One moment it played with the corners of the pages and the next it engulfed an entire column of ledgers—decades of beef prices and chicken sales, measures of flesh and bone, consumed by flames in an instant. Agnes Rose and I watched it burn for a moment; then we turned and walked out of the shop.

News and Elzy were on Main Street already, pretending to evaluate the petticoats in the window of Madame Trumbull's. Elzy wore a blonde wig with her bonnet and a light brown dress cinched close around her narrow waist. Both of them walked differently from the way they did at Hole in the Wall; their steps, as they spotted us and proceeded into the bank, had a careful, tentative quality that, to me, was both familiar and strange. Another woman passed by in the opposite direction with the same peculiar gait, and I recognized it: the walk of women in public, who know they are being watched.

The inside of the bank was very beautiful. The lobby was not large, but it had been made to look more spacious by means of a high vaulted ceiling, on which was painted a blue sky with clouds and cherubs in the old European style. The floor was marble tile, alternating between white with gray veins and black shot through with the subtlest hint of gold. It had probably been salvaged from the house of some rich man felled by Flu—or perhaps the bank had been his house, one of the many cleared of corpses and put to new use in the years and decades that followed the disease. Perhaps the wealth of Fiddleback today was kept in the same room where the wealthiest resident of some prior town had breathed his last some hundred years ago.

On one side of the lobby were four clerk windows behind a high counter—as Henry had said, only two of the windows were manned. On the other side of the lobby was an open corridor leading to the bank's back offices and the vault. The corridor and the windows faced one another, so that the clerks could easily see anyone passing into the corridor—we would have to see to it that their attention was occupied elsewhere.

So far, the clerks appeared to be having a quiet morning. One, his red hair grown long and unkempt over his ears, his glasses marked with fingerprints, was giving an old man in a grocer's apron change for a silver piece in coppers. The other was using an emery board to file his nails. Agnes Rose and I queued up behind the grocer, while Elzy went straight for the fastidious clerk, and News fell in line behind her. I was relieved. With two people ahead of me, one of them Agnes Rose, it was unlikely I would have to put my powers of distraction to the test.

"I'd like to open a savings account for my son," Elzy said to the clerk with the nail file. He was young and handsome, clearly proud of his appearance—his blond mustache and beard were as carefully tended as his nails. Over his crisp white shirt he wore a pair of red suspenders.

"Very good, ma'am," he said to Elzy. "To start, I'll need his name."

"He doesn't have a name," Elzy said.

"I beg your pardon?" the clerk asked.

From where I stood behind Agnes Rose, I could clearly see the bank's front door and the foot traffic on the street outside. Any moment, I knew, Lark would enter, and from that moment he would be in danger, from which it would fall to me, at least in part, to protect him. I was surprised by the force of my fear for him. I had never felt such a thing for my first husband, my spouse before my family and the law. But of course, I had never had cause to fear for him—I could not imagine him in Lark's place now, just as I could not compare any aspect of my old life to its counterpart in the new. The two were connected only by my body, and the failing within it that had made the old life impossible and ushered the new one in.

"You see, his father and I can't agree on a name," Elzy said. "I want to name him Albert, for my grandfather, but my husband wants to name him Christopher, for Saint Christopher. No matter what I say, he won't budge. So I thought, if I open a savings account in the name of Albert, and put some money in it, then my husband will have to agree, won't he? Or my son can't get the money?"

The fastidious clerk cast a panicked look at his colleague, who studiously ignored him, still busily counting coppers for the grocer.

"Ma'am," the clerk said, "I'm afraid there are a couple of problems with your strategy."

The front door opened. A man who was not Lark entered the bank and queued up behind me.

"In the first place, we can't open an account for someone who doesn't exist. And since your son is not, in fact, named Albert—"

The other clerk finished counting coppers and sent the grocer on his way with well-wishes. Agnes Rose stepped up to the counter. A man who was not Lark entered the bank.

"But he will be named Albert," Elzy said. "I just need to make my husband see reason. My grandfather was a great man, you know. He owned two dry-goods stores and was a deacon in his church."

The second man who was not Lark looked at the queues at both windows and left the bank. Agnes Rose removed a torn fragment of a promissory note from her handbag. Cassie entered the bank and stood behind News.

"In the second place, it's not the bank's business to get involved in a dispute between husband and wife. Now, if you'd like to open the account in your own name and simply change the name once you agree—"

Agnes Rose smiled her most winning smile and told the clerk that the remainder of the note had been bitten off by a dog. A woman entered the bank and stood behind Cassie. A man who was not Lark entered the bank. I began to be afraid that he was not coming. Perhaps someone had stopped him in the street and somehow realized what we were planning. Perhaps the sheriff from Casper had come looking for him. Perhaps Cassie was right, and he had betrayed us all.

"But the account isn't for me, it's for my son, who will be named Albert."

The clerk explained to Agnes Rose that she would need more than half the note in order to redeem it. She pretended not to understand him. Sweat soaked the armpits of my blue gingham dress. A man who was not Lark entered the bank.

"Here's what I can do," the clerk said. "I can open an account with no name for now, just a number. And then when you're ready with a name, we can add it to the account. All we'll need is a deposit of five silver liberties.

"Oh, I don't have any money," said Elzy. "My husband keeps track of the money."

Lark entered the bank.

At that moment several things happened at once. Lark and I exchanged a single glance, no longer than the blink of an eye. Elzy's conversation with the fastidious clerk escalated into an argument. Cassie quietly stepped out of line. And the unkempt clerk, having politely but firmly dismissed Agnes Rose, looked at me with a smile.

"How can I help you?" he asked.

I had come with a specific story to tell—we all had—but in that moment, the knowledge that Lark was passing behind me down the bank's corridor, and that his life was in my hands, drove my plans completely out of my head.

"I need to open an account," I said, parroting Elzy.

"Wonderful," said the clerk. He was middle-aged, with a round face and small, warm, gray eyes behind the smudged lenses. "Will you be needing one just for savings, or one you can write notes against?"

I willed myself not to turn around and look at the corridor.

"I don't know," I said. "I've never had a bank account before. Can you explain the different types?"

"I'd be glad to," he said. "A savings account is where you put money for a rainy day. You put money in, and at the end of every month the bank adds a little bit extra on top. That's the interest."

The other clerk raised his voice.

"Madam," he said, "I've been very patient with you. But the fact is, you have no business coming in here and wasting my time with your silly questions when you should be at home with your baby."

The unkempt clerk looked in their direction, so I allowed myself to glance around the lobby. Cassie and Lark were gone. I felt a momentary sense of relief, tempered by the heaviness of the gun in my left skirt pocket and the knowledge that in minutes I would have to use it.

The unkempt clerk shook his head and spoke to me in a low, conspiratorial voice.

"I'm sorry," he said, inclining his head in the other clerk's direction. "The fact is, we're stretched a bit thin today. Some of our colleagues are, ah, busy at the moment, and it's just the three of us here."

My stomach fell.

"Three?" I asked.

The bombs were so much louder than I had imagined. In the valley their force had dissipated in empty air, but inside the bank I could hear them rip through wood and stone and steel. In the chaos that followed I was not sure who was screaming, how the bank's patrons went from racing for the door to lined up against the wall with their hands behind their heads, or when exactly I drew my revolver and began shouting at the unkempt clerk to empty his till. But I was sure of one thing: just before the bombs had gone off, I had heard the sound of gunshots.

Against the wall, one of the women was praying: "Baby Jesus, deliver us from danger. Care for us as your holy Mother cared for you." The fastidious clerk began to cry as he loaded cardboard tubes of gold and silver pieces into a cloth bag. The unkempt clerk wasn't moving.

"I can't give you this money," he said. "It isn't my money to give."

I had no idea what to say to him. His gray eyes were full of defiance, and also full of fear.

"Empty the till," I said, "or I'll shoot you."

"You see those people over there against the wall?" the clerk asked. "This is their savings. They need it to feed their families. If you take it, what will become of them?"

"Don't worry," I said, "we'll take care of them. But first we need the money."

"Just give it to her!" the other clerk shouted. He passed the heavy bag through the window into Elzy's free hand.

"I'm sorry," said the unkempt clerk. "You'll have to shoot me."

I thought of the wagon driver, the way he had crumpled in the dirt, the way his father had keened over his body. I knew I would never shoot this man.

"You don't want that," I said. "What about your family? They need you alive."

I could feel the fear cracking the edges of my voice.

"I don't have any family," the man said. "It's just me. If you're going to shoot me, do it now."

He was looking me square in the eye.

"Andrew," sobbed the fastidious clerk, "please just give them the money."

"Baby Jesus, deliver us into your arms," the woman prayed, "as you were delivered into the arms of your holy Mother."

Cassie appeared in the entrance to the corridor. I took my eyes off the clerk and turned to her. Her face was ashen. Her shirt was covered in blood. The clerk tried to reach for something below the window. Elzy shot him in the chest.

Some people believe that when a person dies, the body is nothing but a shell the soul leaves behind. I have never believed this. The first time I touched a dead body, I was thirteen years old. Irma Love was eighty—had been eighty—the night her heart stopped working and her lungs filled with fluid and she died. The next day, Mama brought me with her to wash and lay out the body.

Mrs. Love had worked in the dry-goods store and taught piano lessons to children. She played very beautifully and was very mean and I and all the other children in Fairchild were afraid of her, but she had a sardonic sense of humor, too, and as I got older I liked to go to the dry-goods store to hear her talk about other adults she thought were stupid or self-satisfied. All of that was still there when Mrs. Love died—the meanness stamped on the corners of her mouth, the laughter in the wrinkles round her eyes, those long fingers still limber after a lifetime of stretching across the keys. Mama taught me to treat a body with respect, like a person, and Mrs. Love was a person to me, her body no less her own just because she was dead.

And so when I saw Lark lying in the corridor in front of the blasted vault, his chest blown open with bullet holes, and when Cassie shouted in a ragged voice to leave him behind, that the sheriff's posse would surely catch us if we delayed any longer, I ignored her, and I bent low and slipped my arms under his limp arms and half-carried, half-dragged him to the wagon, where Texas was waiting to bear us all away.

In the dark back of the wagon, Cassie put her head in her hands.

"I should have been ready for the clerk to be there," she said. "The Kid would've been ready."

The third clerk, a square-bodied, apple-cheeked young man who looked full of life even in death, was likely now being prepared for burial in the Fiddleback churchyard, Cassie's bullet already corroding at his heart. We'd never know what unlucky impulse had made him decide to stay at his post that day instead of drinking with his friends at Veronica's, where he would have been rewarded for his shirking with his life. We knew only that after Lark and Cassie had placed the bombs all around the door to the vault, just as they were lighting the fuses, he had entered the corridor from the bank's back office; that, perhaps having heard a commotion, he was already carrying his revolver in his hand; that on seeing him, Lark reached for his own revolver; and that the clerk shot him three times before Cassie was able to draw her weapon and shoot the clerk. As we carried the gold out of the vault—more bags than we could count, each as heavy as a three-year-old child—we had to step over his body.

"It's terrible what happened," Elzy said, "but Cassie, we did it. We got the gold. I never thought we'd do it, you know that. And at least all of *us* made it out alive."

Cassie raised her head.

"He risked his life for us," she said, "and I let him die."

His head in my lap, Lark looked now as he had in life—slightly sorrowful, slightly amused, very beautiful. But when I'd gotten him safely into the wagon, I'd immediately shut his eyes with my fingers—they were wide and staring, and full of fear.

Cassie looked me full in the eye.

"I'm sorry," she said.

I extended my hand, she took it, and we held each other there.

We had no coffin, but Agnes Rose made a shroud of fine white muslin from Lo's steamer trunk. She offered to help me prepare Lark's body, but I shook my head. I wanted to protect his privacy, even now, and I wanted to be alone with him one more time.

In the bunkhouse, in the early morning light, I looked, once more, at his oldest wound. The whorled scarring, the stub where his penis once had been—they no longer disgusted me. Instead they made me angry and guilty—that Lark should have survived this, only to die by a stranger's gun in a bank robbery gone wrong, all to help me get where I wanted to go. I had not cried yet for Lark; now I shed tears of frustration and self-blame.

There was only one thing I could do for Lark now, and so I washed the blood from each of the wounds in his chest and bandaged them as though he were alive. I cleaned the dirt from under his fingernails. I washed and combed his hair. I treated his body with the same care and attention that I imagined the veterinarian lavishing on his animals, and I swore to myself that from now on I would treat every body I touched that way, living or dead, patient or lover. Then I wrapped Lark in his shroud, and News and I carried him out to the orchard to be buried.

The days that followed were slow, strange ones. The job was half-finished—the gold was piled high in the barn, where the horses periodically nuzzled it and then lost interest since it had no smell except that of the musty burlap bags in which it was stored. Now we had to wait.

Seven days, the Kid had said, would be enough for the bank president to get desperate. If at first the residents of Fiddleback had been sympathetic to the plight of an innocent businessman robbed by thugs, their fellow-feeling would turn to rage once they realized that the president kept his large house on a hill above town while their life savings—the gold that kept food on their tables and cattle in their pastures, that fixed their roofs and shod their horses and paid the midwife when their babies were born—rode away in a stranger's wagon. They would gather outside the president's house with eggs, with rocks, and eventually with guns. The president would be eager to sell.

At least, so the Kid had told us—but now the Kid was gone. On the second day of the week, Cassie rode out to the cowboy shack with a satchel of food and a canteen of fresh water, and returned a few hours later with the news that the Kid was much better and looking forward to rejoining us soon. But when she spoke she looked at a point above our heads, avoiding all our eyes. Later, she followed me to the barn when I went to brush Amity.

"The Kid's sleeping again," she said.

"That's a good sign, right?" I asked as I worked the curry-comb across Amity's flank.

But Cassie looked worried.

"I mean *only* sleeping. Won't eat, won't speak. Barely even looks at me. I almost miss the ranting and raving. Maybe you could come and do an examination."

The cowboy shack contained little—a narrow bed, a pitcher for water, a few old saddles and bridles piled against the wall. When I came in, the Kid was lying facing the wall, wearing a wrinkled, off-white nightshirt.

I remembered all the ways I'd tried to rouse Mama the year that she was sick. I'd made her favorite foods—biscuits and gravy, strawberries with sugar on them, corn pie loaded with butter and cheese. I'd brewed strong hot coffee, teas with lemon balm and hawthorn, broth with beef bones I convinced the butcher to give me for free. Nothing seemed to work and then, one day, she got out of bed for a little while, and the next day a little while longer, and the next day a little while longer, until one day I got up and she was already awake, laughing and playing on the floor with baby Bee. Later, when I asked her what had finally healed her, she shrugged and said, "Time."

Then she thought for a moment and added, "When you talked to me, that helped."

I told the Kid about the weather outside, what Cassie had made for breakfast that morning and dinner the night before, which horses were acting ornery and which people weren't getting along. The Kid said nothing.

"Would you like to take a walk outside?" I asked.

The Kid said nothing.

"Would you like to eat some soup?"

The Kid said nothing.

Then I began simply to talk for talking's sake, telling the Kid the story of my life, from its beginning in my mother's house, through my sojourn at Holy Child, all the way to the moment when I sat at the Kid's bedside.

The Kid said nothing.

Finally I decided to ask the Kid a question to which I actually wanted the answer.

"Why didn't you become a preacher?" I asked.

The Kid sighed, turned to face me, and began to speak.

"I was married at sixteen to a man from our congregation, someone my daddy picked out for me. He was a kind man, and liberal in his thinking. He didn't mind that I was to be a preacher one day. We tried for a year, but we couldn't have a child."

"Did he kick you out?" I asked.

The Kid held up a hand. I saw the burn across the wrist and arm; it had begun to heal, leaving new raw skin behind.

"At the end of the year, my mama took me to see a master midwife. She gave me an herb to regulate my monthlies. I fell pregnant and we had a little girl."

"You have a child?" I asked.

The Kid held up a hand again.

"The birth was difficult. For weeks afterward I couldn't walk. That was when the sickness came for the first time. I was awake thirty nights, then asleep thirty days, at least it felt that way to me. Then my husband's family brought in a doctor from San Antonio. He looked at my tongue and the soles of my feet and the whites of my eyes.

"He told my husband there was nothing the matter with my body, but that my mind was diseased. He said the disease was contagious. If my daughter was exposed to me, she would catch it. So my husband was to keep us apart as much as possible—a single visit on Sundays, at most, was permitted."

"That's horrible," I said.

The Kid held up a hand a third time.

"The doctor said that the best treatment for me would be pregnancy. He said I should continue to bear children as many times as I was able, but they should be taken from me, until such time as I could show myself cured."

This time I did not speak, but tried to look the Kid in the eye. The Kid looked away.

"I made it three months," the Kid said. "Every day I curse myself that I couldn't make it one week longer, to see my daughter a final time. But it was pure torture, lying with my husband, knowing I'd lose whatever child I had. One night in the spring I climbed out our window and hitched a ride to Holy Child, where I'd heard they took in barren women. But the memory of my daughter wouldn't let me rest.

"Years I wandered, cowboying, rustling. I lived as a man and as a woman; no life suited me. Then I met Cassie. As long as I could protect her, I told myself, I would be worth something."

The Kid turned to face the wall again.

"Now I can't even do that."

CHAPTER II

On the morning we'd chosen for the purchase of the bank and the beginning of our careers as landlords, I lay awake in my bunk. The stars were still out, and it was hours before we'd start for Fiddleback, but I couldn't sleep. Cassie had cleared away the blankets that had been Lark's bed, but a clean space remained on the bunkhouse floor where he had slept, the red dust not yet settled over it. His death made me miss my family freshly, the new injury opening up the old wound.

It was Bee's birthday in August—she would be turning ten. I still remembered the smell of her scalp as a baby, the way her tiny fingers wrapped around a hank of my hair. The way her head would grow heavier and heavier against my chest as she drifted into sleep.

As our plan drew closer to fruition I found myself increasingly restless. I visited the Kid every day. Some days were better and some days were worse, but every day I left feeling exhausted, as though the strength had been drained from me.

When Mama attended a birth she often developed a closeness with the mother. When she was sick, many of these women dropped by to help, bringing food or baby clothes. After she got better, she explained it to me. Even if before the birth she'd thought of the mother as silly or small-minded or mean, afterward they had something in common: they'd faced death together, and they'd survived. But the Kid was still facing whatever had to be faced, was not yet on the other side. And so I crawled out of my bed and went to sit by the firepit in the dark.

Night had reached its low point, that time just before dawn when the memory of sunshine is dimmest. The rocks around the firepit were cold, the birds and insects silent. I sat staring at the ashes and found I had an urge to pray. But I had forgotten all the prayers I'd learned at the convent, as though after I left, my mind had expelled them in a kind of protest. Instead I sang to myself, softly, under my breath, my arms wrapped around my knees, rocking myself the way a mother rocks a weeping child.

> In a cavern, in a canyon,
> Excavating for a mine—

A small animal or bird rustled in the alders to the south of the firepit, where the road was. A jackrabbit, perhaps, that had evaded Elzy's snares.

> Dwelt a rich old copper miner,
> And his daughter Clementine—

The rustling grew louder. I got to my feet. The wolves who howled from the mountains at night sometimes came down into the valley to hunt, but Texas had assured me they were cautious and would never approach humans. Bears, on the other hand, were a danger—especially in spring or summer. A mother bear might come down to the flats with her cub, and there was no predicting what she might do if you got between them. The best thing,

Texas had said, was to make a lot of noise, to let her know where you were and give her plenty of time to avoid you.

"She went shopping at the market," I sang, walking back toward the bunkhouse,

> *Every morning just at nine,*
> *Met a man with Flu and fever—*

The gunshot was so close that I felt the wind of it on my cheek. I wheeled around to see, standing among our alder trees, the sheriff of Fiddleback, the barrel of his pistol picking up the first rays of the rising sun.

My mind blanked out and my body took over. My arms pushed open the bunkhouse door, my throat and lungs bellowed out a cry to rouse my friends.

Cassie opened her eyes first. I saw a flash of terror in her face. This was the thing she'd been most afraid of, all her years in the valley—our hideout breached, strange men invading our home. I saw fear turn for a moment to anguish and grief, as though someone she loved had died. Then she swallowed it down. Her eyes hardened. When she spoke, her voice was a command:

"We have to get to the Wall."

Panicked and shooting we ran to the barn. The sheriff was not alone—shots came at us from the pasture, from the grove of trees where, so long ago, I had seen Cassie and Elzy pressed together in an embrace. If I had sat at the firepit a moment longer, we would have been surrounded.

Where we had been caught by surprise, the horses—their ears keen, their muscles tuned to vibrations in the earth—had been ready. Amity was out the door as fast as I could throw a saddle over her back and myself into the saddle, and then tearing along the path to the wall as though the two of us were of one mind. Gunshots rang around us as we rode, and the calls of birds who had lived their whole lives in peacetime, now frightened out of their sleep by the sounds of war. As we crested a hill I heard a cry behind me, a high, helpless noise like an infant in pain, and I turned my head to see Faith dropping to her knees, blood pouring down her flank. I felt pity for the horse, whose tail I had sometimes brushed after I brushed Amity's, who had loved to eat cubes of barley sugar out of my palm. But what sent a spike of icy fear through my mind and heart was what I saw behind Faith, behind Temperance and Elzy, Prudence and Cassie, Charity and News.

As any good outlaw knows, the size of a sheriff's posse changes from one day to the next. It depends on the number of able-bodied men with working pistols and ready horses who can spare the time away from their farms, ranches, or stores, and on the popularity of the sheriff with said men. Perhaps most importantly, it depends on the nature of the crime the posse is gathered to punish. The theft of a cow might raise one or two men; the theft of a prize stud bull three or four. The murder of a derelict or a woman of questionable character might bring out one generous man, or none at all, while the killing of a mother or a pillar of the community might inspire half a dozen.

Behind my friends on the Hole in the Wall Road, pouring over the hill rank upon rank, tall on their horses, pistols drawn, was a posse some two dozen strong. Among them I recognized not only the sheriffs of Fiddleback and Casper, but also Sheriff Branch, wearing his white hat and riding the horse I'd fed as a little girl. To see him alongside these others, after fearing our meeting for so long, gave me a kind of unstable feeling, as though the very ground were buckling and folding beneath me, and distances that had once seemed vast were now so small that my enemies could cross them in an instant. How these men had joined together I did not know, how they had tracked us here I could not guess, but their combined influence had raised a force that outnumbered us three to one, whose horses galloped at our horses' heels and whose gunshots startled flights of meadowlarks into the morning air of our valley.

Elzy rode past Faith, and with her good arm scooped Texas off her back and onto Temperance's. From behind them, Cassie shouted, "Scatter!"

I took Amity off the road and into the tall grass. She bounded, sure-footed as a pronghorn, across the valley floor. Red dust came up in clouds around us, coating my throat and making me choke, but I kept my eyes fixed on the wall. I knew that Cassie, Elzy, News, Agnes Rose, and Texas were all doing the same. If we could get to the hole, we'd have a vantage from which to dig in and defend ourselves, with a clear view of everything in the valley below.

Amity leapt over the creek and in the distance to the east I saw the cowboy shack, the morning sun glinting off its windows. I hoped the Kid would know to stay inside, and that the posse would not think to look there. I remembered how when she was sick, my mama had let a rat crawl all the way up the bedpost and gnaw a hole in the quilt at her feet; I was afraid that if the posse burst into the shack, the Kid would simply let them shoot.

When we reached the stand of alders in the middle of the valley, I let myself look behind me once again. Far in the distance I heard gunshots, but I saw no one. I let Amity slow to a trot, and caressed her gray neck. She was so fast and sure. The sun was already hot, and I wiped my forehead with the back of a dust-coated hand. The air smelled like new grass and sage. All around us the grasshoppers were humming their summer song.

The shot came just as I let myself breathe. Amity bucked and reared and I, unprepared, fell backward into the dirt. I called out to her like she was a child, but she was galloping north, fast as any wild horse. She must be hit, I knew, or she would never throw me. But I had only a moment to worry for her when I heard the other horse approaching, its hooves loud on the hard pan of the valley.

I did the only thing I could think to do—I climbed into the alder tree and sheltered as best I could among the leaves. I was there only a moment before the man came into view. I recognized his narrow frame and blood-colored hat—the sheriff of Casper. I waited until I thought he was twenty paces away. I fired.

The bullet served only to tell him where I was. He raised his eyes to mine and fired, but he missed, too, the lead lodging itself in the bark of the tree. I dropped to the ground. He fired again and missed again, and then I heard the click of an empty chamber in his hands. I looked at his narrow chest and the broad body of his horse bearing down on me, and I knew where my best chance lay. I said a silent apology and fired.

The horse made a sound like Faith had, reared, and crumpled in the dirt. The sheriff came off cursing and running. I aimed at his chest and fired, but this time I felt the click of emptiness in my own fist.

I tried to run through the long grass, but without Amity I was slow, my leg still wounded. I hobbled, and crumpled, and then the sheriff was on me from behind, pinning my hands together behind my back, pushing my face into the dirt. I braced myself for the blow of the pistol butt to the back of my head. I thought of all the people I would never see again—my family, Agnes Rose, News, the Kid—and all the questions I would never answer. I would never know why some babies were born with a cleft lip or a clubfoot, how two brown-eyed parents could have a blue-eyed child, or why I was barren. I was angry at the knowledge the sheriff was stealing from me, and as I realized I was angry, I realized the blow of the pistol had not come. The sheriff yanked me to my feet. Lacking cuffs or a rope to bind me, he had to keep both hands on my wrists and shove me ahead of him, like I was a piece of furniture he was trying to move.

"Where are we going?" I asked.

"We built stocks in the town square just for you," he said. "You'll stay there three days. Then, if you're still alive, you'll hang."

I heard in his voice a kind of contemptuous familiarity. He had been thinking about me since News and Agnes Rose had sprung me from his jail a few weeks before, and I had been thinking about him. Hate, I saw, breeds a kind of closeness. I fell in step with him.

"How did you find me?" I asked.

"Shut up," the sheriff said, giving me a shove.

I tried a different tack.

"Surely the sheriffs of Fairchild and Fiddleback want to hang me in their town squares too. How did you win the privilege?"

"They didn't catch you," he said. "I did. They can hang your friends if they want to. I'm sure Sheriff Donnelly will be excited to string up a gelding in front of his jailhouse."

When he said the word I understood. The wrinkled face of the woman in the jail came back to me clear as if she stood before me on the grass. She must have heard everything I'd said to Lark, and I had said everything to him, about Hole in the Wall and Fiddleback and myself and my family. After our escape attempt she must have traded the information to the sheriff in exchange for her freedom. I almost laughed, almost cried. My marriage had been so costly, and I had barely gotten to enjoy it.

The sheriff and I were the same height, about the same build. But I remembered what Lo had taught me about fighting with men, how I'd have to fight dirty. I broke into a run, as though trying to break free of his grasp. He had to run to keep up with me. Then I stopped short, and when I felt his breath on the back of my neck I brought my head back fast and hard into his face. He yelled and dropped my hands—it was all I needed. I drew my gun and cracked it as hard as I could against his skull. I did not wait to find out if he was dead. I ran.

Soon I had to slow to a walk, then a hop, dragging my hurt leg behind me. The sun seemed to swell in the sky. The birds went silent in the midday heat. Sweat and dust turned to mud on my skin. On foot it would take me another day at least to reach the wall, longer in my injured state. Knowing how much ground I had left to cover made the pain worse; I grew dizzy with it. On a hill above a salt flat I sat down to rest.

I must have been dozing when a sound roused me, a single, high yip from the flat below. At first I thought I saw a wolf crossing the cracked, red earth, and my blood pounded in my ears. But as my eyes adjusted to the sun, I saw from the animal's hunched posture, the sly sneakiness in its movements, that it was not a wolf but a coyote. My heart slowed and I watched the animal without fear. I began to make calculations—if I alternated walking and resting, an hour each, I could make it to the wall in two days, maybe a day and a half. But by then my friends might be dead or captured. And of course, Sheriff Branch or the sheriff of Fiddleback or one of their men might find me before then. The best thing might be to hide and wait the battle out, but the flat open space of the valley yielded few if any places where I could conceal myself. This was part of the strength of Hole in the Wall—from its perch you could see everything and everyone in the open space below. But until you got there, you were totally exposed, vulnerable to whoever might come upon you.

The coyote was nosing its way along the flat, slowly working its way toward the hill. It was a big animal, not as big as a wolf but bigger and more powerful than a dog, the ruff of red-gold fur at its shoulders concealing a girdle of muscle. As I watched, it must have caught my scent on the wind: it raised its head and opened its lips in what would have been, in a dog, a smile of recognition. It began to come near.

I knew a lone coyote would not attack a healthy human. But if it took me for dead, or too sick to move, it might nose around me and take an exploratory bite. I got painfully to my feet. The coyote stopped, but did not back off.

"Hey," I yelled.

The coyote stood its ground. I began to hop-walk in the direction of the wall. The sun was reaching its high point and the shadows on the rock were shrinking, dark giving way to red. I looked behind me. The coyote was following, its mouth still slightly open. It gave another yip, the sound loud in the silent afternoon, and this time I heard an answer—to my left, in the tall grass south of the hill, another coyote was approaching. This one was smaller, and its fur had the soft, bushy look common to young animals. A yearling, I guessed, traveling with its mother.

I hopped faster. The coyotes yipped back and forth to each other, their calls increasing in frequency and excitement.

The third coyote was invisible until I was almost upon it. It stood motionless in the tall grass, silvery where the others were red, and with a heaviness around its head and jaws that marked it as a male. I was close enough to see into its eyes, which were golden, intelligent, and unafraid. I began to run.

The sound that went up around me was one of exultation—high and musical, almost like singing. It would have been beautiful had I not been the injured animal at its center, the prey whose fear-smell set the wild dogs racing through the grass, baying with joy.

The mother and father coyotes were running alongside me, waiting for my first stumble so they could close in, and I felt that stumble in my injured leg, I felt my muscles giving way, when another sound broke through the coyote song.

I did not see the source of the hoofbeats until she was galloping past the coyotes, powerful as a thundercloud, scaring them twenty paces off to either side of her, where they resumed their normal postures, their shamefaced scavengers' crouch. Then she circled back and slowed, just long enough for me to clamber onto her back, where my saddle waited for me as though I'd never left it.

As I gathered the reins and guided Amity toward the wall, I saw blood drying along her left flank. Its source was a raw wound across her gray shoulder, angry red but shallow, easily healed. I thought of the flesh wound Lark had sustained in Casper, and the deeper, more terrible one he'd suffered in Mobridge—I thought of all the wounds that hadn't killed him, and the wound that had. For a moment I bent low to Amity's mane and inhaled her smell of hay and dust and something sweet, like mother's milk. I told her I loved her. She dropped her head and covered the miles of grassland like they were inches, and we reached the rocky outskirts of the red wall with the sun still high in the sky.

The air was eerily quiet, and for a moment I feared the worst: my friends all dead, or, more likely, captured and parceled out among the remaining sheriffs for hanging in their respective towns. But then I saw movement above me, in the shadowed notch where two rock faces met, the Hole in the Wall itself. I tied Amity up to an aspen and began to climb on foot. I rounded a switchback and came face to face with the barrel of a gun.

"Doc, Jesus," said Texas, lowering the pistol. "I thought you were one of them."

"Where are they?" I asked.

"They're dug in down by the sentries."

Texas pointed to the tall outcroppings of rock to the south. There I saw men and horses. Sheriff Branch's hat shone in the sunlight.

"What do we do now?" I asked.

"We wait," said Texas.

Where she and I had sat, many months ago, now the others had set up camp. Elzy gave me bullets for my gun. Cassie gave me a stick of pemmican and a canteen of water. News touched my shoulder.

"We thought you were gone," she said.

The afternoon aged. We watched the men at the foot of the wall as they paced back and forth among the sentry rocks with their guns. A mixture of boredom and fear got hold of me. The valley below me took on the quality of a painting, its greens and reds and golds all flattening out against the sky. Agnes Rose began to sing, very quietly, in her low, pretty voice,

Jesus don't want me for a sunbeam,
Sunbeams were never made like me.

"Hush," said Cassie. "They're on the move."

The men below were fanning out. One group of them had begun to scale the rocks just uphill from the sentries. Another was climbing south, and another made its way straight up the path to the hole. I could no longer see Sheriff Branch.

"Let them come," said News. "We'll pick them off as they get here."

Cassie shook her head.

"They're trying to surround us. We have to split up. Stay high, hide among the rocks and fire on them as they get close. News, Aggie, you go south. Doc, Texas, you take north. Elzy and I will stay here and face the ones coming up the trail."

She paused. "If they take you, keep your head up. Don't beg for your life. Don't confess to any sin. If you die without shame, the shame is all theirs."

I thought of the woman the sheriff of Casper had talked about, who had died in the stocks at Salida. I wondered if she had pleaded for release with her last breaths, or if she'd held firm until the end. To the people gathered round her, hurling stones and rotten fruit and feces, I wondered if it had mattered.

Texas and I climbed the flat rocks north of Hole in the Wall. They were laid atop each other layer on layer, carved and stacked long ago by some great disaster. Some layers were thin as pastry leaves, others thick as tree trunks. As we climbed across them, the valley floor grew hazy with distance. Below us, falcons were diving for their prey.

Near the crest of the wall we reached a notch, smaller than the hole, and just large enough for one person to shelter with a gun. We nodded to each other, Texas installed herself, and I walked on alone.

North of the notch, the layers of rock were stacked nearly flush on one another. I had to turn my body toward the face of the wall and scuttle sideways along a narrow lip, just wide enough for my boots. The wall smelled of old rainstorms, water turning into rock and washing rock away. I knew how fast a determined man could climb, and so every few steps I peeled my face away from the rock to look dizzily over my shoulder for anyone approaching from below.

But I was not prepared for gunshots from above. They shattered the lip of rock behind me, then before me, leaving me trapped on a ledge no longer than my own stride. I drew my gun and looked up to see Sheriff Branch lying belly-down on a layer of rock not ten yards above my head. The sun was dipping down behind him; his hat glittered like a crown.

"Drop your gun," he shouted down the barrel of his own.

Instead I fired, but the sun ruined my aim and the shot sailed wide.

"If you do that again," the sheriff called, "I'll have to shoot you. And I think you know I'm not liable to miss."

The sheriff was famous in Fairchild for his hunting skills; it was said he had once leaned out the jailhouse window and picked a dove off a branch at the end of the street. I holstered the gun and lifted my hands. Then I saw the sheriff had tears in his eyes.

"Ada," he said, "little one, I'm sorry it's come to this."

"Then leave us alone," I said.

The sheriff shook his head.

"Come back to Fairchild with me," he said. "I promise you, the judge will show you mercy. You'll live out your days in the town jail. You can see your sisters on Sundays."

Behind me I heard shouts and gunshots, my friends and his allies at war with one another.

"I don't believe you," I shouted. "The sheriff of Casper wanted to put me in the stocks."

"I never would have let that happen," said Sheriff Branch. "I know you're in pain. I know what it is not to have a child. It can make you do terrible things."

I wanted to tell him I had done nothing terrible. That had been true when I left Fairchild, but it wasn't true now.

"I never hurt Ulla," I said instead. "I never cast a spell on anyone. It's all gossip and nonsense."

The sheriff removed his hat and wiped his brow with his sleeve. Bareheaded he looked older, weary, his bald scalp reddening in the sun.

"I know that, Ada," he said.

"Then why would you do this? Why chase me all this way?"

I felt tears welling in my eyes. More shots rang out behind me. I heard bootsteps and hoofbeats. I heard News shouting but I couldn't make out the words. There was something strange in her voice—it sounded like joy.

"It's such a hard world," the sheriff said. "People need some way of making sense of it. You know that as well as I do. You and your mother, when you said 'rheumatism' or 'hay fever' or 'liver trouble,' half the time the patient got better just from knowing what was wrong."

"I don't understand," I said.

"When a child dies, or two people in love can't conceive, or a man loses his wife in childbirth—these things aren't bearable, Ada, not without help. But if you know why it happened, if you have someone or somebody to blame, then sometimes that's enough to keep going. Do you understand now?"

"You'd let me rot in jail just so Ulla has someone to blame?"

"Not just Ulla," the sheriff said. "Everyone in town was lighter in their hearts when I announced you'd been charged with witch-craft. They'll be lighter still when I bring you back. We all have to make sacrifices, Ada. I'm sorry, but this is yours."

My tears dried and contempt welled up hot in my throat. At the same time I knew he was telling the truth—he wouldn't hurt me. He would take me back to the town jail and let me see my mama and my sisters every Sunday. I would see Bee grow up and have children of her own.

But, I realized, I would not see them born. Someone else would attend my sisters' births and I would be kept far away from pregnant women and babies, even—especially—those who were sick and desperately needed expert care. Women would die when I could save them. And I would sit useless in a cell, my hands aging and curling in on themselves, my knowledge growing outdated, while others, elsewhere, learned what I would never know. I looked over my shoulder at the valley spread out in greens and golds. It was especially beautiful in the late afternoon light, opening up below me like a bowl, like a pair of hands. I could simply step back and drop into it. I would die without shame.

"Please, Ada," the sheriff shouted. "Let me take you home."

I shut my eyes. I took half a step back. I heard a gunshot so close I thought I was hit. And when I opened my eyes and looked up, I saw the Kid standing over the sheriff's body, gazing down at me with a face both alert and at peace.

CHAPTER 12

We fought the posse all night and into the next day, but by the time I saw the Kid, the tide had already turned. The Kid knew all the hiding places in the wall, all the routes and trails, and wherever the men tried to climb, we were there first to shoot them down. The sheriff of Fiddleback was the last one alive. Cassie and the Kid found him at the base of the wall, readying a horse to flee back to his town, and Cassie put a bullet in his chest. Then the Kid staggered and collapsed into her arms.

Weak and skinny, with a mind still weary from illness, the Kid had to be wrapped in blankets back at the camp and fed hearty soups with beetroot and marrow bones. I made a tonic of lemon, dandelion, and nettles boiled to blunt their sting, and I thought of what Sheriff Branch had said. I did not know what ailed the Kid, and I could not promise it would not come again. All I knew was that visiting the Kid's bedside had seemed to speed healing, and so I made sure someone sat with the Kid every moment, reading or talking or simply looking out the bunkhouse window as the Kid slept.

After five days the Kid was feeling strong enough to sit up and eat pemmican and biscuits, and Cassie asked the question on all of our minds:

"What are we going to do now?"

The Kid smiled.

"I was thinking of taking a walk."

"That's good to hear," Cassie said, "but you know what I mean. We can't very well buy the bank now. If any of us go to Fiddleback we'll be shot on sight. And there'll be a price on all of our heads—I'd be willing to bet someone's already putting together another posse, bigger and better-armed than the last."

"I know," the Kid said. "I'll think of something."

But the days went on without a new plan, all of us in a kind of stasis. The nights began to crisp; autumn was coming. We rotated patrol duty up at the pass, waiting for the day when the townsfolk whose sheriffs we'd slaughtered got together a new posse to capture us. It would take time, we reasoned—after the Battle of Hole in the Wall, our gang would be even more feared than before—but it would not take forever.

On the seventh day after the Kid's return, I was kneeling by the side of the road, digging up coneflower plants to dry for the winter. When I heard footsteps behind me I wheeled around, drawing the pistol I now carried with me every day. Before me was a woman, her feet bleeding through flimsy house shoes, her hands empty except for a sheet of crumpled paper.

"Please," she said, "I'm looking for Hole in the Wall."

"Who are you?" I asked. "Who told you to come here?"

She handed the paper to me without a word, and through the red road dust, I saw my own face staring back. Next to mine were the faces of my friends—remarkable likenesses, as we'd appeared the day we robbed the bank. Below the drawings, the poster bore the following words:

WANTED

HOLE IN THE WALL GANG

Held up the FARMERS' AND MERCHANTS' BANK OF FIDDLEBACK on MAY the THIRTIETH, 1895, stealing THIRTY THOUSAND in GOLD and ONE HUNDRED THOUSAND in SILVER COIN.

These VERY DANGEROUS CRIMINALS are known to harbor among them WITCHES and people of MIXED BREED, and to engage in UNNATURAL BEHAVIOR and DRESS. They are capable of all manner of DECEP-TION and TRICKERY and should be approached with GREAT CARE.

A REWARD of FIVE HUNDRED GOLD EAGLES shall be paid for any information leading to the capture of these DEPRAVED PERSONS.

"Please," the woman said again. "They were going to hang me for a witch in Sturgiss. I saw these and I thought maybe you could help me."

Another woman came the next week, and two the week after that. By the end of August we had half a dozen people staying with us, most barren but some run out of their towns for lying with other women or otherwise corrupting moral character. All of them carried the poster in their hands or in their heads. The Kid sent Agnes Rose to Nótkon for enough flour, lard, and ammunition to feed and garrison an army for the winter. We did not have a town, but we had money, and we had land, and now, it seemed, a town might be coming to us.

One night I sat with the Kid at the firepit. Around us was chaos, everyone meeting one another, talking and arguing.

"Cassie was right," the Kid said. "This is dangerous."

"You don't trust them?" I asked, casting my hand around at the new faces.

"It's not that," the Kid said. "Look around you: soon they'll outnumber us. Keeping us together, keeping all of us safe—it's going to be harder than I ever dreamed."

But the Kid was smiling. Every time something had to be decided, some question of provisions or strategy, some feud between two factions of new arrivals, the Kid seemed to grow in stature, shepherding all parties toward a solution with deftness and confidence. The Kid was a born mayor.

"I made you a promise," the Kid said then. "And I'll honor it. But we need a doctor more than ever. Rosie over there, I hear she brought in lice."

I laughed. The truth was, I had thought many times over the last few months of staying at Hole in the Wall. I had not felt so at home since I left Fairchild, and I was loath to give up the feeling for the uncertainty of Pagosa Springs.

"Give me a few nights to think about it," I said. "It'll take that long to wash everyone's hair with turpentine anyway."

The next night, Agnes Rose was combing through News's hair while I searched the brown locks of a new recruit named Daisy. At first Agnes had been chatty with the new women, telling them how she'd liberated two hundred eagles from a lawyer near Spearfish and separated a young deputy in Cody from his billfold and his pride, but as the weeks wore on she'd grown quieter and quieter, and now she was nearly silent.

"What's wrong?" I asked her.

"I can't stop thinking about the butcher," she said.

"From Fiddleback?" I asked. "You said he'd be cheering if they hanged us."

"And that he would," said Agnes Rose. "Still, I thought either we'd die, or we'd come back and put all the gold back into the town. I never thought we'd just take all those people's gold and keep it."

"Aggie," I said as gently as I could, "you've robbed people before."

"Don't insult me," she said. "I'm not stupid, I know what I am." Then her voice softened. "But there's always something you tell yourself, before every job. And in Fiddleback I told myself, if we survive this, we're coming back and repaying these men and women ten-thousand-fold, by showing them a new way to live. And now I know that we won't do that—it just eats at me, that's all."

"I understand," I said. "It eats at me too."

"Ouch," Daisy complained. "You're hurting me."

"Here," Agnes said. "Let me. News is clear anyway."

Daisy got up, scowling. News stood too, but paused, her hand shading her eyes.

"Looks like Cassie found a new recruit," she said.

Cassie had not warmed to the new women, exactly, but she had begun drawing up plans for planting and ranching in the valley to feed a larger number for years to come.

"We have to be self-sufficient," I'd heard her telling the Kid one night.

Now as she approached the firepit, my heart rose in my chest. Behind her in the saddle was the woman with the birthmark, whom I'd met at the patent medicine stall on Easter Sunday, all those months ago. I was dressed in dungarees and a man's shirt; as I helped her down from the horse, I saw recognition in her eyes.

"Sweet Mother Mary," she said when we were face to face.

"My name is Ada," I said. "We have a lot to explain to you."

She looked around the firepit at News, Agnes Rose, Daisy, a few more straggling in to get a look at the new arrival. She gave a little laugh of exhaustion and sorrow and relief.

"I suppose you do," she said. "But you were right. I should have saved my liberties for the wagon ride to Holy Child."

"Did the Mother Superior send you here?" I asked.

"That's right," the woman said. "I didn't mind reading scripture, but I couldn't put aside my anger. Or maybe I could, but I don't want to. The Mother said I wasn't suited to be a nun. She said if I came here, maybe I'd find what I was suited for."

The night after that, I went to visit Texas in the barn. When I arrived she was leaning close to Prudence, combing her mane and singing to her in a low voice.

"Aren't you worried about giving her lice?" I asked.

"Horses can't get human lice," she said. "I'm thinking of bringing my cot out here till the cold weather comes in. It's quiet, it's clean, and nobody asks questions."

I laughed.

"Sorry," I said.

"Too late," said Texas. "What do you want?"

"Are you still going to Amarillo?"

"Yes," Texas said, giving Prudence's mane another brush. "One day. When I'm finished here."

"And when will that be?"

"Hard to say. We have more people now, we need more horses. More horses need more care."

"Someone else could care for them," I said.

Texas moved on to Temperance's stall. The bay horse gave a whinny of recognition and nuzzled her nose against Texas's hand.

"Not as well as me," Texas said.

*

The following night I found the Kid walking the pasture. I hoped the Kid's heart was lighter than it had been; mine was heavy. I would miss my cot on the upper level of the bunkhouse, overlooking the woodstove. But it was as clear to me now as it had ever been: I was not a sharpshooter, a con artist, or a horsewoman. My mastery, when it came, would be of a different sort.

"Keep up the turpentine for another three days," I said. "And make sure Agnes checks everyone over for a week. Lice are tricky."

"I'll pass along your prescription," said the Kid. "Take News and Texas with you to Colorado country, if they're willing. And Amity, of course. She won't let anyone else ride her."

It was September when News, Texas, and I set out for Pagosa Springs. We traveled as itinerant cowboys, heavily disguised with false beards and hats pulled low over our eyes. The story of the Hole in the Wall Gang had preceded us: everywhere we stayed, we heard of our own exploits, already twisted and magnified into legend. The Hole in the Wall Gang had reduced an entire town to rubble. The Hole in the Wall Gang could make rain fall from a clear sky. The Hole in the Wall Gang roasted babies on a spit. The members of the Hole in the Wall Gang were male and female both, with breasts and a penis, and could make themselves pregnant at will. The stories both amused and frightened us—we saw how large a target we made now, how attractive for someone with the ambition to bring down a villain. But as we traveled, even among the posters bearing our likenesses, no one recognized us, because Lo had trained us well to disappear into new suits of clothes so that someone could look right at us and see only the ordinary men we wanted them to see.

After ten days on the road we began to climb through Rocky Mountain country. The air took on a new quality, clean and coniferous, and when I woke in the mornings I thought of Lark and the plans we'd made on our wedding day, no less sweet and sad in my mind for being part of a charade. We climbed up past the tree line where all life was low to the ground, the lichens drinking cloudwater, the marmots and pika scuttling from rock to rock. Only the birds there seemed still to have their freedom—the bluebirds singing brightly in the autumn sun, the falcons hurtling fast as bullets between the mountain peaks.

When we reached the other side of the mountain range, and the trees began to grow again and the forests quicken with deer and moose, I knew we must be close. On the fifteenth day of our journey, I smelled something different on the wind, a mineral scent like liquid rock. The springs themselves ran underground along the road for miles before the town appeared; when we stopped to rest the horses we could hear them, like the whispers of ghosts. Where they bubbled up, finally, in pools and falls, bathers gathered singly and in groups, floating up to the neck in the water, anointing their faces with it, soaking feet and hands, dipping children and babies, wheeling the old and sick down in chairs and cradling their bodies in its warmth.

There was no roadhouse in Pagosa Springs, only a bathhouse with rooms arranged around a central pool. News and Texas and I could not remove our clothes, so we sat in the sunroom, where men and women could sit together on folding chairs and drink tonics made with the town's waters. A young woman, chubby, with very healthy-looking skin, brought us foul-smelling drinks in heavy glasses.

"We're looking for Mrs. Alice Schaeffer," I told her.

The woman shook her head.

"Never heard of anyone by that name," she said.

"Who runs the surgery here?" I asked.

"There's no surgery," she said. "We don't need it. The waters cure everything that ails you."

As she left I sipped my tonic; it tasted like saltwater.

"There was a surgery," said the woman next to me.

She was impossibly ancient, so old she was young again, her skin soft-looking as a baby's, her hair like dandelion fluff. Her eyes, staring blindly into space, were the very lightest blue.

"What happened to it?" News asked.

"It closed down three years ago now. Maybe more. The midwife had to leave town very suddenly."

"Alice Schaeffer?" I asked.

"That might have been her name. She had women coming in and out, you see—women who couldn't have children. There was an outbreak of something—maybe spotted fever, it's hard to remember now. Suspicion fell on her. The sheriff was involved."

"Do you know where she went?" I asked.

The woman fixed me with her blue eyes, and I realized she could see after all.

"Wherever it is," she said, "I imagine she wouldn't want anyone to find her."

The sunroom was lined with glass windows looking out on the pool. A young couple in blue bathing costumes kissed each other ceremonially on the lips, then stepped into the water.

"Where was the surgery?" I asked the old woman.

"On the eastern edge of town, if I remember right," she said, "opposite the school."

It was late afternoon when we reached the spot, and school was just letting out. I saw three girls walking hand in hand in hand, and thought of Ulla and Susie and me. By now both Ulla and Susie must be mothers, I knew; perhaps their children would play with my sisters' children. The thought did not even make me sad anymore. It was like an image seen through very thick glass, its impact muted and distorted.

The building opposite the schoolhouse was low and small, its roof clearly damaged in a hailstorm. But inside, I saw it had been designed for calm and comfort. The windows were large and looked out on the mountains, and even through the dust that lay thick on the glass, the light in every room had a sweetness to it, like cool water.

"We should stay the night here," Texas said. "We can start back in the morning. I'm sorry, Ada. I know you must be disappointed."

I nodded, but I could not quite believe that Mrs. Alice Schaeffer was gone. Her presence filled the surgery. The front room was large with a wide bed, a washbasin, and a variety of cushions of different shapes and sizes. I recognized them from the hand-book—Mrs. Schaeffer had recommended a peanut-shaped pillow for back labor, and a smaller, cylindrical one between the knees to help with the pain of transition, and I saw both set neatly next to the bed, along with others whose uses I had not yet learned.

In the back room was a narrower bed and three dark-wood cabinets. One was full of instruments—a speculum, forceps, a scalpel, an assortment of needles—many now ruined with rust. A second held bottles and jars of tinctures, ointments, and tonics, some familiar and some new to me. The third was full of note-books, ordered by date, each one containing details of observations, operations, births, and deaths. I was reading Mrs. Schaeffer's records of a series of women who had suffered miscarriages in the winter of 1889 when I heard the knock at the back door.

It was past midnight. The woman who stood before me had come on foot, alone. She was young, probably younger than me, with dark eyes and a forward jut to her lower jaw that made her look determined.

"Are you Mrs. Schaeffer?" she asked.

"I'm sorry to tell you," I said, "but Mrs. Schaeffer's gone."

"All right then," the young woman said, quickly as though the words were casual, but with a catch in the back of her throat. She turned to walk back into the night.

"Wait," I called after her. "Do you need a midwife?"

She turned back to me, her face sad and sardonic, the smallest hint of hope playing about her mouth.

"I wish what I needed was a midwife," she said.

"Come inside," I told her.

In the morning the others found us seated together at the desk in the back room. The young woman had told me the history of her family, who was barren and who had many children, and now she was telling me about her town, the illnesses that had passed through when she was younger, and the ones that had sickened her in the past year.

"Who is this?" Texas asked.

"This is Minnie Parrish," I said. "She's my patient."

"Well, you'd better hurry up and treat her," Texas said. "If we don't get on the road soon we'll lose the light."

But I had already stripped the bed and set a pot of water boiling to sterilize the bedsheets and instruments. I had made a preliminary inventory of the cabinets, finding all the ointments parched and the herbs dusty, but a few seed packets tucked behind the camphor from which I could start a little garden. I had found an empty notebook, a fountain pen, and an inkwell with a little ink still liquid inside it, and I had opened the notebook to the first page and written that day's date at the very top. Below it I had written down everything Minnie Parrish said.

I was afraid, and I was uncertain—I thought it distinctly possible that what had befallen Mrs. Schaeffer would also befall me. But I had received, in the preceding months, an excellent education in how to evade suspicion—and, once it could be evaded no further, how to fight for my life. Now, I reasoned, was the time to employ what I had learned.

"Tell the Kid thank you," I said. "If any of your number needs a doctor, you can always send them to me. And if any of my patients needs safety, I hope I can send them to you."

I want to tell you about the years that followed, about the births I witnessed and the deaths, about the women I treated and the books I wrote, about what I learned from the notebooks and what, eventually, other midwives learned from me. But those are other stories for other days. This story ends in September in the year of our Lord 1895, when I came over the mountains a wife and a widow, a doctor and an outlaw, a robber and a killer and ever my mother's daughter, and set up shop in the surgery of Mrs. Alice Schaeffer and got to work.

ACKNOWLEDGMENTS

I owe enormous thanks to Julie Barer for her expert guidance, Callie Garnett for her probing questions, Barbara Darko for her wise help with copyediting, Nicole Cunningham for all her help over the years, and Liese Mayer and everyone at Bloomsbury for their enthusiasm about this project. Thanks to JoEllen Anderson, Andrew Cowell, and Phoebe Hart for sharing their expertise, and to everyone at Willow Creek Ranch at the Hole-in-the-Wall for welcoming me and giving excellent directions. Thanks, as always, to my writing group: Anthony Ha, Alice Sola Kim, Karan Mahajan, Tony Tulathimutte, Annie Julia Wyman, James Yeh, and Jenny Zhang. Utmost thanks to my family, especially Toby, for advising, listening, reading, and driving.